THE SKY

THE SKY PLACE

A Contemporary and Historical Fantasy

LYLA CORK

This novel is a work of fiction. The events and characters are fictitious. Certain places, businesses, and geographical locations are mentioned, but the characters involved are entirely imaginary. Although this novel has historical components and references historical events and figures, the timing of events and the actions of the characters are completely fictitious. Any resemblance to actual events or persons, living or dead, is entirely coincidental.

For my family with love.

Special thanks to my husband, who was my first reader.

Special thanks to my sister for her feedback.

CHAPTER 1 - IXCHEL

Tikal
Maya Lowlands
Mesoamerica
A.D. 562

THE GREAT STAR GLOWED above the city of Tikal like firelight in the black sky. Ixchel stood barefoot on the limestone patio outside her bedchamber and savored the chill in the predawn air. She wore a sleeveless dress of spun cotton, the white fabric dancing about her knees in the damp wind. An indigo shawl of woven hemp warmed her shoulders. From the rim of foliage bordering the eastern walls of the royal complex, came the high, thin squeaks of pygmy fruit bats. Reep-reep-reep. Yick. Yick. Reep-reep-reep. Yick. Yick.

Nervous toucans thudded their bills against thick-limbed trees in the waning dark. But Ixchel was too preoccupied to heed the birds' warnings as they squawked in alarm at the mayhem brewing beyond the palace walls. She eyed the moon and its shimmering companion. Just as it always did, the rising of the Great Star had sent the daykeepers into a state of insatiable panic, and Ixchel was thoroughly sick of it. If she heard the words *portent of evil* once more, she would confine herself to her bedchamber. She had her own troubles to manage. The last thing she needed was to have every meal ruined with talk of *harbingers of death* and *striking serpents*.

"Let the serpent strike. Tikal is the ocelot that rips the snake in two," she'd remarked at dinner the night before when Ajq'ij Kabek, the oldest of the daykeepers, soured the cashew wine and honey cakes once again

1

with his dire chatter. The king's eyes had widened at her impertinence. If she was not his favorite daughter, he would have banished her from the table. Instead, her lord father was satisfied to sip his wine and glare at her. Ajq'ij Kabek was not similarly inclined. He launched into a lecture on the significance of cosmic omens, as if Ixchel didn't already know the whole of it by heart. She was then forced to listen to her cousin and future husband, Lord Jaguar Claw, rise to her defense. Ever the warrior, he diverted the discussion by vowing to cut the lips from the face of any man who so much as sneered in the direction of Tikal. On and on, he droned, spinning his well-worn tales of blood and blade as her lord father looked on and smiled.

Ixchel spent the remainder of the evening struggling to calm her raging heart. She'd been engaged to Lord Jaguar Claw since birth. But just as heat draws sickness from a wound, the approach of their wedding day had drawn out her cousin's true nature. In the past three weeks, she had come to despise him.

Ixchel shook off the events of the night before and focused on the present. She often felt as though she was floating within the heart of the sky when she stood upon the precipice of her bedchamber, at peace with her noble ancestors and the gods. Beneath her bare feet, the floor of the patio disappeared in the darkness. Around her, the red walls of the royal complex, grand and glorious, were shrouded beneath the light of the moon. These predawn moments were usually a comfort to her; but on this day, they brought little relief to her worried heart. The sprawling grandeur of the royal complex, with its high, wide patios and thatched porticos, its spreading staircases and layer upon layer of curtained chambers, felt suddenly confining.

Ixchel left the patio for her bedchamber. She slid the shawl from her shoulders. At the foot of her bed, a cedar chest lined in deerskin gaped open. Soon the sun, brother to the Great Star, would lift the darkness from the four corners of the land, bringing with it the morning's warmth, and she would have no need of the shawl. She fingered its braided hem as she placed it inside the chest. The shawl was her dearest possession. Imbued with the image of One Hunahpu, the patron god of scribes, and ornately embroidered with polished seashells, it was a gift from her lady mother, given to her on the first day of her scribal tutelage.

Almost seven years had passed since she first began her scribal studies with Master Fire Dawn, the instructor who would teach her the tenets of cosmology, mythology, mathematics, and divination. She still had much to learn from Master Fire Dawn. But it would all come to nothing if she could not extricate herself from the clutches of her future husband, Lord Jaguar Claw.

Ixchel returned to the patio to proffer her daily blood to the gods of earth and sky. She unrolled a mat of braided thatch upon the red floor. To her right sat a squat pair of terra cotta pots, their fat little bellies painted full circle with the images of spotted monkeys dancing nose-to-tail in torrents of rain. The first pot was covered and tied with cloth and twine. The second was perforated near the rim and lidded with a slab of polished stone. Between the two lay a small flint blade with a handle of carved bone.

Ixchel untied the first pot, revealing a pool of still water. Taking the blade in hand, she carefully slid the stone lid from the second pot. The mouse squeaked as she cradled its back within her palm and closed her thumb around its neck. With a swift strike to the belly, she bled the mouse into the dry bowl. When the animal was drained, she slipped its body into the pot of water. As she poured its blood into the water, she whispered a prayer into the spreading dawn,

"Heart of Earth, Heart of Sky,
don't let us fail, don't set us aside,
thou gods upon the earth and in the sky,
give us our path, our way.
May there be no worry, no blame,
give us a green road, a steady flame,
thou Sovereign Plumed Serpent,
thou Hurricane,
maker of life, bringer of light.
Calling to thee,
thou noble ancestors,
Xpiyacoc, Xmucane,
Grandfather of day, Grandmother of life,

let us flourish, let us grow,
when it comes to the dawning, the sowing."

Her daily proffering complete, Ixchel covered the pot of water so it may be still again. On a wooden table in the rear corner of the patio sat a shallow basin of water and mint leaves and a collection of cotton rags. After cleaning her hands with the water and leaves, she returned to her bedchamber.

The rains had come hard that season. It was clear to all the palace nobles, from the youngest ah nab to the oldest ajq'ij, that their prayers and offerings had been well-received by the god of rain. Indeed, Chac continued to smile upon the kingdom, even now with the days growing longer and mid-year scarcely sixty days away. But Ixchel wanted more than rain that season. She wanted her freedom. And a private audience with her lord father, King Wak Chan K'awiil, was her only hope.

Wary of the mud pooling in the courtyard, she strapped an unadorned pair of twine sandals to her feet and strode from her chamber in search of her lord father. She descended the wide, shallow stairway beneath the Jaguar's Nest, the family residence of the king, and walked westward through the courtyard. The morning air bloomed thick and full, covering the lower patios and staircases in a film of white.

Ixchel found her lord father atop the Plateau of the Great Jaguar, the rooftop that formed a towering ledge at the western corner of the palace. King Wak Chan K'awiil, known to his people as Lord Double Bird, was a strong, steady man, his royal bloodline written upon his face in high cheekbones, wide eyes, and a rigid brow. His long raven hair was wound about his head in a thick braid, the festooned end falling down his back in a stream of carved jade beads. A loincloth hemmed with shells and feathers draped his hips. Above, a pati of jaguar pelts covered his broad chest and fell to his waist. The pati was knotted at the right shoulder. Beginning at his left shoulder, a massive tattoo of twin gorging hawks decorated his copper skin. The beasts, drawn upon his flesh in black pigment, feasted on the bodies of the slain, their open wings covering the thick muscles on his upper arm and back. The plumed tail of the first hawk curled around his left forearm, ending in a flourish of black beneath the cuffs of gold at his wrist.

He looked every bit the Halach Winic. The True Man. A god-king, who, like his ancestors before him, served as a conduit between the three planes of existence: the upperworld, the middleworld, and the underworld. Each Halach Winic and his descendants was gifted with the divine power to travel freely between these planes of existence. It was a priceless privilege.

Lord Double Bird was facing north, peering into the mist, and he did not acknowledge the presence of his daughter until she touched his shoulder. When he turned, he smiled at her. "There is such beauty here," he said, taking her by the hand. "Ajq'ij Kabek would have me clear the northern canopy and raise another field of rice just beyond the eastern temple of Jaguar Skull, but I believe I will leave the canopy as it is. I have more need of beauty than rice. I trust he can feed the hungry without depriving me of my trees."

"I'm sure he'll groan about it at dinnertime," Ixchel replied. "And foretell all manner of societal decay for want of rice. He'll be predicting riots at the palace steps before he's had his first bite of cassava bread."

Her father chuckled.

Ixchel took this as her cue. "Lord father," she began. "It pains me to say this, but my heart does not want Lord Jaguar Claw as my matchmate. I beg you, please do not make me marry him. He is my cherished cousin, but his ways are not mine. He wants me to abandon my calling once we are married. He says he will insist upon it. And I am so close now, I need to continue...."

Her father refused to hear more. "I know what is in your heart, dear daughter," he interrupted gently. "I have spoken to Master Fire Dawn. You are a keen student, but you seek knowledge as a road to glory. In truth, you and Lord Jaguar Claw are much alike. He has chosen the warlord's way, and he will magnify himself upon the battlefield. His battleglory will outshine the Night Sun. And his glory will be your glory."

"I do not want his kind of glory," Ixchel insisted. Her father seemed oblivious to the truth of the matter but in her mind there was a salient distinction. Secondhand glory was no glory at all. More significantly, a warlord's wife had not the privileges of a scribe. After her marriage, she would be permanently cut off from the sacred writings of the daykeepers, and, without them, she would never learn the secrets of the gods. She would have little hope of magnifying herself in this life or the next.

5

"You are nineteen," Lord Double Bird continued firmly, "old enough to understand the sacred nature of your engagement. You were promised to your cousin on the day of your birth. He is the first-born son of my first-born sister, and you are my first-born daughter. You do not need a matchmaker to divine that he is your destiny. Do not worry me with this, my child. It will not be undone."

"How can you force this upon me?" she cried, her voice high with desperation. Though far less important to her than the first, she threw forth her second objection to the marriage, "You know he has already taken a concubine. He has already chosen his second wife! If you cherish me at all, please do not make me marry him."

"You are my beautiful flower, my most precious daughter." He placed his hand upon her cheek to quell her rebellious tears. "And Lord Jaguar Claw is the greatest warlord in the kingdom. It is expected that many fathers would seek him for their daughters. But you will be his first wife, and, in time, you will see that this is a great honor."

"I will never see that," Ixchel whispered in defeat. She didn't mention her third objection to the marriage. It pained her even to think about it because it cast her lord father in such a dark light.

Ixchel watched in silence as her lord father descended to the courtyard and made his way back toward the Jaguar's Nest. She did not follow. Instead, she exited the royal compound through the southeast passage and headed for the deep green canopy beyond the market square to seek the sanctuary of the sacred tree. The morning's mist was only just beginning to rise. She did not sense the Yax Xook amid the gossamer. Thinking back now, they must have been there, lurking just beyond the southeast wall. The first sharks. Shadow warriors that sneak forth before the madness of full battle and rifle for royal captives.

When she reached the massive trunk of the sacred tree, Ixchel curled her body upon the moist earth and rested her head against its ancient roots. Marriage to Lord Jaguar Claw would mean the end of all her hopes. And the lingering gossip among the old nobles only made things worse. Twenty years later, they still whispered that her lord father did not gain the throne with honor. The palace gossips hinted that he had a hand in the mysterious death of his first-born sister, Queen of Tikal. The queen, Lord Jaguar Claw's mother, died suddenly in the prime of her life. If the queen had lived, Lord Jaguar Claw would be heir to the throne. Instead, Ixchel's father claimed the crown, and her infant cousin was cut from the line of succession. If her cousin even half believed the gossip, it would be impossible for him to love her.

Ixchel cried and prayed until the sun was bright in the sky. Before long, pangs of hunger brought her troubled mind into the moment. It was time for the morning meal, and she knew her lady mother would be looking for her. She sat up and wiped her streaming tears. Ominous sounds blew in from the west. She strained to hear but could make little sense of the noises that met her ears. Unsure of what was happening, she hurried toward home. Moving quickly along the rainforest floor, a rising sense of panic bloomed in her heart, and the feeling intensified with each forward step. The ominous sounds grew wilder, until the weak noise became a maelstrom of terrible cries. By the time she broke free of the rainforest, it seemed the whole city was screaming. And when she approached the eastern border of the market square, she saw the truth of it. War had been brought to Tikal.

The market square was situated in and around the Red Plaza. The plaza itself was a large stone rectangle, it's low walls painted crimson. The land surrounding the plaza was a floor of turned black soil and knitted thatch, lined with merchant's huts, pens, and stalls. Ixchel sped to the relative safety of an abandoned hut. From the cracks between the slatted pine she stared, terrified, as the sounds of battle thundered in her ears. The air rang with a cacophony of booming drums, shrill whistles, and desperate cries. Amid it all, at the center of the battle lines and flanked by foot soldiers, stood the daykeepers of Caracol. Raised on litters in a triad formation, the daykeepers of Caracol, painted blue from foot to forehead, sang out their prayers to Buluk Chabtan. And it seemed the war god was indeed on their side.

They are attacking us! They are bleeding us dry! The horrifying reality before her was more than she could stomach, and she choked back bile as the men of Tikal fell before her eyes. Painted warriors with feathered helms and armor of salt cotton owned the field. With brutal force these men drove club to bone and spear to flesh in a bloody dance that soon turned the market floor as red as the walls of the plaza. Her own warriors were unadorned, taken by surprise as they welcomed the dawn, half must have been at their morning meal or proffering their daily blood.

Slim as it was, there remained a chance of victory. And win or lose, Ixchel wanted to be with her family. But the invaders were slashing their way west toward the palace, and she would have to dare a perilous run home. If she was lucky, she might be able to make it back safely. If the invading host was not divided; if they'd made a full assault from the southeast, then the palace would still be untouched, but not for long. She sprinted for home, cutting hard west.

She was intercepted at the Spider's Mound by a warlord of Caracol. The man was a fearsome sight. His eyes blazed beneath a wooden helm adorned with a shower of quetzal plumes that framed his painted face, the black and red ink smeared with blood and sweat. A jade collar protected his neck from chin to chest. The worst of it pivoted in his right hand, a war club spiked with flint blades.

He lunged for her, but she sprang back, just out of reach. The effort sent her flailing to the ground. He was on her before she could blink. She curled her body like an upturned crab and pushed against his chest and hips with her palms and knees. But he was a heavier load than she could bear, and her limbs shuddered beneath him. She knew she could not hold him off long.

She spied the massive flint dart mere seconds before it tore through the warlord's face. He howled as his lower jaw fell free from his face and his tongue lolled from his mouth. He rolled off her in agony, clutching his ruined face in his hands. In an instant, the Tikal warrior who saved her life was at her side. "Run!" he screamed and heaved the spiked club from the ground as a second plumed warlord descended from the Spider's Mound, spear in hand.

The spear came raging through the air. Her warrior broke its course with the club, then turned to face his old foe who'd risen for revenge, tattered face and all. The wounded warlord held his helm in hand, and he swung it like a drunken baboon, dizzy from pain. Her warrior cleaved his club into what was left of the warlord's face and ended the man's life in an explosion of bone, blood, and teeth. Turning to face his second foe, who'd reclaimed his spear, her warrior ordered her to flee. This time she did not hesitate, running home with all the speed she could scavenge from her trembling limbs. As she ran, she begged the gods to keep her family safe. She was desperate to see her father's face again, to feel her mother's arms around her.

When she arrived at the palace, she found her enemies tearing into it from every direction. In that moment, she knew her father, mother, and sister were gone. Despair fell heavily upon her; her knees turned soft and weak. Somehow, she found the strength to keep moving, and circled back toward the hidden reservoir.

It was there her eldest brother, Lord Red Hawk, found her. His battle-axe and spear still dripped, and there was fear in his voice as he spoke, "Our lord father and our brothers, the twins, have fallen. Jaguar Claw fights on, but soon he must flee north as we all must, for there is no hope, dear sister. Our lady mother and our sister have gone to meet our noble ancestors in the upperworld; widow's bark has sped their final flight to the goddess Ixtab."

"Then you are king, lord brother," Ixchel blurted frantically. "You must flee at once. If you are captured the men will yield, and Tikal will be lost." She did not say the worst of it. They both knew that dark truth too well. The blood sacrifice of a captured noble, particularly a king, was the most horrific death imaginable. The longer the defeated king suffered, the more power Buluk Chabtan bestowed upon the victorious king who turned the blade in the war god's name.

As children, their grandmother, Lady Hand, had terrified them with tales of Lord Kinich Ehb, the defeated boy-king of Yokib, who was tortured for seven days and nights by his conqueror, King Moon Skull. When he died, the boy's limbs were all but shredded, his eyes, lips, and ears torn from his head.

Panic seized Ixchel as she clutched her brother's arm. "We must go now! We must flee to safety!" she begged.

He shook his head. "I must find my lady wife. She left the palace with her mother before the siege to proffer parrot's blood for our unborn babe. I will find her within the Cave of Lady Skull, and we will make our way northward to Uaxactun."

"The cave is south of the palace walls," Ixchel protested. "They clamor like cockroaches to the south!"

"That is why you must go north," Lord Red Hawk commanded. "Run hard, for once you clear the rainforest and break the jungle north, they will not follow you."

Her face a mask of tears and terror, Ixchel embraced her brother, then ran northward, her legs pounding forward more fiercely than she would have thought possible. She only hoped it would be enough.

CHAPTER 2 - IXCHEL

TIKAL HAD FALLEN. Ixchel ran like a wild animal, the terror in her chest a living thing, driving her onward. Behind her, painted bodies flashed red amid the green of the rainforest. The men were gaining ground.

Her only hope was to push northward. *Breach the borders of the rainforest*, her lord brother had said. *They won't follow you into the jungle scrub.* But the rains had turned the black earth to sludge, and her sandals slid beneath her with each forward lunge. She was gasping now. Her shins burned.

It took her a moment to realize she'd fallen. On her belly in the mud, fear sent spasms through her insides. Almost instantly, she felt hands beneath her shoulders, hot breath against her face. They lifted her roughly. Fingers pushed the small of her back, and a voice bid her, "go."

There were four in the war party, and they walked in a tight formation around her, two forward, two behind. Winded from the chase, the sound of the men's quick, shallow breaths came at her as from the four corners of a cage. Ixchel sized up the two in front. They were dressed in the common style of the warrior. Loincloths of red and black were wound about their waists and through their legs. One of the men wore a deerskin strap across his chest fashioned with a slip to sheath his knife.

They wore no battle scars. *War rats sent to gather the women*, Ixchel thought with contempt. She bit the inside of her cheek until it bled and spat the blood upon the earth, sending with it a prayer to Kinich Ahau that at least one of her men would come upon them as they led her through the rainforest. She was certain that even one Tikal warrior could slaughter these four with ease. But no one came, and she shivered as all hope fell away. She nursed her aching cheek with her tongue and choked back the sorrow swelling in her throat.

Though the sun was still high, they walked in shifting grey light beneath a canopy of green. Here and there, sunlight tore through the canopy like massive blades, making its way past the thick shoulders of mahogany and ceiba. They walked in silence, the only sounds the soft padding of their sandals upon the damp earth and the heavy breaths at their lips. But as they neared the plaza, voices of despair came braying upon the wind, and Ixchel soon found herself amid the chaos that comes with the wrapping up of war.

The men tied her wrists and bound her to a human chain of captives. As she stared in disbelief, warlords bellowed orders to their warriors, who gathered and bound her people like animals in preparation for the southbound journey to Caracol.

Ixchel felt herself stifling beneath the weight of defeat. The anguish on the faces of those bound with her was as raw and wet as a seeping wound. Women wept for their husbands, called out for their children. But there would be no further resistance. Young voices called back through the din, and the women would trudge forward, clinging to the hope of finding their children on the other side of the journey. Ixchel knew she would find only death. She was Lady Ixchel, daughter of Lord Double Bird, King of Tikal. And her bloodline would be her doom.

Behind her, a broken voice cried out a prayer,

"Heart of Sky, Heart of Earth,

give me courage, give me strength...."

But Ixchel could not listen, nor could she pray. A single thought smoldered in her mind. *How can this be?* She could not fathom how the invaders had cleaved through her city's military muscle, for there were none who could challenge the might of Tikal.

Ixchel knew Caracol's king hungered for vengeance. Two years earlier, her lord father abruptly ended their long alliance and then summarily executed Ajq'ij Kan Mo of Caracol when he arrived at Tikal demanding an explanation for the sudden about-face. But Caracol's military was nothing to Tikal's. The lords of Tikal had always assumed they'd be safe from any retribution by Caracol, yet Tikal had been overrun in a single day. *How did Caracol succeed where all others had failed?*

Above, the sun was at the height of its life, and it blazed in a cloudless sky. Soon it would begin its slow decent into the underworld. Ixchel stood motionless in the stifling heat, gaping at the madness surrounding her. The sun was near death by the time the warlords commanded their warriors to drive the captives south.

As they journeyed, the sun was born anew in the sky eight times. They traveled the white road. It was the merchants' route, a hard-packed limestone passageway winding through the heart of the jungle. The procession moved quickly along the broad road. The warlords set the pace, with their foot slaves just behind. The daykeepers came next, carried in litters of silvered teak, and accompanied by temple slaves and royal guards. Behind the powerful and the blessed followed the others. The warriors and the captives, the domestics and their slaves.

Each day was harder on Ixchel than the one before. Her heart ached for the past as much as her legs ached from day upon day of near-constant trudging. The captives' provisions were not much less than the warriors'. But the masa had run out days earlier, and they were all subsisting on jungle meat—peccary, tamandua, and coati. Ixchel felt herself growing weaker in body and spirit with each forward step. Beneath the weight of the merciless sun, her lips grew dry and chapped. Water was portioned among the captives throughout the day, but Ixchel always found herself thirsting for more.

At least the warlords have held onto their honor, Ixchel thought. It was meager solace, but as long as the captives kept walking, there was no violence, no brutality. The welfare of the captives was no small thing. They were the king's sacred bounty, his currency with the gods, and a warlord's battle glory was measured by the number of living bodies brought back to the king in his war retinue.

On the eighth day of their journey, the sight of terraced mountains in the distance animated the warriors, and their raucous chatter could be heard up and down the length of the caravan. Ixchel raised her eyes and scanned the unfamiliar landscape. Gently sloping mountains rose from the jungle floor in terraced waves. In her heart, she was still hiding beneath the billowing skirt that was Tikal's rainforest canopy, and the image of giant earthen stairs in layers of green and yellow brought her hard into the moment. Tikal was now forever beyond her reach.

13

Lyla Cork

The return of the triumphant warlords sparked a frenzied celebration. As the procession of warriors and captives approached the city-center, the masses swarmed. The procession moved through the crowd like a fish swimming through mud, slowly making its way toward the king's palace. The crowd closed in around them, and a wave of nausea washed over Ixchel. They were calling for blood, and she could feel their mad energy on her skin, crawling and burning like fire ants.

Instinctively, she fought against her restraints, but the effort brought its share of pain. Over the course of her dark journey, the twine cuffs at her wrists had rubbed her skin raw. A film of tears made indistinct the jeering faces before her, drawing them together into a single lurching animal, grotesque and sodden. She lowered her head as she cried, unwilling to let the masses glory in her pain. With fierce determination, she gathered her memories about her, a shield to encircle her wounded heart—her mother's thick tumble of hair, black as a starless night; her little sister's ringing laughter, sweet as birdsongs at dawn; her twin brothers' endless antics, and her eldest brother's shining eyes, an exact copy of their father's, with long lashes and smiling corners.

Ixchel's heart broke anew as she thought about her family and what they must have suffered. Once the palace was surrounded and her lord father was killed, her lady mother and sister would've had no choice but to fly to the goddess Ixtab. If they'd been captured, they would've been sacrificed, and Caracol's king would have magnified himself twice over by offering two royal women to the gods. Death by suicide preserved their honor and left nothing for the invading king to take from them.

In her mind's eye, Ixchel saw her lady mother and sweet sister gathered within the blue walls of the sacred chamber. She could almost smell the clean, crisp scent of pom burning upon the altar of Heart of Sky.

But the sky god had forsaken her family, as he had forsaken her.

When the procession reached the base of the king's temple, a massive structure towering above the plaza in three broad levels, each more elaborately painted than the one below, the warlords, warriors, and captives made their way around its staunch perimeter until they were full rear, and Ixchel soon found herself mounting a long rise of shallow stairs. Tied as they were, waist to wrist, it was a challenging climb for the captives. If one stumbled, at least two more felt the hard bite of stone against their limbs.

Once inside the temple, the royal guards took charge of the captives, leading the procession toward the king's ceremonial chamber. Ixchel knew what was to come. Caracol's king would assess the captives. Most would live out their lives as slaves. A few prime specimens, chosen with care to please the gods, would be sacrificed during the Festival of Conquest.

Ten at a time, the captives were taken inside the chamber, a wide room adorned with murals in shades of red, yellow, and black. What Ixchel saw when she was led through the doorway brought a mountain of rage down upon her. The mural covering the eastern wall was still bright red, having not yet given over its vibrant pigment to the effects of time and sun, which would eventually turn the red hue from bright crimson to a muted red orange. Here, from floor to ceiling, the images and inscriptions described an alliance between Caracol and Calakmul.

That explains it, Ixchel thought bitterly. *They united with Calakmul and came at us like a serpent with twin heads!* Anger swelled inside her until her chest ached with it. She turned from the eastern wall, brought her gaze forward, and trained her eyes upon the king.

King Yajaw Te' K'inich II, known to his people as Lord Water, was perched upon a raised platform that extended from the far wall of the chamber, his body rigid beneath wood racks affixed to his torso. The racks served as support for his massive headdress of carved jade, spun cotton and quetzal plumes. The headdress was an explosion of blue, copper, green and gold, and it increased the king's height by two and a half feet.

As the captives were brought before him, Lord Water made his pronouncement for each—slave or sacrifice—with the royal indifference of a farmer selecting his produce for market. When Ixchel was placed before him, he did not ask her name, nor did he acknowledge her as her father's daughter. He simply declared, "She will honor us in sacrifice." He then eyed Ixchel as if expecting her to thank him for the honor.

She stood motionless, her face as blank as a stone. *He does not know me,* she realized, thankful she'd been humbly dressed on the day of her capture. *It is a small victory. My death shall be quick, and he shall gain little by it.*

The guards moved forward to guide Ixchel away.

15

"Wait," Lord Water declared, leering at Ixchel. "In two days, we celebrate our conquest. Let my brother Lord Itzamna have this woman until that time."

At this, the king's squat face seemed almost to smirk, and Ixchel would have let Seven Death himself bathe in her blood in exchange for an obsidian blade and five minutes alone with the traitor rat.

Ixchel turned her eyes from the king lest he glory in the anger burning there. The guards took her by her elbows, but she ground her heals into the stone floor, her body stiff with rage. One of the guards reached for her wrists and jerked the twine lead, causing her to stumble to the ground. Quickly, he tried to right her, but he was not quick enough. Lord Water approached the edge of the royal stage. His movements were slow and calculated, hampered by the weight of his massive headdress.

"Stop," he commanded in a monotone of measured restraint. With a flick of his finger, he beckoned the guard to come forward. When the guard knelt before him, he growled, "I have declared that this woman belongs to Lord Itzamna, yet you treat her like a scavenging coati."

Ixchel eyed the guard as she rose to her feet. He made no sound. His shoulders trembled.

"You dishonor my brother with your actions!" the king bellowed, his mouth a violent curl. Rage seized his features like a storm and all restraint fell away. The blood came full to his face until his splendid headdress appeared to be sitting atop a rotting cashew apple.

The guard bowed fiercely, a string of apologies tumbling from his lips.

Lord Water waved away the guard's apologies, as if swatting a fly. "The games commence in two days," he said. "You will play, and perhaps you can regain your honor on the ball court. Play fiercely, for if you fail, you will lie upon the altar, and reclaim your honor in death."

With a stern warning against mischief, Lord Water commanded the remaining guard to carry out his orders. The guard took Ixchel by the arm and led her through the corridors of the royal compound to the chamber of the king's brother. But when Itzamna appeared at his doorway, he would not allow them entrance to his chamber.

"Take this woman back to my lord brother," Itzamna said. "Tell him I will not force her into my bed, and that he should know better."

The guard refused to deliver the message and hurried away.

16

Itzamna sighed and turned to Ixchel. "What do they call you?"

"Hix Nik," she lied.

He cradled her wrists in his hands and examined her injuries. "I am Itzamna," he said as he gently loosened her bonds. "Come inside."

CHAPTER 3 - MITCH AND MANUEL

Cayo District, Belize
Present Day

MITCH HUDSON HIT THE BRAKES and a spray of limestone dust flew from the tires of his rented Suzuki. Just ahead, four men crouched in the middle of the jungle road. At the center of the group, a fifth man writhed in the dust. Mitch told himself to hightail it back the way he came. Something didn't feel right, but he couldn't leave an injured man stranded in the middle of nowhere, or back-a-bush, as the locals called the sparsely populated western jungles.

Mitch cut the engine and stepped out into the thick humidity. It was late January, but Belize heat thrived year-round. To his left and right, the long fingers of scrub grasses hemmed the margins of the road while the thin necks of saplings bobbed in the hot wind. Beyond this narrow line of lowland scrub, a towering rise of green bordered the road like the ramparts of a verdant keep, enclosing Mitch within merlons of mahogany, pine, and ceiba.

Mitch thought about his young patient Sena and her father, Manuel. They were expecting him for a follow-up visit less than half a mile ahead, and he hoped this wouldn't take long, hoped it wouldn't require a three-hour drive to the nearest hospital. Lifting his hand to shield his eyes from the afternoon sun, he approached the group. "Do you need assistance? I'm a doctor."

One of the men stepped forward. "Yes, gracias."

As Mitch knelt to examine the injured man, the first blow came, a fist to the lower back. Mitch arched against the pain and old instincts took over. He plowed into the man in front of him, reared back, and slammed his forehead into the bridge of the man's nose. The man howled beneath a shower of blood until Mitch landed a right hook that sent the man to the dirt, silent.

Two of the men scattered into the bush, and Mitch was left to deal with the remaining two. They came at him side by side. Mitch put his shoulder into the neck of the man on his right, grabbed the other by the throat, and threw his weight forward. They landed hard, Mitch on top. The guy on the bottom, who'd just absorbed 210 pissed-off pounds, lost consciousness on impact. The other guy squirmed like a worm on a hook, his neck caught on the end of Mitch's closed fist. Within seconds, Mitch squeezed the fight right out of him.

Mitch darted toward his vehicle. But the ambush wasn't over. At the sound of feet on gravel, he scanned the perimeter, never slowing. The two who'd fled had returned and they were coming at him head-on, one from each side of the Suzuki, like a V formation zeroing in on its point. Focusing his attention on the greater threat—the asshole on his right was now wielding a machete—Mitch charged, knocking the man off his feet. The machete spun out behind them and landed in the dust. Mitch scrambled for it, but a burst of wind sent dust roiling like a wave of hot ash. Half blind and off-balance, Mitch turned to face the last man and immediately took a blow to the gut from a makeshift bat. The choking pain brought him to his knees. The next sound he heard was a sickening thud as the blade of the machete sunk into his skull. The world pulsed around him like a beating heart, and his body was no longer his own. There was nothing but wild, ringing pain. For a moment, it seemed the earth itself was screaming, until Mitch realized the screams were coming from his own lips.

His eyelids slid shut. As he fell away from consciousness, a final thought slipped through the agony. The thought was not borne of fear or rage. It was something older, something Mitch had never learned to live with. It was guilt. He thought about his wife, and how he'd betrayed her.

***

Less than 200 meters westward, Manuel Cocom and his nineteen-year-old son, Evan, sat on folding chairs within the shade of their covered porch. Father and son were hiding from the heat and anticipating the arrival of Dr. Mitch Hudson when a wail of agony cut through the air.

"What was that?" Evan asked, his hand reflexively gripped the sliding blade he'd taken to wearing at his belt.

19

"Maybe one of the dogs," Manuel replied doubtfully. "Probably got hit on the road. I'll tell your mother we're going to check it out."

When Manuel returned, they left the porch, and together they ran to investigate. At the sound of raging voices in the distance, they stopped short. A hard left in the road and a wall of overgrown foliage afforded ample cover for the time being, but once they took the turn, they'd be face to face with whatever mess was on the other side. Abandoning the road, they sought cover in the high brush then picked their way forward until they found themselves just shy of the ambush. As they peered through the trees, they glimpsed Mitch's blue Suzuki. It was barely six feet in front of them. Then they saw Mitch curled on the ground on the far side of it, his bleeding head resting near the driver-side tire. He was surrounded by five men. Two of the men were unconscious, their faces bloodied. Another two were trying to revive their fallen companions. The fifth man was standing over Mitch, holding a watch and a wallet in one hand, a machete in the other. The weapon was a slipshod thing, a curved blade secured to a rough wooden handle by frayed twine. But when the man moved, the metal of the blade came alive in the sun, shimmering silver white.

The men were unnerved, arguing with each other. The fifth man raged and gestured toward the vehicle with trembling arms. In response, his companions loaded the unconscious pair into the Suzuki.

"Border raiders," Manuel whispered to Evan. His son had bloodied a few noses in his time, but this fight would be different. Manuel was confident in his own abilities; he'd earned his stripes the hard way, and he'd taught Evan how to handle himself in a fight, even a dirty one. He only hoped his son was ready.

Manuel held back, but only for a moment. If Mitch was badly wounded, the Suzuki was his lifeline. Manuel knew they had to act fast. Swooping forward like birds of prey, he and his son stormed the road.

The man on the far side darted away at the first sign of reinforcements. Evan chased him into the brush.

Manuel tore the machete from the fifth man's hand and chopped him with swift, brutal strokes, driving the weapon into the man's body as if felling a tree. As the man crumbled, his cries grew shrill then choking, until the death blow—a penetrating strike to the side of the neck—silenced his cries altogether.

The others escaped in Mitch's vehicle. As the Suzuki disappeared in a cloud of dust, Manuel scanned the perimeter for his son. Evan, wide-eyed and panting, his knife dripping, was making his way back through the scrub grass. A few paces later he was standing next to his father. Manuel dropped the machete and hugged his son. Then he knelt over Mitch's body. The moment he set eyes on Mitch's damaged head, Manuel knew exactly what he had to do, the only thing he could do. Just thinking about it kicked his fear level up to high alert, but he owed it to Mitch to try. "Lady Ixchel," he whispered, "we are coming to find you."

Manuel removed his shirt, tore it into strips, and bandaged Mitch's head. Then, methodically, he soaked a single strip in the blood of the fifth man. Carefully, he folded the bloodstained fabric in on itself and secured it beneath the leather strap of his belt. Resting Mitch's head upon his knees, Manuel spoke to his son as the boy crouched to retrieve Mitch's watch and wallet from the ground. "We must take him to the Sky Place."

The boy froze. "Have you done this before?"

"No, but I have seen it done, once by my father, and once by my grandmother. I know what is required. Run and get Carlita. Tell your mother what's happened, but don't breathe a word to Sena. And hurry back."

Evan ran to the house and returned quickly, bareback on Carlita, the old mare. He'd brought a fresh shirt for his father and two pouches of water. Mitch was still unconscious, his wound bleeding freely through the strips of cotton.

"Take his legs," Manuel said to Evan. They lifted Mitch onto Carlita. Manuel cradled Mitch's head, and Evan lead the horse northward. The Sky Place, a towering temple that crowned the ancient kingdom of Caracol, was almost a mile away. They struck out from the limestone road and made their way up a rough-cut path that shot straight through the jungle. As they walked, the hot white of day submitted to the cool violet of dusk. When they reached the temple, the real work began. Arms trembling, backs aching, they carried Mitch up the temple stairs. They entered the uppermost chamber of the Sky Place after dark. Evan fished his phone from his pocket and quickly illuminated the sacred chamber.

There, within the stone walls of the ancient temple, Manuel knelt beside Mitch. The gravity of the moment settled upon Manuel's shoulders like a silent storm. His breath went shallow; his heart pumped quick and wild.

He began to chant in the Yucatec dialect of his ancestors,

Lady Ixchel,
Mother Goddess,
may you hear, may you speak,
noble ancestor, noble provider,
thou guardian of the sky passage,
calling to thee among the clouds and light,
come out now, fly out now,
to the sky-earth,
the four sides, the four corners,
let there be sowing, let there be dawning,
may there be only light...."

As his voice filled the temple chamber, Manuel felt the pulse and pull of the upperworld. The air in the narrow room grew heavy. He retrieved the blood-soaked strip of cloth from beneath his belt, cradled it within Mitch's palms, and folded Mitch's hands over his chest. The ritual had begun, and Manuel prayed that on the other side of the long night ahead, Mitch would open his eyes.

CHAPTER 4 - MITCH

Houston, Texas
Eleven months later

IT WAS TWO DAYS UNTIL CHRISTMAS and the Galleria mall was crowded that evening, but Mitch barely noticed the chaos of holiday shoppers around him as he made his way to Tiffany's. He was distracted by the letter in his hand. It was from the man who saved his life in the wilderness of Belize almost one year ago, Manuel Cocom, the man Mitch hoped could perform another miracle.

Mitch quickened his pace and stuffed the letter inside his jacket pocket. Manuel had two bad answers for him. The first, Mitch would deal with later. The second lived right here in Houston, and like it or not, he would have to deal with her soon: Emily Stillman. Manuel's letter confirmed that Mitch needed Emily to save his wife, and since Emily would never come with him to Belize if she knew what was waiting for her there, something would have to be done.

Mitch felt guilty about his plans for Emily. He had loved her after all, in a way, as much as one can love a fantasy or a beautiful creature in a fairy tale. But his love for his wife, Maggie, was firm and true. It was the unshakable foundation of his life.

Mitch was tired of worrying; Christmas was approaching, and he wanted to feel lighthearted for a change, if only for a little while. He smiled as he walked through the silver and glass doors at Tiffany's and recalled how Maggie had lingered over a diamond necklace in the winter catalog the night before. As he'd watched her trace the outline of the necklace with her finger, he'd decided he was going to slip that blue box into her stocking on Christmas Eve. The price didn't concern him, for he had a point to make. Diamonds are timeless, and he would do anything—buy the whole store, barter his own life—for just a little more time with his wife.

He approached the display cases and scanned the suede interiors for his prize. There it was, practically greeting him at the door, eight flawless carats set in a curling vine of platinum. *Not much of a hunt*, Mitch thought. The necklace, abundant and self-assured, was poised on the elongated bust of a neckline and stood regally apart from the other offerings hesitantly gathered around it, as if they were aware of their inferior claims to beauty. Mitch rapped the glass softly with his fingertips and smiled down at the necklace. Two of the diamonds seemed to wink back up at him. "I'll take this one, right here," he said to the nearest salesperson without looking up.

"Yes, of course," replied a young woman, tall and lithe. She completed the sale, boxed and wrapped the necklace, then hooked a single delicate finger through the white chords on the blue shopping bag. She presented the item to Mitch with a smile befitting the price tag. Mitch collected his offering and, for a moment, felt the meager significance of it. He'd spent the second half of his marriage making up for the first, and now he needed to do so much more. He folded the bag around the box and closed his palm over it. For now, it was enough. He would just have to take things one at a time, first Christmas then Belize.

After his visit to Tiffany's, Mitch climbed into his Range Rover and headed home. It had been a long day. December was always a busy month for him. Whether it was the use-it-or-lose-it vacation days that tend to sink to the bottom of the fourth quarter, or the idea of starting the new year with a new face, he did not know, but his patient list always doubled around the holidays. He'd also cut his hours in half recently so he could spend more time with Maggie, which meant he had no downtime when he was at work. He'd started his day with a rhinoplasty and ended with a consult on a Brazilian butt lift. Everything in between was now a blur.

Bypassing Westheimer Road, which was always jammed in the evenings, Mitch jumped onto the Loop 610 access road, then exited onto San Felipe, which would take him straight home to River Oaks. As he drove, he thought about Manuel's letter. There was enough information in its pages for him to move forward with his plan to save Maggie. Lady Ixchel was the key. Mitch had known this all along. What he hadn't known,

24

until now, was that he needed Emily to reach her. As it turns out, you can't secure the aid of a 1400-year-old Maya princess turned goddess without getting your hands dirty.

When Mitch arrived home from the Galleria, he hid Maggie's gift in the butler's pantry and made his way to the living room where he expected to find Maggie either reading or watching TV. But the living room was dark; the tree wasn't even lit.

"Maggie," he called.

She didn't answer. What came instead was a loud SNAP then BANG from the direction of the master bedroom. Mitch hurried down the hall. He found Maggie in the master bathroom standing in front of his side of the sink. Her eyes were red, her makeup a streaked mess. "Are you okay?" he asked.

She glanced at him. "I'm fine," she replied. "I'm just making a few adjustments." She opened the cabinet door beneath his side of the sink. The child-safety lock on the door gave less than an inch. She pressed the tab, swung open the door, and grabbed the plastic latch. With a quick twist, she snapped the latch off the door, leaving behind a plastic cleft and two screws that seemed almost to sneer at her. She scowled down at them and kicked the cabinet shut. As she tossed the latch into the trash, she said, "You're just in time. That was the last one. The kitchen took forever."

She looked exhausted. Her sorrow filled the room like a tempestuous cloud, and his heart ached for her. Ever since her oncologist served them the last, and final, course of bad news two months earlier, she'd spent each day vacillating between despair and rage. Mitch couldn't stand it. He wanted to drive a wedge of hope into the machinery of her misery and break the downward cycle before it got anywhere near full throttle. But all he could do was bide his time and offer her a shoulder to cry on, a chest to pound her fists upon.

"I'm fine," Maggie insisted and walked over to him. "Don't look at me like that. I know I'm never going to have children. I'm never going to need child-safety latches. I've accepted this fact. And I don't need those nasty little buggers reminding me of it every time I reach for the damn toothpaste." She dabbed at her eyes with her fingertips, wiped the snot from her nose. "I must look terrible," she said.

Mitch wrapped his arms around her. "You look gorgeous, as always," he whispered.

"I look like E.T.," she countered. "No breasts, bony limbs, and a potbelly."

"A supermodel with a little beer belly." He rubbed her shoulders, then cradled her damp face in his palms. "And I love you just the way you are."

"I love you too." She smiled slightly, the storm of despair quelled for now.

While Maggie freshened up, Mitch collected her gift from the butler's pantry and brought it to the living room. The Tiffany's box was too big for her stocking, so he lit the Christmas tree and placed the box beneath the tree's twinkling boughs. Each ornament on the tree was a mini treasure. Maggie had been collecting ornaments since childhood, and she carried the tradition into their new life together. Their most recent acquisition, a pink ribbon of blown glass purchased during her painfully brief remission, caught Mitch's eye. He touched it gently. Time was folding in on him, and he prayed this Christmas with Maggie would not be the last.

CHAPTER 5 - EMILY AND HUNTER

AT NINE IN THE MORNING on Christmas Eve, Emily Stillman trudged into her office and set her satchel on her desk. Her office smelled vaguely of wasabi, and she scanned the room until she spotted last night's supper on the windowsill. After she walked her leftovers to the kitchen trash, she settled behind her desk and opened Outlook, pulling up her To Do list.

"Slim pickings," she muttered. She'd already burned through most of her workload thanks to a recent string of late-night hauls. "This isn't enough." She frowned at her desktop. "I jumped the gun." What she wanted was to be buried in work, swamped to the point that it was physically impossible for her to think about the holidays. But it wasn't even Christmas yet. She'd never make it to New Year's Day.

"Damn you, Mitch," she whispered for the fifth time that morning. She almost chuckled. If my life was a song, "Damn you, Mitch," would be the chorus.

She scanned the remaining items and estimated about twenty hours of work, give or take. Twenty hours wasn't much. Still, twenty plus the time she'd already logged that month would add up to a heck of a lot of hours. The end of the year meant the end of the billing cycle, and Emily knew that most of the other associates were annoyed with her for setting the bar so high this year. She cringed. She hated to upset anyone, and she felt guilty about the added pressure she'd created. But she hadn't done it on purpose. She just needed a little something to look forward to each day, and work was better than nothing. At least she'd be getting a nice bonus come January, and maybe that was reason enough to wish away the rest of December.

Emily had just finished reading through the first few emails of the day when her secretary buzzed her with a call on line one. "Who is it?" she asked.

"Plaintiff's counsel on the Del/Mar case."

"Okay, put her through." Emily picked up the line. "How can I help you, Judy?"

"Hi Emily, I just wanted to see about getting an extension on our expert deadline. You know how it is with the holidays; I just haven't been able to get it nailed down yet. And I'm going on vacation tomorrow. Can we do mid-January?"

"Look, Judy, you know my client is pushing to get this thing dismissed, and the sooner we hear what your expert has to say—or doesn't have to say—the better. I'm going to need you to have the report ready for me by the first week in January at the latest. And I'll need an extension on our deadline as well."

Judy sighed with relief. "Thanks, Emily. I appreciate your helping me out on this one. I can make the new deadlines work. I'll send the Rule 11 right over. Can you get it back to me by close of business today?"

"That shouldn't be a problem," Emily replied. "Enjoy your vacation."

Emily rolled her eyes as she hung up the phone. *Of course, Judy's taking a Christmas vacation*, Emily mused. Stout, bustling Judy and her family of four would be spinning in teacups at Disneyland or shuffling down a bunny hill in Colorado; this was paradise compared to Emily's plans, which would undoubtedly include watching her mother and newly minted stepfather feed each other three-bean casserole in their remodeled, eat-in kitchen.

A real vacation would be nice, Emily thought. *Some place tropical, some place where stress meant choosing between a Margarita and a Mojito.* She drummed her fingers on her desk and tried to refocus her thoughts on work. But her mind was a sieve that morning and work fell right through the holes. What remained in the round belly of her consciousness was everything else. Her life and what it wasn't.

These days she hated interim moments, slivers of time between one focused thought and another. Interim moments were treacherous because she never knew when memories of Mitch would slither in and poison her thoughts.

And there they were. Not memories this time. A question asked and never answered: *Why her and not me?* Emily often pictured them together; she couldn't help it. Mitch and the woman he preferred: Maggie, his wife. Almost a year had passed since the day Mitch broke Emily's heart by ending their three-month affair with a ten-second phone call. But Emily couldn't move on. She still thought about Mitch constantly.

Even after all this time, Emily couldn't understand what had happened. A happily married man doesn't open doors for you, take you dancing, buy you flowers. A happily married man doesn't make promises like that....

Shake it off, Emily, shake it off, she told herself. Her motivation had dwindled to nothing. What she needed was a little interoffice field trip, so she headed down the hall to Hunter Marlow's office. Hunter had started working at the firm six months after Emily, and they'd become close during the last two and a half years. He had a kind of casual confidence that Emily admired, and there was something intriguing about him just below the surface, a latent energy, that Emily found appealing.

She had once failed to resist his many charms. And, in one of her more vulnerable moments in the months following her breakup with Mitch, she'd kissed him. To this day, she couldn't say exactly why she'd done it—too much wine, too many nights coming home to dark, empty rooms. Nothing had ever come of it, and sometimes Emily wondered if she'd imagined the whole thing. But too much time had passed to broach the issue. She couldn't very well come out and say, "Hey Hunter, remember the time you kissed me and then pretended like it never happened? What was the deal with that?" He was, after all, her friend. He listened. He encouraged. She didn't want their friendship to change, but she hoped that someday Hunter would give her a clue as to why their nascent relationship fizzled out faster than a sparkler in a downpour.

As she approached Hunter's office, she noticed he was hunched over his keyboard and clutching his mouse like a lifeline. She studied his face as she drew closer. It had always been difficult for her to predict Hunter's moods. And, as time passed, he'd become nearly impossible to anticipate. He seemed to be transforming into a full-fledged surly person. *Maybe it's the weather this time,* she thought. *Too much gray sky can make anyone crabby.* Hunter looked more stressed than usual, and Emily briefly considered walking by with just a wave. But she stopped at his open door instead.

"What are you still doing here?" he asked when Emily appeared in his doorway.

"I've got some work to finish up." She walked over to one of the chairs in front of his desk and sat down.

"Yeah, sure you do. I know you've got your hours already. Why don't you take a vacation or something? If I didn't have this Motion to Dismiss hanging over me, I'd be out of here like everyone else."

"What, and leave all this? I wouldn't know what to do with myself. Besides, billable hours are like potato chips ... you can't have just one." Emily wasn't expecting outright laughter, but she'd hoped Hunter would at least crack a smile. He didn't. Instead, he continued sliding his mouse in short strokes with one hand and started rummaging through the papers on his desk with the other. Hunter generally responded to Emily's jokes (the good ones and the silly ones) with more enthusiasm, and she wondered what was bothering him, but decided not to ask. She hated talking about anything personal at the office; people were constantly skulking around the halls, and sensitive conversations always had a way of magically attracting the wrong people into earshot.

Glancing up from his desk, Hunter asked, "Hey, did you hear about Bill's new medical client and the blood drive? I paid my visit to the blood mobile this morning. It wasn't that bad."

"Yes, I heard about it, and I think it's ridiculous. I can't believe Bill would agree to something like that."

"Apparently, it's for a good cause. And the client was adamant about getting everyone's participation."

"I don't care. I hate needles. I'd rather get fired."

"You might," Hunter warned her. "Rumor has it the client's agreed to prepay for 2000 hours if he gets full participation for the blood drive. Otherwise, it's just the standard retainer."

"That's unethical," Emily insisted. "I'm not doing it."

"It's your call, but I think you're going to regret that decision."

Emily ignored him. She leaned forward, swiped a pen from his desk, and rolled it between her palms. A moment later, she asked, "Do you need help with your motion? I can go through the expert reports."

"No, I'm almost finished," he replied. "But thanks anyway. Besides, I need to cram at least another twenty hours in before January to seal the deal on my bonus. I'm not letting that sucker get away from me after the year I've had."

***

Hunter forced a laugh. He always tried to be lighthearted about work, but he hated the billable hours race so much he couldn't fake it, and he resented Emily a little for constantly out-billing everyone. Which he knew was unfair. Emily always found time to help him when he was running behind, and she usually gave him whatever easy billables she could spare.

He looked at Emily. She'd put on a little weight. *Good,* he thought. She looked better with some weight on her. At least it made her somewhat recognizable as a woman beneath her figure-killing, double-breasted suits. He didn't blame her. If she didn't encase her ample chest in two layers of worsted wool, nobody would ever look her in the eyes. *But does she have to wear pants 99 percent of the time? It really is a shame to keep those great legs under wraps....*

"....at your apartment tomorrow night ... Hunter, are you listening to me?" Emily's voice floated through Hunter's thoughts, and he realized he was staring at the place where the ends of her dark hair rested on the fullest part of her chest. And he hadn't heard a word she'd said.

"What?" he asked. His eyes focused on her face at last. He smiled. Although she didn't know it, he always thought of her as "my Emily". If she ever found out, he knew she'd accuse him of Laches (sitting on his hands; failing to state his claim within a reasonable time). And she would be right. For the time being, there was no way around it. But he was planning to change all that, very soon.

"Why weren't you listening to me?" she half-scolded, half-pouted. "I was asking you about your party tomorrow night."

"You're coming, right?" he asked eagerly. "The food is going to be incredible. I'm preparing everything myself." As he talked about his party, Hunter felt a surge of anticipation, and he could tell from Emily's smile that she was happy to see the change in his demeanor.

"Yes, I heard," she lilted and raised an eyebrow at him. "Very impressive. Of course, I'm coming." She began walking toward the door. "Since you seem to be preoccupied with work, I'll let you get back to it. I'll see you tomorrow night. Nine o'clock, right?"

"Yeah, nine o'clock." Hunter threw Emily a quick wave and wrapped his hand around the mouse again. As soon as she was gone, he regretted not being open with her about the changes he had in store. *Better not to rush,* he told himself, feeling a small measure of consolation. *Besides, timing is everything.*

CHAPTER 6 - MAGGIE AND MITCH

MAGGIE STARED AT MITCH as the morning sun brightened the taupe walls of their kitchen. It was Christmas day. She'd opened the necklace and was wearing it with her nightgown as they enjoyed cinnamon rolls, omelets, and gingerbread spice tea at the breakfast table.

She rubbed her shoulder. She was shocked at how tired she felt all the time, how much of a struggle it was to keep the constant pain from wearing her down to nothing. At least the chemo and radiation were over for good. It was a dire boon. It meant her doctors had given up on her, but it also meant she could cook and eat again without constant nausea.

Hard as it was, she was determined to make the most of the months that remained. It was one thing to die; it was another thing entirely to wither away while still alive. *That,* she thought, *would be too painful to endure.* Now that time was an angry sliver, she felt a desperate hunger for everything around her—the sun, the sky, the damp soil in the back yard. She wanted to eat the earth, consume it, wrap her arms around it, and somehow hold on.

It is a peculiar kind of torture, she thought, *to be forced to forsake your life while you are still living it.* Sometimes she'd let the melancholy seep into her heart until she was saturated with it. On those occasions, she pictured all her hopes and dreams scampering out into the darkness, searching the city to seek out her grave, settling in, waiting for her. To Mitch she offered a small smile. "How are the omelets?"

"Delicious," he replied. "And the cinnamon rolls are out of this world. You've outdone yourself." Mitch finished his breakfast, walked his plate and fork to the dishwasher, and came back over to her. He took the teacup from her hand and placed it on the counter. She wrapped her arms around his waist and pressed her weight against him. All she wanted was more of this, more time together. But it was the cruelest kind of Catch-22. She couldn't savor Mitch's embrace without simultaneously anticipating the loss of him.

There is no Heaven bright enough to console me, she thought bitterly. She was terrified of death, and she was afraid she would go mad from the expectation of it. What she needed was a little hope, something to push the darkness out of her mind and allow her to appreciate the rest of her life, short as it was. Mitch pressed his cheek against the top of her head and hugged her tightly. When he released her from their long embrace, she picked up her cup and watched as he checked the kitchen clock.

"What time are we heading over to your parents' place?" he asked.

"They're serving lunch at one o'clock."

Mitch eyed the clock, an iron monstrosity they'd picked up at an art fair in Beeville. It was almost eleven. "I'm going to grab a shower."

"Okay," she said. Then added, "I think I'll get dressed and head over a little early. Maybe I can help my mom with the preparations."

"Really?" Mitch asked warmly before planting a kiss on Maggie's forehead. "They have a chef and a housekeeper, and your mother is the queen of entertaining. Wouldn't you rather stay here and get some rest? It's going to be a long day."

Maggie shook her head. "I want to be included. I don't want to miss out on anything."

"Alright," Mitch conceded. "I'll come with you. Meet me at the front door in twenty."

Maggie followed Mitch down the hallway to their bedroom, stopping at the walk-in closet while he headed for the bathroom. As she searched the racks of clothes for her new red dress, she smiled as she thought about spending Christmas day with her family.

***

Mitch locked the bathroom door behind him and fished his cell phone from his pocket. He caught Bill Walters, the managing partner at Emily's firm, on his way home from church.

"Sorry to bother you on Christmas Day, Bill, but I was just wondering if you'd made any progress on the blood drive?"

"Well," Bill paused. "Truth be told Dr. Hudson, we got all but two. And I'm afraid that's as good as it's going to get."

"Which two?"

"I don't see why it matters?"

"We're talking about an awful lot of money here, and perhaps we can still make a deal beyond the standard retainer. But I need you to tell me who's missing."

"Don Eldridge and Emily Stillman," Bill said.

Mitch sighed. "I'm sorry to hear that. It's just the standard retainer then, nothing more. I appreciate the effort. Believe me, it was for a good cause. Merry Christmas." Mitch shook his head as he hung up the phone. He'd gone to a lot of trouble and put a huge chunk of money on the line with the charity blood drive. But Emily hadn't fallen for it, which meant he had to physically get his hands on her. His stomach churned. He never thought he would find himself here, on the precipice of evil.

"I don't have a choice," he whispered, like he always did, when the reality of his plan twisted like a knife in his gut. "I don't have a choice."

Mitch let the shower steam up a bit before stepping inside. He flipped open the cap on the bodywash and poured a generous portion into his palm. The scent of eucalyptus filled the shower stall, a cavernous retreat constructed of reclaimed Italian marble and brushed nickel. As he lathered his hair, Mitch traced the contours of the scar, a thin crescent high above his ear, which once claimed over five inches of space along the side of his head. It was now only a shadow of itself. Once a thick rope of knots, his scar had faded to almost nothing in less than a year. There was no way to explain it. He knew his friends and family assumed he'd had it removed, which annoyed him to no end, along with the fact that they kept insisting he'd had work done, which he hadn't. Irritating as it was, he couldn't fault them for their mistaken assumptions. Although the stress of Maggie's illness was overwhelming, his face had nothing to show for it, not a furrow, not a line. Even his hair had stopped turning grey. It was as mystifying as it was frustrating. Each time he spoke to Manuel, he pressed him for answers. But Manuel was as tight-lipped as a filler addict.

Mitch stepped from the shower and toweled off. Whenever he thought about Belize and the secrets that lay hidden there, adrenaline surged through him until his skin bristled. Almost a year earlier, Belize made him a better man. What he experienced at the Sky Place, as he found himself suspended between life and death, changed him beyond anything he could have imagined. Lady Ixchel saved him that day. He still saw her in his dreams.

Mitch had faith in his dreams, and he had faith in himself. If there was one thing he knew how to do, it was turn things around for the better. He was raised in Gary, Indiana, the youngest of four brothers. His father put in long days at the steel mill, grabbing whatever overtime he could, but there was never enough. The boys learned early not to complain. Learned by example from a blue-eyed farm boy all grown up, who somehow found the gumption to dance his wife across the living room floor even after double shifts at the mill. Their mother would dust off the apron she wore like a uniform and smile as she hummed in time with the radio.

There was always love, but there was also despair. Winters were hard. In the summertime, the boys could scrounge a little fun, but winter brought nothing but cold and envy. In the early hours of morning, when night still pressed itself upon the day, Mitch would half walk, half run to the bus stop, the bitter wind curling like frigid cuffs around his wrists and ankles. By the time his older brothers' threadbare, hand-me-down clothes found their way to him, they were always too short for his long limbs.

Mitch learned early how to fight. It was the only way to keep what little money he had in his pockets. And the thing he valued most those days was money. He saw it as a lifeline, and he was determined to use it to pull himself out of Gary, Indiana. His older brothers had done fine for themselves. Their father was strict about grades, and books were the one thing their mother was willing to spend money on. But Mitch wanted to be more than fine, and by the time he enrolled at college, he knew exactly how to get there. He was 35 when he finished his plastic surgery fellowship. He set up shop in Houston, Texas, determined never to suffer through another hard winter.

A year later, Mitch met Maggie at a silent auction when they both bid on a piece of art by Natalya Romanovsky. The painting, an oil-on-canvas titled Home, was a color-blocked jubilee. Apples in shades of ruby, sapphire, and emerald were gathered center right—red delicious resting on a ledge of blue, granny smith falling through amber. In the center of the painting, a window broke through the blocks of color to lend a view of a summer sky and smokestack, a fat apple in place of the chimney.

Mitch made sure he won the painting then finagled Maggie's address from the host of the silent auction and had the painting delivered to her. When she called to thank him, he asked her out. She accepted. A year later, when they bought their first home together as Mr. and Mrs. Hudson, they hung the Romanovsky above the fireplace in their living room.

The first year of their marriage was perfection. But Mitch had been too vain and foolish to stay the course. Emily had worshiped him in a way Maggie never did, never should. And back then, he wanted very much to be worshipped. But that changed when he returned from Belize. He'd confessed and made amends. The real miracle was that Maggie had been generous enough to forgive him. He would be eternally grateful for that blessing.

And now he was planning to invite the one person Maggie despised back into their lives. He hated the thought of it. But losing Maggie would be too much to bear. When he thought about the long, blank years of loneliness that might lay ahead, day upon day, month upon month, with nothing to salve the biting pain, his mind lurched for any sliver of hope, any possible solution.

There was only one solution. After Christmas, he would pay a visit to Emily Stillman, and he would have to play his hand with precision or there would be nothing left to hope for.

CHAPTER 7 - IXCHEL

Caracol
Maya Lowlands
Mesoamerica
A.D. 562

ITZAMNA'S CHAMBER was comprised of two rooms. The entryway opened into a large living area, the floor of which was strewn with braided mats, screenfold books, and brush pens. Behind the living area was a small bedchamber with a raised surface for sleeping.

Itzamna collected the books and pens from the floor, placed them in a corner of the room, and gathered the mats together to form a seat for Ixchel. "Rest here," he told her and walked into his bedchamber. He returned holding a ceramic bowl, a small flint blade, and two strips of cotton cloth. He cut the twine from her wrists, treated her skin with salve from the bowl, and wrapped her wrists with the lengths of cotton.

Ixchel could feel the warmth of the day ebbing from the stone floor beneath her. Beyond the white road, below the whispering canopy, Tikal lay vanquished. Her lord father and lady mother were gone, as was her younger sister and her twin brothers. She had no idea if her eldest brother, Lord Red Hawk, was still alive or if he was also a prisoner.

"Your feet," Itzamna said. "They need tending."

Ixchel stretched her legs out in front of her and Itzamna removed her sandals. The soles of her feet were blistered and bloody, and she flinched from his touch.

"I'm sorry," he said. "But I must clean your wounds, or they will fester."

She nodded, and he cleaned her feet gently before wrapping them with clean cotton strips.

"You are tired," he said. "You have journeyed far these days past."

"Yes," she whispered. Exhausted, heartbroken, and homesick, she began to cry. Itzamna touched her shoulder, tried to comfort her, but she turned away, her sobs growing fierce and choking. He stepped away and let her cry.

When her sobs gave way to small shudders, he gave her a cloth to dry her face and water to drink. She gulped every drop from the clay cup, and Itzamna filled it three times before she was satisfied.

"Are you hungry?" he asked. "I can bring you something to eat."

"Yes," she answered weakly.

As soon as he was gone, Ixchel darted for the doorway. Silently, she slid aside the thatch door and peered out into the hall. A guard paced the floor, and Ixchel retreated into the chamber to await the food. Her stomach was a hard knot and she found herself growing wearier with each passing moment. They had journeyed over 50 miles. The pathway of the dead sun had marked their footsteps. Ever forward they had trudged until it seemed to Ixchel they might walk past the fourth corner and fall away from the earth altogether. For five days they'd tracked the path of the dead sun before turning eastward to follow the sun reborn.

And now she was at Caracol, bound to another man she did not love. *At least he is kind*, she consoled herself. *And our time together shall be short, for in two days I shall be with my family in the upperworld, and he shall be nothing more than a memory.*

Itzamna returned with bowls of cassava bread, basted deer, and kakaw with honey on a wooden platter. He set the food in front of Ixchel. She scooped the shredded meat up with a wedge of the thick, crisp bread and took several large bites, gulping the kakaw as she chewed. But she soon found she did not have the stomach to finish the meal. Her eyelids grew heavy, and she felt as though she might collapse into sleep as she chewed.

"I am so tired," she said. "Can I sleep here, on these mats?"

Itzamna led her to his bedchamber and gestured toward his bed, a raised stone rectangle affixed to the wall and covered with thatch and cotton batting. Ixchel began to panic, fearful that his declaration to the royal guard had been a lie. Then he said, "You can sleep here. I will not disturb you. I will remain in the forward room."

Ixchel thanked him and climbed into the bed. Her limbs aching, her heart heavy, she fell asleep as soon as she placed her head upon the cotton batting of the bed.

Ixchel awoke the following morning to find Itzamna asleep on the gathered floor mats in the main room. Carefully, she made her way around him and eased open the door. The guard still paced the hall.

"Kinich Ahau be damned," she cursed, and closed the door. Itzamna stirred, began to snore, but did not wake. Ixchel walked past him and sat in the corner next to a pair of screenfold books. Sitting cross-legged on the floor, she cradled the nearest of the books within her lap and gently turned the pages. The inscriptions told the story of the father of the Hero Twins, One Hunahpu, a celestial being who became a god.

The Hero Twins were known throughout Tikal, and Ixchel was no stranger to stories of their battles with the lords of the underworld. This story detailed the exploits of their father, however, and it was altogether different. Intrigued, she read on. But Itzamna remained asleep only a few more minutes. When he began to wake, she closed the book, having barely scratched the surface of the tale.

Itzamna reapplied the medicine to Ixchel's wrists and feet, then left the chamber to see about breakfast. He returned quickly with two bowls of corn tamales and roasted guava, and two cups of vanilla bean tea.

Now that she was rested, Ixchel's appetite returned, and she ate greedily. When Itzamna noticed her empty bowl, he handed over his. After a moment's consideration, she took it gratefully, and finished it all.

Clearing the empty bowls from the floor, Itzamna placed them near the doorway, and returned to the center of the room where he opened one of his books.

"You are a scribe," said Ixchel, her fear and anger forgotten for a moment. "I have also studied the sacred books."

"Yes, I have been following this course of study for almost two short cycles now. It is demanding work."

"It is," Ixchel agreed, her mind filling with memories of her home life.

"I saw you reading my books earlier," Itzamna said with the hint of a question in his voice.

"I did not mean to intrude," she replied.

"I am not upset. But I am curious to know what you thought of my work, for it was not my first calling. I once studied the sacred rites of the daykeepers. I learned many great things from my holy master, and I performed several ritual offerings to Yum Kaax. But I turned away from that path the day they asked me to drain the blood of a man as an offering to Chac. I could not make my hands cause the death of the man who stood before me. I could not waste his life, for I do not believe mortal sacrifice is the design or desire of the gods. A blood sacrifice must be offered, of course, but death is not always required."

As he spoke these words, Itzamna looked intently at Ixchel, and she could tell he was trying to divine her thoughts. "I hope you do not think I am weak," he continued. "I know there are times when a man must kill to defend his home and his family. And I understand the gods would not bestow their kindness upon us if we did not demonstrate our devotion with proper offerings, blood offerings, but there is no need to destroy the body and end a life. I do not believe the gods, who took such care to fashion human beings into living flesh, would wish or yearn for human destruction."

Ixchel shook her head, and the ebony curtain of her hair fell back, revealing wide dark eyes. "I do not think you are weak. In fact, I agree with you," she said. What she did not say, however, was the one thing she wanted most to say—the words rising and falling inside her chest with every breath—that she had no wish to honor the gods with her own death.

"I am relieved you feel this way," he said, the beginnings of a smile rising at the corners of his lips. "Not many would agree with, or even understand, my way of thinking."

"You must have at least one ally," Ixchel said. "Surely the woman to whom you are promised has adopted your thoughts and your way of thinking."

A flush of red mottled his cheeks. "I am no longer promised."

Ixchel lowered her eyes. She wasn't sure if he was embarrassed or heartbroken.

Itzamna closed the question immediately. Awkwardly, he explained that he had recently been passed over by his matchmate. The girl had made clear her preference for Itzamna's cousin, and the girl's father had pursued the connubial exchange. "I agreed to release her from our engagement," he said. "My cousin is a warlord, battle-worn and unforgiving. We are as different as a parrot and an ocelot. If she could rest her heart in his hands, she could find no happiness in mine."

Ixchel could divine the bitterness in his heart, and she was sorry for it, but she could find no words to fill the silence that suddenly made the room feel cavernous.

When she did not respond, he spoke again, the warmth returning to his voice, "I learned the truth about One Hunahpu not long ago."

"He is the patron of scribes," she interjected. "Did you know that?"

"Yes. I was told this by my uncle when I first began my studies. On that day, my uncle gave me a whistle; upon it is carved the face of One Hunahpu. Would you like to see it?"

"Yes, I would."

Itzamna retrieved the ceramic whistle from beneath his shirt. It was secured to a twine necklace, and Ixchel inched closer to admire the detailed carvings on the small object. The carvings were finely done, like etchings on a sparrow's egg, and the whistle was painted deep red.

She smiled. "The whistle is beautiful. You must be very dear to your uncle. But you were telling me a story about the father of the Hero Twins, please go on."

He slipped the whistle beneath his shirt and said, "The World Tree was the work of One Hunahpu in his incarnation as the maize god. Standing at the center of the sky-earth, he fertilized the soil with his blood, causing maize to spring. The maize grew into a stout tree, doubling and redoubling in size until its branches reached the upperworld and its roots descended into the underworld. This is the World Tree, which stands at the center of the sky-earth."

"I have never heard that story," Ixchel countered, "I have always known that the World Tree was born from a conversation between Heart of Sky and Heart of Earth. Hurricane came down to meet Sovereign Plumed Serpent, and their words combined to create all life in this world, including the World Tree."

"Then I have opened your eyes to the truth," Itzamna said with a smile.

"You have opened my eyes only to your truth," she replied. "But I am happy to have heard it just the same."

"Heart of Sky joined with Heart of Earth to create life from the darkness. That truth is clear as dawn, but it was One Hunahpu who created the World Tree," Itzamna said as he placed his hands upon the pages of his book. "Heart of Sky is a powerful god. He is the bringer of life; he can even bring life to the dead. Within the Council Books, you will find many stories of death and rebirth. I have studied these stories carefully, and I believe I am close to understanding the secrets hidden within the texts."

"That is fascinating," Ixchel said.

"You must continue to read and study. There is much more …." Itzamna paused. "I'm sorry, I wasn't thinking."

Ixchel lowered her eyes to the floor and straightened the hem of her skirt. "My education was coming to an end anyway," she confessed. "The cause would have been marriage not death, although before this war I could hardly tell the difference between the two. My cousin, a warlord to whom I was betrothed, barred me from my studies. He was determined to transform me into a warlord's wife, and I was determined to have none of it. I believe my cousin is much like your brother, and I could never love such a man. For him, there is only one way, the warlord's way, and a warlord's wife has only one role." Covering her face with her hands, she continued mournfully, "On the morning of the invasion, I pleaded with my lord father to call off the wedding, and I ran fuming from the palace when he refused. I was headstrong and selfish. The last words I spoke to my dear father were words of anger. It is my deepest regret."

She paused. Itzamna's gaze was fixed upon her face, a mixture of sadness and concern within his deep brown eyes. Amid all this misery, he somehow made her feel a little better. He listened to her with compassion and empathy. No other man had ever been so attentive to her. No other person, really, except her lady mother, had ever taken such good care of her. She was overcome with the desire to tell him everything, but she held back, revealing instead a single secret. "I prayed desperately to Kinich Ahau," she whispered coarsely, "begging him to change my fate and free me from the bonds of marriage. And now it has been done in the cruelest possible way. I only wish I could have it all back again. I would have celebrated my wedding day, surrounded by my loving family, at the end of the Tzolk'in cycle, had I not found myself here." As she spoke the last few words, her voice cracked, and her eyes flooded with tears. "Your wretched brother and the snake king of Calakmul, have torn my family apart," she sobbed. "I pray they meet the same fate before long. May Kimi take their hearts!" Her hands curled into angry fists, and she hugged them to her chest as she cried.

Itzamna frowned but said nothing.

Ixchel uncurled her legs and stood to walk the room. After a few paces, she dried her eyes and turned to him. "I am sorry I spoke badly of your brother. You cherish him, of course, because he is your family. But I can never see him as you do. He is the one who destroyed my home and murdered *my* family. And tomorrow he will close the circle when he spills my blood to honor Buluk Chabtan."

Itzamna walked over to her. "I am sorry for your family, and I am sorry for this war," he said. "In truth, my lord brother had no choice. Tikal abandoned us, and our kingdom was vulnerable. Lord Sky Witness offered my lord brother a place within the Calakmul dynasty. Lord Sky Witness is a power-hungry king, to be sure, but he was our only option. We tried to realign with Tikal. My uncle traveled there with tokens of allegiance, but Lord Double Bird took his life without ceremony. My family was devasted by the loss, and we were desperate to protect our kingdom. Calakmul set their terms. Joining them in war was the price for our protection by the snake kingdom." He paused, then added softly, "I know this meager explanation will not bring you any comfort, but I hope it will help you understand why we find ourselves here. I am truly sorry you have been caught in this web of war and blood."

There was genuine anguish in his voice, and Ixchel blinked back another bout of tears. "I am not afraid," she said. "Soon I will lie upon the altar and honor the gods in sacrifice. Then I will fly to the upperworld where I will find myself in the arms of my lady mother, and I will see all my dear family again." She turned toward him to show him there was no fear behind her eyes. He closed the space between them and drew her close. She did not pull away. In her heart there was a deep sorrow, and she welcomed this small comfort. Strange as it was, she felt she could trust this man she hardly knew.

What she wanted most before she died was news of her eldest brother. But she dared not test her newfound trust, not yet. If she started asking questions about the royal family, he would surely be suspicious. And she had no desire to bleed long upon the altar, simply because she was the flesh and blood of a king.

CHAPTER 8 - EMILY AND HUNTER

Houston, Texas
Present Day

EMILY ARRIVED ALMOST THIRTY MINUTES LATE to Hunter's party. She hated being late, but the delay could not be avoided. While searching her closet for her sequined cardigan, she'd come across a pair of strappy wedge sandals that rivaled her new platform slingbacks. It had been quite a showdown, but in the end, it was the slingbacks that clicked their way down the sidewalk toward Hunter's Christmas shindig.

Emily climbed the short flight of stairs at the entrance to Hunter's apartment complex and walked into the main lobby. After signing in with the doorman, she headed to the elevator.

When the elevator doors opened on the eleventh floor, she made her way down the hallway and knocked on Hunter's door, but there was no answer. She knocked again and pressed her ear to the door. The low hum of music reverberated through the door, followed by a muted clanking sound. The doorknob jiggled a few times, and seconds later, Hunter greeted her with a smile. He was holding a spatula in one hand and a jingle-bells dishtowel in the other. On the floor at his feet was a smattering of items: a pewter platter, drink stirs, and a corkscrew.

"Oops." Emily giggled and knelt to collect the items. She placed the stirs and the corkscrew onto the platter and walked them into the kitchen.

"Thanks," Hunter said as he followed her into the kitchen. "My attempt at multitasking failed miserably."

"No worries," she said, "you can make it up to me with a glass of wine."

"Now that I can handle. Red or white?"

"Red, please."

"I've got a Merlot and a Cabernet open, but I can open a bottle of Shiraz if you prefer...."

"Merlot would be perfect."

Hunter crossed the kitchen and pulled a wineglass from an upper cabinet, grabbed the bottle of Merlot, and walked toward Emily as he poured. "I hope you're hungry. I've got Christmas cheer on a platter—or ten—out in the dining room. All of it is homemade and none of it is good for you."

"Excellent," she said. "I'm starving. Are there plates in the dining room or should I grab one from here?" She stood on her tiptoes and tried to see through to the dining room, but her view was obscured by three matching pots of poinsettias adorning the counter.

"I've got plates out there." Hunter nodded in the direction of the dining room. "Go ahead and fix yourself something. I've still got a few things to finish up in here. I'll be out in a minute or two...." After a brief pause, he added, "Actually ... come to think of it ... while you're here, there's something I've been meaning to...." He stopped short.

"What is it? What's up?"

"Never mind, you're hungry. Go ahead and eat. I'll tell you later."

"Okay, but don't forget." Emily grabbed her glass of Merlot and headed for the buffet. The table was loaded with a bevy of Christmas treats: sliced honey ham and roasted turkey, fresh-baked rolls with thyme butter, cranberry relish, southern dressing with gravy, smashed potatoes, poached pears, pecan and mincemeat pies, and gingerbread cookies.

Setting her wineglass on a small width of space on the crowded table, Emily grabbed a plate and made a sandwich with one of the rolls, the cranberry relish, and a few slices of honey ham. She immediately realized there was no way she could carry her wineglass and the plate while eating her sandwich, so she gobbled down her sandwich and ditched her plate with the idea of doing a little mingling on the balcony. But Hunter's food was too good to abandon. She made herself another sandwich, this time savoring each bite before making her way outside.

Hunter's apartment complex was a high-rise on Main Street, and the balcony offered an exquisite view of downtown. A sea of lights flowed outward to touch the curve of the horizon, and in the distance twin towers winked into the night sky—green, yellow, green, yellow. As Emily watched pairs of white headlights navigate the asphalt ribbons of Highway 59 and Loop 610, a ghost of a thought floated through her mind. In that moment she realized this was the first time she'd felt content all day. And, as usual, it had been a very long day.

The jolt of someone bumping into her broke through her thoughts, and she came to her senses just in time to keep her black pants from catching a splash of Merlot.

The pants of the man who was now crushed up against her were not as lucky. He slapped at his chinos with one hand and tried to pocket his phone with the other. "I'm sorry," he said to Emily. "I was trying to take their picture and I didn't see you." The apologetic faces of his three friends smiled back at her.

"Don't worry about it," Emily chirped. "It looks like you got the worst of it anyway."

"Yeah, well, that's what I get, right? I'm Andrew, by the way."

"Emily," she replied with a smile and a toss of her hair, "nice to meet you."

"And this is my wife, Maureen, and my friends Bill and Susan."

Emily's smile cooled. "Nice to meet all of you," she said. "I think I'm going to head inside and get some more wine. Merry Christmas."

Emily walked inside to a chorus of "Merry Christmas" behind her. Returning to the kitchen, she found Hunter opening another bottle of wine. She worked her way between the barstools at the counter, made an exasperated sigh, and rested her elbows on the granite. Wineglass still in hand, she pressed it gently against her forehead as if it were a towel of ice to cool a headache.

She studied Hunter as he uncorked the wine. He was at his best in the kitchen. When he was cooking or entertaining, his innate intensity felt positive and focused. At the office, his seriousness was always negative, and when things got intense, he became scattered and frustrated. Emily hated those days. Whenever she sensed Hunter was about to lose it, she knew her day was shot. She'd be spending the rest of it trying to help him get matters in order.

***

Hunter was happy to have Emily back in the kitchen with him, but he'd been dreading this moment since she walked through his front door. He had something to tell her, and she wasn't going to like it. He was quitting the firm; he was moving on. His heart was never in it, and he'd always known his passion was elsewhere, though it had taken him years to do anything about it.

He knew Emily was struggling too. But he also knew that she was too stubborn and proud to give up the game, the social snakes and ladders. He didn't know how to explain to her how much he hated going to work every day. How much he despised those rooms with their vanilla-pudding walls and somber carpets. Worst of all, he feared Emily would never understand that a life lived in that florescent haze was no life at all, no matter how big the paycheck. He would go and she would remain, slowly becoming an echo, like the wail of a phantom ocean within a conch shell, audible only after the living organism has been scraped out and consumed.

Not knowing how to begin, he finally blurted out, "I'm leaving the firm. I've been accepted to the Culinary Institute … I want to be a professional chef."

She laughed. "I don't believe you. You're joking, right?"

"No. I'm dead serious." Hunter folded the handle on the corkscrew he'd been turning and slid the cork from a bottle of Syrah.

Emily eyed him from across the counter. She scooted a poinsettia out of the way and thrust her empty wineglass across the divide. Hunter closed his fingers over hers as he took her glass, let them linger a few seconds longer than necessary. He gave Emily's glass a quick rinse before filling it.

"Well? What do you think about culinary school?" he asked and handed her the wine.

"Work is going to suck now." She gulped down most of the wine in her glass and continued, "What brought this on? I mean, I know you love to cook, but you can always find time for it on the weekends; no need to quit your day job."

"That notion," Hunter said, leaning in, "is exactly what got me into this mess in the first place." He caught Emily's gaze, held it for a moment, and then turned to fill his own glass.

"I'm sensing a story here." Emily set her glass on the counter and slid onto the empty barstool beside her. With a nod, she motioned for Hunter to join her. He sat down on the stool next to hers.

"It's not much of a story," he said. "You know I've always loved to cook. I used to dream about owning my own restaurant. But the whole idea just seemed too risky. I figured I would play it safe and go to law school. Besides, I could cook as much as I wanted on the weekends, right?"

"Sure," Emily agreed. "What went wrong? Why the sudden change of heart?"

"I hate my job. I just can't do it anymore."

"Everyone hates their job." She chuckled. "That is not a good enough reason to go from financial security to financial oblivion in sixty seconds flat."

"Hey!" Hunter jostled Emily's shoulder in feigned defensiveness. "This is my dream. And dreams are meant to be followed, damn it!" He moved closer, dropped the humor from his voice. "Besides," he added, "you don't understand what it was like for me. It's not just that I hated things from nine to five. Work was always hanging over me, making it impossible for me to enjoy anything else around me." The last line Hunter spoke in earnest, hoping Emily would catch his meaning, but her eyes were beginning to glaze, and he could tell she'd had too much wine to appreciate subtle hints.

"Well, I'm very happy for you, Hunter" she replied. "But don't forget about me when you're off at school. Please come back and visit on the weekends. Promise me you will."

"Oh, I'm not leaving Houston. I'm going to school right here in town. And don't worry. We'll see each other all the time. I promise."

Emily raised an eyebrow, accused him of abandoning her without saying a word.

"Don't look at me like that," he said. "You're making me feel guilty.'

"Good."

"You look nice tonight, by the way. I like your outfit, very sparkly."

Emily smiled and straightened herself on the stool. "Thank you. Flattery will get you everywhere. But what do you think about the shoes? It took me forever to decide."

"Very nice. But I don't know much about shoes."

"Fair enough." A moment later, she added, "Hunter? My glass is empty."

"I can see that. I'll get you some water." He left his stool and walked to the fridge.

"Do you have anything more festive than water?"

"How about club soda with a twist of lemon?"

"That'll work. I love club soda with lemon."

"Yes," he said. "I remember."

CHAPTER 9 - EMILY AND MITCH

FOR EMILY, Christmas day passed uneventfully. Her mother smiled ceaselessly, her stepfather quipped jovially, and the three-bean casserole turned out better than expected.

Emily was tired when she walked into the office after the Christmas holiday. She'd dreamt about Mitch again the night before, and she always had trouble getting back to sleep after one of her Mitch dreams. This time she'd stayed up until three in the morning reading Persuasion and eating sour skittles until her jaw hurt.

But now she was back at the office, and it was time to focus on work. As she walked past the receptionist's desk, she noticed that Ronald Nielson, a chronically obnoxious associate, was chatting up Madison, the firm's young receptionist, yet again. That morning, he was employing the thin guise of pointlessly shuffling papers as a cover for his ungainly flirting. To Emily, he remarked, "Look at you rolling in at ten o'clock."

"I'm tired Ronald, keep it to yourself, please," Emily said and continued down the hall. She could still hear the tail end of Ronald's sarcastic witticisms as she trudged into her office. As soon as she walked through the door, the phone on her desk began to ring. Lifting the receiver, she was immediately accosted by a surly client who was flatly refusing to have his deposition taken.

"I understand your feelings," Emily said in her most soothing voice at the end of her client's tirade. "But as you know, this deposition has been scheduled for some time now, and it would be almost impossible to reschedule at this late date." Emily was certain she could talk her client into submission in a few short minutes, but she needed all her concentration to do it, and Charlotte happened to be barking at someone just outside her door. Emily was about to plug her free ear with her finger when something familiar caught her attention. The other voice, it sounded like....

But she could only make out Charlotte's side of the exchange, "Okay, fine ... your name ... Dr. Mitch Hudson ... I'll tell her you're here."

At the sound of Mitch's name Emily froze and almost lost her grip on the phone. The voice on the other end of the line said, "Hello? Emily, are you still there?"

"Yes, uh...." she responded quickly, "I'll have to call you back on this." She hung up the phone and stared in disbelief as Mitch walked into her office and shut the door.

"Emily," he said, "your secretary told me you're busy, but I had to see you right away."

Emily folded her arms across her chest and glared at him. "It's been almost a year, Mitch. And suddenly you need to see me right away? What the hell are you doing here?"

"I'm sorry to bother you at work." He cleared his throat, but his voice was high and nervous just the same. "I'll get straight to the point. I want us to be together again—I want a second chance. I know this is a lot to ask, and you don't have to say anything right now. I'm going to Belize City for a week right after New Year's, and I want you to join me. It's a tropical paradise. We can talk things through, reconnect, and start fresh. Everything can be the way you wanted. You were right about us all along."

Emily clenched her jaw and inhaled sharply. "Get out before I call security."

Mitch did not oblige. Instead, he moved toward her desk, then eased around the corner of it to stand next to her. He was so close she could smell the scent of eucalyptus on his skin. And, for a moment, her determination faltered. There he was, right there, the man who broke her heart. The man who still owned what was left of it. Mitch was staring at her so intensely that, against her will, her chest warmed with hope and eagerness. But she checked herself and compressed her sudden hope into an imperceivable speck. *He'll only disappoint me again*, she reasoned, *and I'm tired of being disappointed.*

"Are you deaf?" she asked. "I just told you to get the hell out of here." She was beginning to recover from the initial shock of it all and was

53

determined to have Mitch out of her sight before he had a chance to crack her resolve. But Mitch seemed determined to stay.

"Emily," he whispered, "just hear me out."

Tersely, she replied, "I'm going to get a cup of coffee, and when I get back, I want you to be gone." She turned away from Mitch and walked toward the door.

He came around to meet her, grasping her arm as she walked away. "Please say you'll meet me in Belize," he begged. "We'll have a perfect week together. It'll be absurdly romantic," he added, smiling awkwardly. "It'll be the kind of vacation you always talked about when we were together. You and me in paradise."

Emily shook her head and wrenched her arm free from his grasp.

"Can I call you later?" he asked.

"No," she answered and hurried out the door.

Emily lingered in the kitchen for thirty minutes before returning to her office, which she was happy to find empty. But work was impossible with Mitch lingering just below the surface of every phone call, status report, and email. After struggling against distraction for the rest of the morning, Emily decided to walk to the hotel restaurant across the street for lunch.

As soon as she entered the hotel lobby, she spotted Don Eldridge at the lobby bar and tried to sneak past him without success. When he waved for her to come over, she sighed and tried not to roll her eyes as she walked toward him. She didn't know much about Eldridge, but what she'd heard about him wasn't good. He was the firm's founding partner. Two decades earlier, he'd started the practice that would eventually become Eldridge, Kealey, Moorehouse & Walters, L.L.P., with only two attorneys, a law clerk, and a paralegal. He was a seasoned litigator. He was also rumored to be crazy.

Eldridge was sucking down something on the rocks, probably Bourbon. His mouth began to move but his vacant stare remained. "Have a seat," he offered, his eyes struggling to find their mark.

Emily suppressed a sardonic smile. *Drunk in the early afternoon*, she mused, *this should be interesting.*

She ordered a sandwich and a Diet Coke. At first, she told herself it would be a relief to have something to take her mind off Mitch while she ate. But thirty minutes and almost half as many Bourbons later, Eldridge was rambling at a steady clip. He'd explained (twice) that he'd been working in excess of 2500 hours a year for decades, but now he was certain "those young sons of bitches coming up the ladder" were trying to steal his clients and squeeze him out of the firm. But the joke was on them because he wasn't giving up without a fight, "no siree … a long, bloody fight … if that's what they wanted, that's what they'd get...."

Emily only responded with periodic nods. There was a loud whooshing sensation inside her head, and all she could focus on was Mitch's sudden reappearance. Mitch's proposition made it impossible for her to think about anything else. He wanted her back. It felt like a bizarre dream.

Eldridge continued, "Who are you working with these days? And what do y'all have going on, anything good?"

"I'm in the litigation section with Bill Walters. We have a couple of big cases, but most of them are quiet right now. We have a string of depositions starting in February." Emily drummed her fingers against the bar. She wanted to be alone with her thoughts, and this incessant chatter was making her restless and agitated.

"Well, that's something at least," Eldridge said. "These baby lawyers nowadays don't know shit about how things work around here. It's all about finesse, you've got to have connections, know the right people. Back in my day...." Eldridge tilted his head back and Emily could almost see the memories floating in his eyes before he shut them tightly. "Let me tell you something...." he muttered while shaking his empty glass. Apparently, the glass shaking made him forget the something he was going to tell her, and he asked, "What kind of depositions do you have lined up in February?"

"Mainly toxic tort cases, some oil and gas stuff. I think the first one is the plaintiff's expert in a down-hole loss, an engineering expert."

"Who is he?"

How presumptuous, she thought. *Of course, he assumes the expert is a man.* "Mr. Mahmoud," she answered, irritated at not being able to prove his assumption wrong by saying Misses something or other.

"Make sure you know your stuff, young lady, before you go in there and start asking questions. Don't half-ass it. And don't let Walters take all the credit for your hard work. He'll cut you out of your share without a second thought. That jackass doesn't have an ounce of integrity. I've been saying it for years! Ever since he made partner, everything's gone downhill! And those young sons of bitches are trying to squeeze me out! But I'm not going without a fight!" Eldridge's voice was growing louder with each passing syllable. He was practically shouting now.

Emily placed her glass next to the remnants of her sandwich and leaned away from her companion. She was utterly disinterested in this conversation, but it wouldn't pay to be openly rude to the firm's most senior partner. If she could pay her tab, she could make a break for it. But escape was not in the cards. The bartender had gone missing, and Emily was further annoyed by Eldridge's repeated attempts to speak despite being lost in a drunken fog.

Finally, the bartender returned and ran Emily's card. As soon as she scrawled her signature across the credit slip, she sprang from her seat like a rabbit from a cage. "I have to get back to work." She tossed the words into the middle of another of Eldridge's slurred rants and sped toward the exit.

Outside the hotel, the December air cooled Emily's flushed cheeks. She let the wind work the heat from her face for a moment before wrapping her scarf around her neck and tucking her chin against her chest. She took a deep breath and tried to rub the frown from her forehead as she quickened her pace toward her office building.

She had invested three years and sixty thousand dollars in her law degree and most of the time she was proud of her work, especially when she nailed a deposition or prevailed on a contested motion. On those days, she felt like a badass. But some days, like the one she was drudging through at present, she felt like the whole legal profession was comprised entirely of cutthroat bullshit. *What a morning,* she thought wearily. *Surely it can't get any worse.*

Emily made her way to the street corner and stopped at the light. The streetlight for cross-traffic turned from green to red, but the crossing light stayed fixed on red, the words "DON'T WALK" glaring back at her. Emily sighed. The streetlight at the corner of Ambassador Way and Post Oak Boulevard was her nemesis. It never turned green, and, regardless of the time of day, vehicles tore down Post Oak like it was the turnpike. Emily always dreaded the long sprint across the six-lane expanse. She would be easy pickings for any of the monster vehicles prowling the Houston roads.

At the first break in traffic, she clutched her satchel to her chest and dashed across the street, narrowly escaping the full-on charge of a Chevy Suburban. From the safety of the sidewalk, she threw a few choice words into the Suburban's wake before making her way past the water fountain, then up the shallow flight of stairs leading to the lobby of her office building.

When she walked through the revolving doors, she stopped cold. Mitch was seated on a bench between the two banks of elevators, waiting for her. Briefly, she considered running straight back the way she came, but the thought of bumping into Eldridge as he stumbled his way back to work was too much for her. She squared her shoulders and walked toward the elevator. Mitch was on his feet now, staring at her. She hurried past him.

"Emily," he said. "Please wait."

Emily's index finger was glued to the UP button, and she pressed it furiously as Mitch closed in on her.

"I know this seems sudden to you," he said. He was standing at her shoulder, speaking softly to her. "But I never stopped thinking about you, never stopped loving you." He touched his fingers to her arm, but she shrugged him off.

"Get away from me," she whispered harshly. "I am not having this conversation with you. Not now, not ever. Do you understand? How dare you show up here, at my office, and throw this on me. I mean, for crying out loud, Mitch…." She shook her head angrily.

He hesitated. Emily had never seen him this nervous. "I was trying to do the right thing," he explained desperately, "trying to make it work with my wife. I felt obligated to her. Don't you understand? We'd only been married a year when I met you, and …. Emily, you know I never meant for this to happen. It's been killing me that I hurt you. But I'm here now, and I'm begging you to give me another chance. Please. I've loved you for eleven long months, and I can't live without you one minute longer."

The elevator came and went. Emily's eyes were fixed on the steel doors in front of her, but her heart was floating in her chest. Mitch had just said the words she'd been longing to hear, and although she couldn't let herself forgive him, she couldn't seem to make herself walk away either.

Just then, Eldridge stumbled into the lobby and offered a thunderous greeting to the security guard. Emily hit the elevator button with the heel of her palm, and the doors snapped open.

"I have to go," she said to Mitch as she hurried into the elevator. Once inside, she hit the CLOSE button with her thumb and the doors slid shut. *Safe at last,* she thought. *Safe from Eldridge and safe from Mitch.*

But something told her Mitch wasn't about to give up. There had been a look of fierce determination in his eyes that Emily had never seen before, and she was certain she would see him again. She just hoped it wouldn't be today.

That evening, Emily returned home to find her fridge as empty as she'd left it and her favorite show waiting on the DVR. She fished through the junk draw in her kitchen for the takeout menus and spread them on the counter. Her options were Italian, Chinese and Mediterranean. She immediately decided against Italian. Ever since the fiasco that was her twenty-ninth birthday, she'd given up pizza, and she didn't want spaghetti. After waffling back and forth between the chicken pad Thai and the hummus platter, she finally decided on the pad Thai and made the call.

While waiting for her food to arrive, she changed out of her work clothes and into a pair of pink-and-white-striped flannel pajamas. She pulled her hair into a sloppy bun on top of her head, washed her face, and slipped her favorite pair of fuzzy, non-skid socks onto her feet. The whole process took less than twenty minutes, and Emily estimated she still had at least another twenty-five minutes to wait before the delivery guy arrived, so she walked to the kitchen and poured herself a glass of wine.

She had just settled on the sofa with her tattered copy of Persuasion when the doorbell rang. *That was fast,* she thought as she schlepped toward the kitchen for her wallet.

"Coming," she called. She unzipped her wallet and pulled out some cash. Without so much as a *who's there?* she pulled open the door. Mitch was standing in the hallway with a bouquet of red roses and a bottle of wine.

"You can't be serious," she said.

"May I come in?" he asked.

"Not a chance."

"Please, Emily. I've got a great bottle of wine here, and we can talk things out." He nodded toward the bottle and thrust the bouquet into her hands.

"I'm already drinking," she said. "And I don't want your kind of company."

He moved closer. "Thirty minutes. Just give me thirty minutes. Then I'll leave you alone forever, if that's what you want."

Emily paused and considered his offer. "Fine. You've got thirty minutes. But you're wasting your time." She led Mitch through the entryway, stopping at the kitchen to toss the bouquet of flowers into the trash.

When they entered the living room, Mitch set the bottle of wine on the coffee table. Emily turned to face him; her arms folded across her chest. "Your time started at the door, by the way."

"Can we sit down?" he asked.

She moved toward the sofa and tucked herself into the far corner. Mitch sat down beside her.

"Emily," he began, "I can only imagine the pain you felt when … when things between us fell apart. But you must believe me when I say I felt it too. Only worse—because I had to live knowing I'd hurt you—the one person who means everything to me."

She lowered her eyes, stared at her hands folded in her lap. "Then why, Mitch?" she asked. "Why did you leave me without any explanation? You went on your trip to Belize, and then all I got was a phone call. Ten seconds. You ended everything between us with a ten-second phone call. How could you do that to me?"

"I felt trapped," he replied. "You can't imagine what it was like for me. Maggie's parents spent a fortune on our wedding, and there I was cheating on her after only a year. How could I tell them all I'd fallen in love with another woman—an amazing, beautiful woman? I wanted to be with you…. You don't know how hard it was, day after day, thinking about you, missing you. And I refuse to do it any longer. Please don't let anger keep us apart. You knew going into this thing that it wouldn't be easy. And, yes, it's taken a lot longer than you thought. But I'm here now, and I'm begging you for a chance to be together, the way you always wanted."

The doorbell chimed and Emily started in surprise.

"I'll get that," Mitch said. "Take a couple minutes to think about what I've said. Really think about it, and then think about how good we were together. It can be that way again."

As Mitch walked toward her front door, Emily sat motionless on the sofa. She *was* thinking about it, and it was making her heart drum inside her chest like a wild parade. Everything Mitch said made sense. She knew he was the kind of man who wanted to do the right thing, even when it hurt. And the truth was she hated being without him. The one thing she wanted more than anything was someone to love. And here was Mitch, the only man she'd ever loved, asking her to let him back into her life.

She tried to compose herself, tried to think things through. *Could she start over with him?* Their time together had been the best of her life, but he'd left her in the end. Then again, maybe that wasn't the end, and this wasn't a new start. Maybe this was the middle and Mitch had loved her through the long months they were apart until he couldn't take it anymore—just like he said—and when they tell their story to friends and family in their new life to come, he would say he'd always known Emily was the one; it just took him awhile to prove his love.

In the span of thirty seconds, Emily constructed thirty years of wedded bliss. She pictured Mitch's hands clasped over hers as he slipped a ring on her finger. Her wedding day would be exquisite. Mitch, the one person who always spoiled her, would certainly give her as lavish a wedding as her heart desired. And surely her father would show up to walk her down the aisle.

By the time Mitch returned with the food, Emily was ready to be convinced. They split the pad Thai, opened the wine, and talked for over an hour, Emily's happiness growing by the minute.

***

As Emily's enthusiasm grew, so did Mitch's guilt. But he reminded himself how high the stakes were and pushed forward with his plan. As he piled lie upon lie, the charade became a little easier for him, but it was still a brutal struggle. He was relying on the one thing he knew for certain about Emily—she was a hopeless romantic. Her heart was her Achilles' heel. When they were together before, she'd convinced herself they were in love, and she'd believed, against all evidence to the contrary, that they were heading toward happily ever after.

Mitch cringed at the memory of those months. He hated the man he was back then, and he hated the game he was playing now, but he had no choice. He had to get Emily on a plane to Belize, whatever the cost.

In the end, he couldn't get a firm commitment from her to come with him to Belize. But she promised to think about his offer and call him before long with her answer. He left her apartment disappointed but hopeful. And, as he maneuvered his Range Rover through traffic on his way home that evening, he felt almost certain that Emily would agree to his proposition within the next day or two, provided nothing happened between now and then to make her change her mind about him altogether.

CHAPTER 10 - ITZAMNA

Caracol
Maya Lowlands
Mesoamerica
A.D. 562

ON THE DAY BEFORE THE FESTIVAL OF CONQUEST, Itzamna made the most difficult decision of his life. He would lay his feelings at the feet of his lord brother and ask him to bestow a single favor. But before he could proceed, he had to be certain of one thing.

"I have a question to ask you," he said to Ixchel when they'd finished their morning meal.

"Yes?" she replied. They were seated together on a pair of stitched cotton matts, their empty bowls gathered between them.

"What is your real name?" he asked, his voice almost a whisper. She trembled, and he instantly regretted his thoughtlessness. "Don't be afraid," he added quickly. "I've no intention of exposing you in any way. I would sooner sacrifice my own life than cause you greater harm by revealing the truth of your birth." He rose and took her hands, pulling her toward him. Her palms were damp with fear, and he wanted desperately to comfort her. "Please believe me when I say I only want your safety. My deepest wish is to free you from this poisoned web. When we spoke yesterday, you mentioned Kinich Ahau, the patron god of nobility. You also mentioned that your father is a lord and you resided in the palace. Please, tell me who you really are."

Ixchel straightened herself up to her full five feet two inches and looked him in the eyes. "I am Lady Ixchel, daughter of Lord Double Bird, sister to King Red Hawk."

Itzamna squeezed her hands, which were still nestled in his. "I suspected as much. I met your lord father when he championed the accession of my lord brother ten years ago. It pains me to tell you this, but I have dire news of your lord father's fate. He has fallen into the hands of the snake king, Lord Sky Witness. He will be sacrificed at Calakmul."

"No," she insisted. "My lord father fell in battle; my lord brother told me so. Lord Sky Witness has captured another, and he intends to pass him off as my lord father to magnify himself before his people, for Lord Sky Witness is truly a snake. But the gods will know the truth, and the serpentine lord will be punished for his deception. I am sure of it. Now, please tell me, do you have news of my lord brother? Does he live?"

"Yes," he replied. "Lord Red Hawk has returned to Tikal. Your military force was greatly weakened by the battle. Lord Red Hawk has brokered an agreement with Lord Sky Witness of Calakmul. Tikal will submit to the Calakmul alliance and there will be no further bloodshed on either side."

"He has agreed to be dominated by the serpentine king? I don't believe it!"

"It's a good deal," Itzamna insisted as he approached her. "Your lord brother is a wise man. He knows one alone cannot fight two. He will bide his time and keep his people safe while he rebuilds and regroups. Believe me when I say this is not the end. Tikal will rise from the carnage, and your kingdom will be stronger than ever."

"I wish I could live to see it."

Itzamna placed his hand upon her shoulder. "You have not asked me about your cousin, the one to whom you are betrothed."

"He is Lord Jaguar Claw," Ixchel said thinly.

"Lord Jaguar Claw is alive. He has also returned to Tikal as King Red Hawk's military advisor."

Ixchel lowered her head. "Oh," she said.

"Do you wish to return to him?"

"I wish to return home."

"But what does your heart want? Is Lord Jaguar Claw your cherished matchmate?"

"He was my lord father's cherished match for me. I would seek now to honor my father's wishes. If I was able to return home, I would marry Lord Jaguar Claw without quarrel."

"I understand." Itzamna pressed his palms together and began to pace the floor. "I told you before that I want to keep you safe." He paused and glanced nervously at Ixchel. When he spoke again his voice was tentative. "With your consent, I will try to secure your safety by asking my lord brother, the king, for your hand in marriage. If he agrees, you will have a choice to make. You can abandon your past and stay here with me as my wife. Or you can remain here only temporarily. In the weeks leading up to our wedding, I will divine a means for your escape, and you will be free to return to your cousin. You don't have to decide now. I only need to know if you want me to proceed with the first part of the plan."

"Yes, certainly!" Her eyes were bright with hope. "Do you think the king will agree? Do you believe he will spare my life?"

"I don't know," Itzamna replied softly. Ixchel's face fell, and Itzamna wished he could raise her spirits again, but he did not linger. He wanted to find his brother as soon as possible. He kissed Ixchel's cheek, then strode swiftly from his bedchamber in search of the only man who could save the woman he'd so recently come to cherish. She was everything he'd always wished for in a wife, beautiful, strong-minded, and decidedly unimpressed with warlords and their shiny weapons.

Itzamna knew the king and his courtiers would be in the courtyard that morning enjoying the Long Performance, a divine theatrical exhibition that always preceded the Festival of Conquest. He thought it best to sit with them through the course of the performance and display at least some brotherly affection before the morning was over. After steadying his nerves with a cup of cashew wine, Itzamna entered the courtyard and joined the royal family in the stands.

Below, a stage of packed clay had been constructed in the courtyard. Upon the stage a single dancer leapt and pranced. It was the Dance of the Armadillo. The dancer's head was covered in a mask of scales and plumes, painted to resemble an armadillo's head. In his hands were a flute and a rattle. The low beating of drums offstage guided the dancer's movements. He crept and leapt, shaking the rattle when he was low, trilling the flute when he was high. The dance was a prelude to the Long Performance, a

64

series of readings and reenactments delivered by the daykeepers of Caracol, which recounted the tale of the beginning of life on earth.

When the dance was over, the performer removed his mask and bowed to the king before exiting the stage. Within moments, the oldest of Caracol's daykeepers, Ajq'ij Dark Fox, shuffled onto the stage. Dressed in a heavily embroidered tunic, plumed sandals, a delicate plumed headdress, and layer upon layer of jade beads, he was resplendent from foot to forehead. He bowed low before the king, then raised his arms to the sky and began,

"Here is the account of the lighting of all the sky-earth, the four sides, the four corners, by the Maker, the Begetter, mother-father of humankind."

At this point the daykeeper was joined by three others, all regally attired, and together they spoke the story of The Dawn of Life,

"Now it ripples and sighs,
It hums, empty under the sky.
There is not yet
one animal or bird
one person or tree.
Only the sky is there. The form of the earth is unclear.
Nothing stirs.
Only the Maker, Sculptor, the Bringer, Begetter are a shimmering light in the sky.
They are there in the stillness.
There is Hurricane. He came in the blackness. He is called Heart of Sky.
In the early dawn he spoke with Sovereign Plumed Serpent. He is called Heart of Earth.
They joined their thoughts and reached agreement in the light.
Then humankind was created.
They created life in the blackness.
They created plants and shrubs, jungles and lakes, animals and birds.
When they joined their thoughts and words."

The performance continued through the morning as Itzamna stewed anxiously in his seat. He'd greeted his brother Lord Water warmly and received a wide smile in return, but he was uncertain about his chances of success. For now, all he could do was sit and wait.

Finally, at mid-afternoon, the exhibition ended with The Dance of the Weasel. When the last of the nobles left the stands, Itzamna sought a private audience with the king.

"My lord brother," he said when they were finally alone. "I have come to thank you for the gift you bestowed upon me. The female captive has brought the warmth of fire to my bedchamber, and I now intend to ask you to spare her life. I wish to take her as my wife."

Lord Water's dark brows arched in surprise. He said nothing and seemed to be basking in the glow of self-satisfaction.

Itzamna frowned impatiently.

"What you ask is impossible," the king replied at last. "She is a peasant. You cannot marry a peasant."

"Then I shall take her as my concubine."

Lord Water shook his head. "The girl will eternally be seeking an open doorway, always sniffing the air for a chance to run."

"That notion is ridiculous," Itzamna countered. "Tikal is more than 50 miles away. No man would attempt such a journey, let alone a girl."

"Yes, she is a girl. Guided by the heart and not the head. She will run and take her chances like a fool. And it will mean your humiliation and mine."

Itzamna pressed his point. "I promise you I will keep her close. I have never worried you for anything, lord brother. Bear me this single favor."

"The stone has been thrown. It cannot be undone," Lord Water said firmly. "Her blood belongs to Buluk Chabtan."

"The white stones of Caana will bleed rivers tomorrow," Itzamna said, his voice thick with anger. "And the war god will drink his belly full. One girl will make no difference."

There was irritation in the king's black eyes, and he raised his palm for silence. "Do not worry me with this. There are more sweet girls in this kingdom than guavas on the vine. If you would only lift your eyes from your precious books, you would find much to satisfy you. Trust me, you will soon forget this Tikal flower. She will wither in your memory when you find your true matchmate, who will be a noble woman of Caracol, not a peasant from the kingdom where your uncle was killed. Truly brother, how can you ask this of me? It cannot be done."

The Sky Place

Itzamna clenched his jaw. He had taken his chance, and he had lost. Now there was only one path open to him. And if he did not walk it carefully, Buluk Chabtan would feast on his blood as well.

CHAPTER 11 - EMILY

Houston, Texas
Present Day

WHEN EMILY AWOKE the morning after Mitch's sudden reemergence into her life, she felt a shift in her perception of the world. A kind of jittery anticipation had settled in overnight. Inside her chest, wild excitement grew like the swell of a rising wave. She waited for the wave to break, anticipated the crescendo, but it did not come. The wave kept rising, and her thoughts swirled.

Emily's odd mood followed her to work and lingered through the morning. She found it difficult to subdue the nervous energy building up inside her. She rose from her desk and began to pace the floor, but the files littering the carpet made pacing more of a stop-and-go process than she could endure. She stooped to gather the files. Her office was not large, and she quickly collected the files into a neat stack and placed them onto one of a pair of chairs facing her desk. With a sigh, she flopped onto the other chair and began to drum her fingers on the surface of her desk while simultaneously tapping her foot against the desk's back panel.

It was in this state of emotional disarray that Hunter found Emily at twelve thirty in the afternoon when he walked through her open door to invite her to lunch.

"Am I interrupting?" he asked, leaning against the door jamb.

Emily turned. "Yes, thank goodness."

"It's one of those days, is it?"

"Ugh—yes—this day is killing me already. But what are you doing here? You quit, remember?"

"Stacy said I had to come in and pick up my paycheck in person, something about having to sign off on the final check because of the bonus and vacation payout."

"That's weird. I've never heard of that."

"It's no big deal. Besides, now we can have lunch together, right?"

"Absolutely, I'm dying to get out of here."

Hunter and Emily made their way down the hall, which lead to the receptionist's desk and the front door. But before they'd cleared half the distance, Stacy came cantering up behind them calling, "Hunter, there you are, hold on a minute please."

Stacy Goodwyn was the youngest (and prettiest) office manager Emily had ever worked with. And even though Stacy was as competent as she was pretty, it didn't stop Ronald, the office ass, from jokingly speculating with some frequency about the manner in which Stacy had secured the privilege of presiding over the support staff at Eldridge, Kealey, Moorehouse & Walters, L.L.P.

"Where're y'all running off to?" Stacy asked, smiling up at Hunter while ignoring Emily as much as her Southern charm would allow. "You know I have a tradition," Stacy continued, a little breathless, "of treating every associate to lunch on their last day at the office."

This was the first time Emily had ever heard of this alleged tradition, and she wondered what Stacy was up to.

"Oh, you don't have to do that," Hunter said. "Really Stacy, it's very nice of you but it's too much. Emily and I are just going to grab some Subway or something."

"It's nothing," Stacy insisted. "And you are not going to Subway on your last day here. I mean, are you kidding me? I'm taking you to Maggiano's, and I won't take no for an answer."

Emily stood quietly and listened to the exchange. She had no intention of returning to her office. If Stacy wanted to railroad Emily's lunch plans, she would have to work for it.

After going back and forth with Hunter for a few minutes, Stacy finally offered to treat both him and Emily to lunch.

"You don't have to treat me," Emily said as soon as the offer was made. "But I'm happy to join you."

At Maggiano's Stacy deftly maneuvered her way into the booth next to Hunter, leaving Emily to sit alone at the opposite side of the table. Emily was inexplicably irritated by Stacy's behavior and, feeling her cheeks begin to flush, she stared down at her menu in annoyance.

Through the course of their meal, and for the first time in twenty-four hours, Emily did not think about Mitch at all. She was too busy trying to divert Hunter's attention from the volley of compliments and questions Stacy lobbed softly at him during the appetizers, threw steadily at him during the main course, and spiked furiously at him during dessert when it looked like Emily was gaining ground.

When the waiter came to collect their dessert plates and drop off their checks, Emily was suddenly struck by the fact that Hunter had really and truly quit the firm. Amid her earlier anxiety about Mitch, the full weight of Hunter's departure had somehow been lost on her. Now, she was keenly aware of how much she was going to miss him. Struggling for something meaningful to say, she lifted her glass, "Let's toast," she offered, "to Hunter and his new adventure. May your future be bright and filled with success."

Hunter smiled. "Let's toast to all of us," he added, "may all our futures be filled with success."

Stacy giggled. "Oh Hunter," she chided, bumping his shoulder playfully with hers.

Emily tried to recall whether Stacy's voice had always been quite so grating, and then she began to wonder whether she was missing something. Stacy was being infuriatingly odd. Her comments to Hunter were little more than a series of non sequiturs, as if she and Hunter shared a running secret or joke, and, at times, it seemed impossible that Emily and Stacy were taking part in the same conversation. *Either I'm nuts or she is*, Emily thought.

As soon as the trio returned to the office, Stacy insisted that she needed to steal Hunter for a minute so she could give him his check. Emily relented, unsure of how she'd gotten sucked into this game of tug-of-war in the first place.

Back in her office, Emily forced herself to get to work. She was determined to finish every single assignment she'd scheduled for herself that day. But she'd barely made a dent in her first task, an email summarizing the outcome of a recent hearing, when Hunter stopped in to say goodbye.

"Wow," she joked, "that was fast. I'm surprised you're not missing any buttons."

Hunter pocketed his check and sat down. "Jealous?" he asked and settled himself nonchalantly in the chair.

Emily studied Hunter's face. He was smiling, obviously joking, but confident charm was oozing out of every pore, and for a moment she believed he was actually expecting a confession. They sat in silence for several seconds while Emily wondered what she should say.

Finally, Hunter spoke up, "I'm joking, Emily. Are you okay?"

"I'm just kind of out of it today. I'm sorry," she replied with a quick shake of her head. In an effort to lighten the mood, she added, "What are you doing New Year's Eve? Any big plans?"

"No big plans, besides working my magic on some black-eyed peas. Why don't you join me?"

"Sounds great," she said, "I'll bring the wine."

Hunter flashed a smile. "Alright, I'm going to make my escape before Stacy gets ahold of me again."

CHAPTER 12 - EMILY AND HUNTER

THE NIGHT OF NEW YEAR'S EVE was crisp and clear. The morning's cold drizzle had vanished into a cloudless sky with a bright crescent moon. Emily pulled into the parking lot at Hunter's apartment complex at eight o'clock sharp; she'd anticipated more traffic and now found herself unfashionably on time.

She shut off the ignition and reached behind the passenger seat for the wine. She'd bought two bottles, Pinot Grigio and Shiraz, and trimmed them in silver ribbons to make things more festive. She'd also splurged on a gift for Hunter to commemorate his new career move. Wrapped in red and gold, the gift was a set of knives, the kind that slid into a thick fabric sleeve like the ones she'd seen on Top Chef.

Emily arrived at Hunter's apartment door with her arms full—she was cradling the wine within the crook of her right arm and hiding Hunter's gift behind her back with her left—so she rapped on the bottom of the door with the side of her heel. Hunter greeted her with a hug, then eyed the bottles of wine.

"Wow, two bottles," he joked, taking them from her hands. "We'd better start drinking."

"I didn't know what we were having, so I brought white and red."

"We're having pork; let's go with white." He glanced at the labels. "What did you bring?"

"The white is Pinot Grigio," Emily replied. She was still standing in Hunter's doorway with his gift behind her back. When he finally turned for the kitchen, she pulled the door closed behind her. As she followed Hunter into the kitchen, she noticed that everything (Hunter included) seemed different, more put together, more polished.

While Hunter was preoccupied with the wine, Emily wedged his present behind the coffee maker, and moved toward the dining area. She set her purse down on one of the dining chairs and surveyed the festive décor. Hunter had really outdone himself with the New Year's Eve ambiance. The table was set with candles, fine dinnerware, and pewter chargers.

"What're we having?" she asked. "Whatever it is, it smells delicious."

With obvious pride, Hunter gave Emily a rundown of the night's menu. The food was as extravagant as the décor. He'd prepared spinach salad with feta and fresh berries followed by braised pork chops in a butter and cider sauce accompanied by rice and black-eyed peas, and a chocolate raspberry tort for dessert.

***

Hunter's go-to dish for company was usually tenderloin, roasted or broiled, with a nice pan sauce, but he'd made it once before when Emily was over for a dinner party, and he wanted to serve something special. Everything had to be perfect. He was finally going to open his heart to Emily, and he wanted it to be a night they'd both remember forever. He'd planned his menu carefully and had been fully prepared to execute every item to perfection.

But his menu was ambitious, and the food prep took longer than he anticipated. The first issue was the sauce. On the initial try, he made the roux slightly too thick. When he spooned it over the pork, it didn't drizzle down the sides quite the way he wanted, and, by that time, it was too late to thin it with oil, so he started over from scratch. The second time, it was perfect.

Hunter's next frustration was the fresh berries. They were too heavy for the spinach leaves, which meant they either rolled to the bottom of the serving bowl or flattened the leaves when placed on top. He decided to portion the salad onto the salad plates in advance, creating a nest of berries in the center of each plate and arranging the remaining ingredients around the perimeter.

In the end, it all turned out beautifully, and Hunter was glad he'd reserved an extra window of time for unexpected setbacks.

"This salad looks amazing," Emily said. "I love raspberries."

"Thanks," he replied, joining Emily at the table with two glasses of wine.

"Did you make the dressing from scratch?"

"I did. I hope you like it." Hunter placed the wine on the table and walked over to Emily.

"I'm sure I'll love it," she said.

Hunter eased her chair from the table and waited for her to slide in.

Emily eyed the chair. "Thank you," she said as she sat down.

Hunter rounded the table and seated himself across from Emily. He placed his napkin on his lap. "Well, dig in."

***

Emily started on her salad. "Wow, this is really good," she said between bites.

"Thanks, I'm glad you like it."

"By the way, thanks again for fixing the bathroom door at my place last weekend; it was really bothering me that it wouldn't close properly."

"No problem … it was easy … I just adjusted the strike plate so the knob would catch," Hunter said before sipping his wine.

"I never knew you were so handy. How'd you acquire those fix-it skills?"

"I got it honest, that's for sure. My dad's the king of do-it-yourself repairs. There isn't anything he can't fix. In case you've forgotten, I grew up on a farm outside of Bandera, which is about twenty miles from the middle of nowhere. You need to be self-reliant living in a place like that.

"I meant to tell you," he added, "I like the way you changed up your living room; it looks really cozy."

"Thanks," Emily said, "but I can't take all the credit. I stole the idea from a bed and breakfast in Richmond. I used to go there during law school to escape from all the stress. The woman who owned the place was very friendly, and all the rooms were decorated to feel homey and comfortable. I would completely relax as soon as I set one foot on the front porch.

"You know," she continued wistfully, "I used to imagine how nice it would be to own a place like that. What a cool job, right? Anyway, I called the other day to make a reservation, and the woman's voice on the machine said she'd closed the place down … retired or something…. I had no choice but to create my own relaxing retreat in my living room."

Hunter finished his salad then rubbed his palms together, a curious gleam in his eyes. "So, Emily, you never told me your story. You know, the burning question every lawyer should consider thoughtfully in retrospect … why'd you go to law school?"

"Oh geez!" Emily laughed. "I don't know. It's a weird story."

"Well, I'm sure it's better than mine so let's have it."

"Okay. I think I mentioned once or twice that my dad's a doctor."

"Yes, you mentioned it," Hunter interrupted playfully, a note of sarcasm in his voice.

She smiled down at her food. "Anyway, when I was younger, I really wanted to go to medical school because I wanted to follow in my dad's footsteps. But when I told him my idea, he said I wasn't meticulous enough to be a doctor."

"That's harsh," Hunter defended. "And wrong. You're the most meticulous person I know."

"Well, my dad didn't think so," Emily said curtly, "I don't think he was trying to be mean. I think he honestly wanted to help me pick a career I would be good at. He suggested I go to law school. He'd been through a couple lawsuits at the time, you know, just run-of-the-mill stuff, and he really liked his lawyer. When the time came to make the choice, I decided to go to law school and become a litigator, medical malpractice defense, of course."

"Then med mal went to shit. Great timing," Hunter teased.

"I still get a couple of med mal cases a year. And I don't mind doing other things."

"That wasn't a weird story by the way. I mean, I chose law school as my ticket to sellout city because I couldn't think of anything better to do with my history degree. And I suck at math; otherwise, I would have gone to business school."

"I didn't realize you majored in history; you never talk about it."

"You'd be amazed how infrequently the Pequot War comes up in casual conversation."

Emily laughed and drained the last of the wine from her glass. As Hunter poured her another, she said, "Well, about my story, I suppose it's not that weird. I guess it was my relationship with my dad that was kind of … I don't know … different. I know I talk about him all the time, believe me. I don't mean to. I just miss the life I never got to have with him. After the divorce, my mom and I moved into this little bungalow. But my dad bought a freaking mansion, and he remarried right away. My stepmother was really pretty. I mean, she's still pretty, but back then she was *really* pretty. And I ended up with two half-sisters, you know, Jenny and Lizzie.

"I would stay at my dad's place about one weekend a month; and when I was there, I would flip through their photo albums. I would do it casually, like I was just looking for a distraction, but then I'd see these pictures of all of them having so much fun. They'd go to all kinds of places on the weekends and on vacation. I always looked at the dates. My stepmother wrote little notes in the albums under the pictures, like *River tubing with Mom and Dad. Jenny and Lizzie had a blast!* and she would always mark the dates underneath her little captions. I would think back to that date and recall that I hadn't been busy or anything, and I always wondered why my dad never invited me to go along with him on any of their trips."

Emily caught the tone of her voice at the close of her remarks and realized how sad she sounded. She looked up from her plate to find Hunter staring at her, the same sad-sweet look in his eyes that made her kiss him once before.

Hunter leaned forward, and Emily thought for a moment he might take her hand, but instead he adjusted the edge of her placemat.

"It was your dad's loss, Emily," he said, his voice soft but serious. "You're smart and sensitive, and I'm sure Jenny and Lizzie put together aren't nearly as funny as you are. Don't let it get you down, Em. Memories like those belong in the past; just try to let them go." His eyes searched her face. He reached for her hand, but she pulled it away. Surprised and embarrassed, Emily searched for a change of subject. But Hunter beat her to it.

"You haven't told me if you like the pork chops. I hope the sauce isn't too rich," he said, his tone flat, almost curt.

"No, it's perfect, just delicious. What's in it?" she over-enthused, her voice now cheerleader-chipper.

"Believe me, you don't want to know." Hunter flashed his easy smile. "Lots of butter, lots of heavy cream, but worth it, I think."

"Yes, definitely worth it," she replied, her voice and feelings returning to normal.

After dinner, they settled on the couch to watch the ball drop and finish their glasses of wine.

Emily slid her shoes off and curled her legs beneath her on the sofa. "Are you excited about your culinary classes?" she asked. "When do they start?"

"Next Monday," Hunter replied. "I'm really excited, but also a little intimidated; I hope the place isn't a pressure cooker. No pun intended. I just want to focus on improving my technique and expanding my repertoire. I'm not interested in dealing with a bunch of ego-stroking bullshit. You know what I mean? I'm not trying to do law school all over again." He lifted his legs to the coffee table, swirled the wine in his glass.

"Yeah, I know what you mean," she said, "but I'm sure everyone will be cool. I can't imagine it being anything like law school. Besides, the program isn't that long, right?"

Emily slipped her feet back into her shoes, left the couch to find her purse, and returned with a scrunchie to tie her hair back. As she pulled her hair back into a sloppy bun, she could feel Hunter's eyes on her. It was a strange sensation, and for a moment, Emily thought he was about to kiss her, but instead he picked up the conversation where they'd left off.

"The program ... right," he said. "They have a fast-track plan. I'll be in and out in about a year, which is one of the reasons why I chose the school here instead of the one in Austin. I'm just ready to get on with it, you know? I'm tired of being in limbo. For the last few years, I've felt like I was holding my breath, waiting for the day when I'd wake up and realize it was all worth it. But each day I just woke up to more of the same. I got so tired of waiting to be happy."

"I know the feeling," Emily said, but Hunter didn't have her full attention. Her mind was working through various scenarios for coming clean with him about Mitch. She'd all but decided to give Mitch a second chance, but she couldn't pull the trigger, not yet. Not without Hunter's approval. Hunter had been against Mitch from the beginning. Now that Mitch had come crawling back to her, Emily felt self-satisfied and

77

vindicated. But she didn't want Hunter to be angry with her because of Mitch. If she had Hunter's approval, she could return to Mitch with a clear conscience.

***

If Emily was distracted, Hunter didn't notice. Something had been brewing beneath the surface for a while now, but the timing had always been off. Although he'd been miserable at the firm, Emily was its saving grace. And he regretted blowing his chance with her, all because he was too busy sulking about his job. There was so much he wanted to say to Emily, but she seemed to be suffering from willful blindness. When he'd planned this night with her, he'd hoped it would be magic, but now he was worried the whole thing was shot. Still, he wasn't ready to give up. He'd made enough compromises for one lifetime.

"Emily, I want to ask you something, and I'm being serious here." He set his glass on the side table and focused on Emily's face. Her cheeks were flushed from the wine, and she'd been inadvertently biting at her lips, which were now deep pink.

"I've spent the last few years being a total fake," he continued, "and hiding my real feelings about … basically everything. I'm moving on with my life now, and I feel like things are finally falling into place for me. I want a chance to be with you … as more than a friend. We've known each other for a long time, and I think it's kind of natural that we take things to the next level."

Emily began to slowly shake her head.

"Nothing too drastic," he offered. "We can start slow and see where it goes."

Emily's eyes were wide beneath her furrowed brow. "I think you're just caught up in the moment, Hunter," she said. "You're on a high from quitting, so this is all coming out. But you don't really mean it."

"I do mean it, Em. I'm serious," he insisted.

Emily rose from the couch amidst a flurry of head shaking. "It's not that I don't care about you Hunter, I do. But this is just … very bad timing … I need to tell you something. You see, Mitch came by the office, and he…."

78

Hunter didn't let her finish. "Are you kidding me?" He was shocked at how disappointed he felt, and he was certain his feelings were written all over his face. He stared in agony as Emily's confused frown transformed into a mournful look of pity. She reached for him, but he flinched and brushed her off. "You're not happy unless someone is screwing you over, is that it?" he asked. "It's like you and this piece-of-shit firm. At the end of nine years, after you've busted your ass for them, what do you think is going to happen? You think they'll just roll out the red carpet and make you a full partner? I mean that's why you're doing it, right? You want the corner office and the word "partner" after your name on the website. But it all turns on a whim, on how they feel about you when they wake up that morning."

"You're exaggerating. You know that's not how it works," Emily retorted.

"You're right, that's not how it works at most firms. At most firms, you work hard, and you get what you deserve. But you don't work at most firms; you work at our firm—your firm." Hunter was on his feet now, frowning as he tried to keep his voice below a yell.

"I know it's a gamble," Emily asserted. "I'm not blind. But I'm good at this game, and I plan to win." She scowled, obviously ready to leave.

Hunter could tell she was livid at having to defend herself, and he knew she didn't understand where he was coming from.

He clarified, "Just because you're good at the game, it doesn't mean you have to play. You're living somebody else's life, Emily. You've got this picture in your head about the perfect job, the perfect man, and sooner or later it's all going to backfire on you. Mitch and his money won't make you happy. Money isn't everything you know." Hunter turned away from Emily, and his reflection in the glass of the sliding door scowled back at her.

"And what?" she countered. "You're going to culinary school to be poor? If you love cooking so much, why don't you waltz down to the homeless shelter and 'work your magic' for people who would really appreciate it. You're just jealous because I succeeded where you failed. Nobody likes to fail, Hunter, not even at something they hate."

Hunter whipped around and glared at her for a moment before responding. "At least I'm not acting like a damn fool, begging some lying, cheating asshole to come screw me over. Again." He winced inside as he landed the final blow, but he couldn't make himself regret it.

***

Emily left in tears. As she drove, a din of horns and whistles announced the arrival of the New Year. But all she could hear were Hunter's stinging criticisms. She swiped at her eyes. Her vehicle moved steadily down familiar streets, but Emily felt lost and out of place. Hunter's words tumbled through her mind, and she refused to find any truth in them. Instead, she grew defiant.

He doesn't know Mitch like I do, she thought, trying to steady the mix of emotions swirling through her mind. But the world had turned upside down, and she could find no solid ground on which to rest her aching heart. Hunter was her closest friend. He listened to her silly stories and work complaints; complimented her when she looked good, sometimes even when she didn't; and he always saved her a seat when she was running late for meetings. But he was also her most earnest critic. And now she had let him down in every possible way. The look of disappointment in his eyes when she rejected him came back to her, made her miserable. Then there was his anger at hearing Mitch's name again. Emily shook her head at the steering wheel, fretfully chewing on her lower lip. *What a mess*, she thought, *I'll never fix this.*

Determined to set things right, Emily searched for an opening in the median to turn around and drive back to Hunter's apartment, but when the opening came, she passed it by. She was distracted by a flurry of hopes and dreams. She saw herself on the arm of her father, walking down a long white aisle covered with pink petals, Mitch waiting for her down front at the altar. And she saw herself in a beautiful house with leather-bound albums on the shelves showcasing her smiling family and happy life, her own sloping script spelling out the captions beneath the glossy photos of her perfect life.

CHAPTER 13 - MITCH

IT WAS TEN O'CLOCK ON NEW YEAR'S DAY. The temperature had risen into the high 50s overnight, and the sky was blue and clear. The community of River Oaks, nestled in the flatlands just south of Memorial Park and Buffalo Bayou, was hushed and still. Lazy Lane earned its name that day, as the owners of massive mansions and graceful gardens slept off the indulgences of the night before.

Mitch was at home when Emily called and accepted his invitation to join him in Belize. As Emily chattered away about her affection and excitement, relief spread through Mitch's body like a warm wave, awakening a focused energy inside him. As soon as the call was over, he pocketed his phone and darted down the hall.

From the bookcase in the library, locked inside the bottom cabinet, Mitch retrieved a thick letter written on notebook paper, the left sides still frayed at the edges where they had been ripped from their spiral rings. Sections of the letter were underlined in red, and he scanned the underlined portions quickly. When he found the page he was looking for, he folded it in half and set it aside before locking the rest of the letter away again.

A few minutes later, Mitch searched the house for Maggie and found her reading in the living room, fresh from her afternoon nap. He slid into the matching leather chair across from hers. The generous contours of the leather absorbed his weight easily, cradling him like a pillow. But Mitch was a ball of excitement and agitation, and he would not be content until Maggie knew the entirety of his plan. He'd delayed this long because he needed to be sure of Emily's compliance, and now that he was, he could hardly contain himself.

Mitch fidgeted as Maggie closed her book and looked at him. He squirmed in his chair and balled his fist around the page clutched tightly in his palm.

Maggie placed her hand on his knee. "What is it?" she asked.

"Do you remember the story I told you about the men who attacked me in Belize the day I drove down to check on Sena?"

"Yes, of course. How could I forget?"

"Well, I didn't tell you everything that happened that day. You see, Manuel didn't take me to the hospital, not until much later, not until the wound on my head had already closed."

Maggie's face toyed with a frown, and she moved her book from her lap to the side table before she asked, "What do you mean, Mitch? Did you sew it up yourself? I don't understand."

"Look, I need to tell you something, and I need you to just listen. No questions until I'm finished, okay?"

"Okay," she agreed, a note of suspicion in her voice, but she kept her word and sealed her lips.

Mitch inhaled slowly. He began.

"After the attack, Manuel and his son, Evan, carried me on horseback through heat and dust for what felt like a vast distance, but I now know it was less than a mile. I passed in and out of consciousness, and each time I awoke, the pain was like cannons firing inside my skull. Manuel had my shoulders. I couldn't see his face but each time I opened my eyes, I saw Evan's fear staring back at me.

As we journeyed, the sun began to set. I remember the white light of day shifting into the orange haze of twilight then to the dim gray of dusk. We began to climb stairs. Or rather they climbed while I diverted the last of my strength to my neck to try to keep my head from lolling with each upward lunge. But I had nothing left. My strength was gone and each time my head moved I suffered a fireball of pain. We did not climb long before I lost consciousness completely.

The next thing I remember was the sound of chanting. The chanting had no beginning and no end; it seemed to stretch on forever as an infinite river of sound connecting me to the sky and the sky to me. This "river" pulsed through my body, through my veins, and seemed to take on the rhythm of my beating heart. I felt myself rising as if I was being pulled up through the layers of the atmosphere. All the while I could see a woman standing before me. She was as real to me as you are now, but she was not rising with me. She was just … there.

The woman was young with wide eyes and black hair, and she wore a red flower behind her ear. When I stopped rising, she smiled at me, and I could no longer hear Manuel's voice. An ocean of light surrounded me, a milky blue-white churning with energy. Its warmth was palpable, like summer sun on my skin.

The woman came closer and took my right hand in hers. It was then I noticed I was holding something in my left hand—a strip of fabric, which seemed to be dyed red. I didn't give it a second thought, though, because the woman started speaking to me.

"Hello," she said. "My descendant seeks your safe return from the upperworld. This chore will challenge us both, but it has been done before, and I will see it done again."

She reached over and took the fabric from my hand. "We will need this," she said, "when we meet Kimi in the sky world. We are approaching the fortress of Akna. Shield your eyes."

The light surrounding us flashed bright white for no more than a second, but I was temporarily blinded by the wattage for at least a minute. When I could finally focus, I found we were standing knee-deep in grass so verdant I wanted to stuff handfuls of it into my mouth. It was so perfectly green and fresh; I couldn't take my eyes off it. The woman let me run my fingers through the ribbons of green for a few moments before taking me by the hand again.

"Come," she said. "We must go inside."

"Wait," I replied. "Who are you?"

"I am Lady Ixchel, sky goddess of war. You may call me Ixchel."

"Ixchel," I mumbled as I raised my eyes and looked ahead. The fortress of Akna all but glowed before us. It was a broad fortification anchored by twin temples, a massive wall connecting one to the other. The only diminutive thing about it was the entrance, which was a single doorway in the center of the wall. It was barely two feet wide and not even six feet high. I had to crouch down to keep from hitting my head. Ixchel slipped through ahead of me with ease. She was a sliver of a girl, barely more than five feet tall.

There were no guards at the entrance. There wasn't even a door to close off the doorway. I instantly saw why. It was the entrance to a stone maze, each whitewashed passageway seemingly an exact copy of the one before it, beside it, beyond it. On and on the passageways ran like a riddle. But Ixchel guided me through the maze in minutes. I knew I would never find my way out again without her.

The maze ended in a small chamber of gleaming stone furnished with two pairs of polished wooden chairs. The chairs were delicate concave constructions, and the chamber itself reminded me of the waiting room of the Houston Memorial children's wing. The walls completely covered in brightly painted murals. I could tell the paintings told a story, but I didn't have time to make it out.

Suddenly there were others in the room. A young man and an older woman were standing at the far side of the room talking to Ixchel. The new arrivals were dressed regally in oiled skins and strung jade. The woman was much older than Ixchel, and she wore a blue leather tunic with red embroidery at the hem, and shimmering green feathers in her white hair, which fell in a shower of delicate braids to the small of her back. A green jade choker encircled her neck; and jade piercings at her nose and ears gave her grandmotherly features a slightly menacing quality.

The young man was terrifying. He wore a plumed crown as black as ink, and he carried a massive flint knife in a leather harness that crisscrossed his bare chest. His feet were clad in elaborate sandals of woven leather knotted at the ankles and festooned with carved coins of obsidian and white jade. The only actual clothing on the man was a loincloth constructed of the same woven brown and black leather as his sandals but interwoven with red fabric and small red beads. Black skull tattoos in various shapes, sizes, and degrees of agony (some were merely wincing, others clearly screaming) covered his entire torso.

I was in awe. Ixchel, by comparison, was dressed plainly. She wore a short dress of white cotton, a single braided cotton strap crossing one shoulder. A braided leather belt encircled her waist. Her long black hair was pulled back with a white cotton headband and was otherwise unadorned. Still, she was breathtaking. There was a glimmering quality to her, which made her features come to life in a way that can only be described as magical.

I watched as Ixchel gave the piece of fabric I'd brought with me to the man. He folded it, placed it on his tongue, and closed his mouth around it. When he closed his mouth, his body began to vibrate. This lasted about thirty seconds, maybe less. He handed the fabric back to Ixchel and spoke to the woman. The woman shook her head, then seemed to argue with Ixchel briefly. Ixchel looked at me with a frown before leading the man and woman over to me.

"I present Kimi, sky god of death," Ixchel said. The man nodded his greeting. I bowed deeply, eager to please the god who I believed held the keys to my fate.

Ixchel gestured toward the woman. "I present Ixazaluoh, goddess of healing and medicine." I bowed again. Ixazaluoh smiled.

"Ixazaluoh has claimed your soul," Ixchel explained. "It is hers by right, and only she can release your soul back to your body. I had hoped to bargain an exchange. The man whose blood soaks this fabric has been killed in your name. Kimi has divined that the man's soul has been claimed by Cizin, a god of the underworld, as a trifle for the lords of blood. I have offered to take you to the underworld and steal his soul, so Ixazaluoh may take his soul in place of yours. But she does not want this man's soul. He is a killer and a coward. And it's not a fair exchange."

Ixazaluoh spoke up. "You are a brave man," she said, "and a worthy soul. I intend to keep you."

I shuddered at the compliment, and all I could think to say was, "Please. I need to go home."

Ixchel took me aside. "There is a way," she said. "I happen to know that there is a soul Ixazaluoh wants far more than yours. The man she desires has been trapped in Xibalba for more than a decade. If we free him for her, she will grant your release. And then your soul will be mine."

"I hate to argue with you," I replied, "because I know you're trying to help me. But that doesn't exactly improve my situation. I want to go home."

"And you shall," Ixchel said. "For though your soul will be mine, I will not claim you today. I shall return you to middleworld as my descendant begs. But you shall be mine when next you meet your end. Until that time, you shall be my ward, indebted to me, but free to live your life."

"Just to be clear, when you say you will return me to "middleworld," do you mean the earth? Houston, Texas?" I asked.

She smiled. "I do not know Houston, Texas, but I will return you to the land that you have very recently departed. Do you accept my offer?"

"Yes," I replied.

Ixchel walked back to Kimi and Ixazaluoh and made the bargain. With a wave and a smile, the god of death and the goddess of healing and medicine disappeared in a swirl of black and a flash of red, respectively.

Ixchel returned to my side. "Come," she said, "we must make our way to Xibalba." She took my hand and led me back toward the entrance of the maze surrounding the fortress of Akna.

"How do we get to Xibalba, and who, exactly, are we looking for?" I asked as we started winding our way back through the labyrinth of white stone.

"We are looking for a man named Edward. He's a chiro--." She frowned as she struggled to find the right word. "A chiropractitioner or something like that."

"A chiropractor," I corrected.

"Yes, thank you. A chiropractor. Or at least he was when he lived in middleworld. Ixazaluoh is the goddess of medicine, you know. That is how she met him."

"Her definition of medicine is rather generous."

"Why do you say that?"

"Bad joke. Please continue."

"It was the beginning of the 20th century. Ixazaluoh tells me she met him in a place called Iowa. He was one of the first in the land to take up the profession. Edward was just beginning to find his footing in the medical community, and Ixazaluoh loves a good beginning, as do I. She's not keen on endings, though. On this point, we disagree. I love a good ending. One does not rise from the ashes of a good beginning. It's the ending of one's life that matters most."

I nodded.

"According to Ixazaluoh," Ixchel continued, "there was something about this man, Edward, that drove her to reveal herself to him one evening in June. He was in harmony with all the world around him, a true and noble soul who wanted nothing more than to offer honest aid to every other human being. Ixazaluoh appeared to him just as he was locking the door to his office for the day. They fell in love and remained together for a hundred years. Ixazaluoh was able to prolong his life, but she couldn't stave off death forever. That is beyond her province. She would've had to answer to Kimi, the god of death, if she'd tried. You see, it's all one big power struggle with a lot of competing egos, and we have to be careful not to stray beyond our bounds."

Ixchel released my hand when we reached the gleaming grassland at the fortress's exterior. "From here we will travel to middleworld," she said. "We will then enter Actun Tunichil Muknal, the Cave of the Crystal Sepulcher, and follow the cave passage to the underworld."

The goddess wrapped her arms around me. "Close your eyes," she whispered.

With a flash of blinding light, we were off. It was utter free fall of the amusement park variety. But somehow, I didn't feel nauseous at all. In fact, I'd never felt physically better in my life. Moments later, we touched down in a sweltering jungle.

"The entrance to the cave is just through here," she said. "Stay close behind me."

"Will do," I replied as we picked our way through the underbrush. I could hear rushing water nearby. Ten paces later we were standing at the bank of a river, its churning tail feeding into the mouth of a large cave.

"Whatever happened with Edward and Ixazaluoh?" I asked as we walked the rocky riverbank and made our way toward the cave's open mouth. "How did he end up in Xibalba?"

"Eventually, Ixazaluoh had to let Edward go. He died peacefully in his sleep, which meant he gained no honor in death. He would have to be tested in the underworld and earn his honor there. Sadly, Edward was a good man, too good to get the better of the lords of Xibalba. They crushed him like a bug, literally and figuratively. Ixazaluoh learned that the Demon of Filth turned him into a bark beetle and stomped on him repeatedly for about a half-dozen years. He's been returned to human form now, and Ixazaluoh has learned he's been imprisoned in Bat House for the last five years. We'll free him and bring him back to her."

"Ixazaluoh's a goddess, right?" I asked. We'd entered the cave moments earlier and were now following the path of a gently flowing stream toward a smaller opening in the distance. "Why doesn't she rescue him herself?"

"She can't, not without great risk. There are three planes of existence within the cosmos. The upperworld, middleworld, and the underworld. Ixazaluoh is a goddess of the upperworld, and so she has always been. Like all upperworld gods, she can take human form and travel freely from the upperworld to middleworld. But she may not breach the borders of the underworld without debasing herself to the lords of Xibalba. If they got the better of her, they could confine her to the underworld and diminish her.

Only humans, who are the spawn of the creator gods, may move between the three planes. Some of the oldest gods, like Kimi, first among the death gods, may enter Xibalba with impunity. Of course, Kimi may also take human form and enter middleworld, but he hasn't done so in some time. It goes without saying that the creator gods themselves, Heart of Sky and Heart of Earth may also come and go as they please. They are among the very oldest of the gods and the most powerful. They do not concern themselves with the power struggles of lesser gods."

"I see."

"There's more. Most humans have access to only one of the three planes at any point in time. They are born in middleworld and, when they die, they either rise or fall, depending on the manner of their death. Those who die with honor—in battle, through sacrifice, or by their own hand—fly to the upperworld. All others fall to the underworld. And they remain there unless they can defeat the lords of Xibalba at their own game. It is a daunting challenge, but many have prevailed and flown free to the upperworld. However, these days, not as many make it out as before. In this new age of machines and materialism, far fewer souls are capable of besting the lords of Xibalba. Most modern humans lack the skills to defeat the nefarious gods below. You must possess stealth and speed. These qualities are common enough. But you must also be cunning and cruel, capable of outwitting every creature in your path or willing to cut your enemies down if they cannot be outsmarted. Unfortunately, skullduggery is a lost art. And bloodlust has fallen out of favor. While this bodes well for the living, it has dire consequences for the dead."

"It's true," I conceded. "Most people lead very busy lives these days. Skullduggery is so time-consuming. It gets short changed."

"Their lives are busy the way an ant's life is busy. Over and over, round and round. It is always the same. There is no glory anymore, no triumph." She shook her head. "I shouldn't criticize. Ixazaluoh believes the world is a better place these days. She takes nourishment at the bosom of peace and harmony, and I used to feel the same a long time ago. But the snake king changed my mind when he and his ilk destroyed my home and my family.

"I miss the days when kings and queens cured controversies with war. Whole city-states prayed to me and Buluk Chabtan. I would transform into the jaguar goddess of war, and Buluk Chabtan into Yax Muwaan, the first hawk. We would descend upon the fields of battle and sharpen our teeth and claws upon the bones of our foes. It was a thrilling time."

I watched as a strange combination of bloodlust and wistful melancholy gathered in her eyes. When we approached the mouth of the cave, I asked, "I don't mean to second guess you, but I'm confused. I'm human, which means I can only access one of the three planes at a time. And you're a goddess of the upperworld, which means you can't, or shouldn't, access the underworld at all. How are we going to get down there?"

"Ah, yes. I left out the most important part. I was once human, and my lord father was a Halach Winic, a god-king imbued with the power to bridge cosmic realms. This power is bestowed by the creator gods upon each Halach Winic and his descendants. It is a great honor, a sacred birthright, which allows me to travel freely between the planes." She took my hand as we approached the mouth of the cave. "Are you ready?"

"I assume you've got a plan."

"Indeed. I have been preparing for this moment for fourteen hundred years."

CHAPTER 14 - HUNTER AND EMILY

HUNTER WOKE ON NEW YEAR'S DAY to a nest of needles behind his eyes and a stomach that wouldn't settle. After Emily left, he'd finished the bottle of wine then chased it with half a bottle of whiskey before calling it a night. When he pulled the blanket from his eyes that morning at ten, he shrank back from the sun at his window as shafts of light broke free from the edges of his closed curtains. He decided to stay in bed.

His physical pain coupled with his wounded pride were enough to keep him in bed for most of the morning. But at eleven fifteen, he showered and dressed then schlepped to the kitchen for a cup of coffee.

On the kitchen counter, tucked behind the coffee pot, he found his gift from Emily. He wiped clean a section of granite and spread the knives out in front of him, examining each in turn. They were excellent quality, and when he pictured Emily browsing the store to find him a gift (and a very nice one at that), then wrapping her selection with care, his heart quickened with happiness. But the feeling didn't last. He soon pictured Emily in Mitch's arms, and his thoughts devolved from there.

In an effort to divert himself from the Emily situation, Hunter called Stacy Goodwyn. "Hey, it's Hunter," he said when she picked up.

"Hi there!" she chirped, and Hunter could sense a smile in her voice. "What's up?" she asked.

"Seeing as its New Year's Day and all, you probably have plans already, but I was wondering if you might be able to grab a bite to eat later today."

"I'm having a late lunch with my parents," she replied. "I'm heading over there at two."

"And I'm having dinner with the family at six," Hunter said. "Hey, do you want to join us? The Marlows are known to make a great New Year's feast. We're all here in Houston this year, at my sister's place in Montrose."

"Thanks, but I'm doing dinner with my grandparents tonight. It's a tradition. But why don't you meet me for coffee before I head over to my parents'? I'm out of the good stuff here at home, and I sure could use a big ole dose of New Year's cheer this morning. We can meet at the Starbucks on the corner of Gray and Shepherd."

"Which one?"

"The one that's not next to the bakery ... with the outside seating."

"Do you think they're open today? It's New Year's Day after all."

"They're always open. Trust me."

"Sounds good. What time do you want to meet?"

"How's about high noon?"

"Noon it is. See you there."

When Stacy arrived at Starbucks, Hunter was already seated at an outside table reading a day-old copy of the Houston Chronicle.

"Hey there!" she said as she walked over, "I'm going inside to grab a coffee and a cranberry muffin; do you want anything?"

"No," he replied, pointing at the large coffee in front of him. "I'm fine. Thanks."

Stacy walked inside to place her order, and Hunter half-heartedly returned to his paper. Moments later, he smiled warmly as Stacy, coffee and muffin in hand, approached the table and set her plate on the wrought iron surface. He stood to greet her with a hug, but she was already reaching for her chair, which caused them to collide in an awkward embrace. Surprised and clearly nervous, Stacy muttered a quick apology and slid into her seat, licking a trickle of spilled coffee from the lid of her cup.

While Stacy fiddled with her napkin, muffin, and coffee cup, Hunter shook his head and struggled for something to say. "Crummy weather we've been having lately," he offered, "but at least the rain's let up."

"I know what you mean," Stacy replied, "I'm a sun girl myself. The hotter the better. Although, I have to say the humidity DOES A NUMBER on my hair. But I found the most AMAZING straightening balm last month. It has, like, ninja straightening powers." She tossed her hair so Hunter could take in the full effect.

"Absolutely. Amazing."

She smiled. "All I can say is, bring it on Houston humidity. This girl can take it."

Hunter chuckled, then chugged his coffee as Stacy launched into an oral dissertation on the pros and cons of wet/dry ceramic flatirons versus tourmaline ionic hairdryers as a countermeasure to the Houston heat's frizzing effects on thick (but not course), wavy hair.

She's funny, Hunter acknowledged as Stacy chatted, giggled, and smiled. But that didn't change his baseline opinion of her. Although Stacy was a beautiful woman, and he was happy to spend time with her, he didn't trust her. He'd always suspected there was mercenary intent lurking beneath her perfectly polished facade. He'd seen her turn on the charm at holiday parties, luncheons, and summer socials. Usually, her target of choice was one of the wealthier partners, young or old, it didn't matter. Now that he was merely an unemployed associate, he found her sudden over-the-top interest in him baffling and a tad disingenuous. He wondered what was going on with her, but there was no polite way to ask.

As Hunter watched Stacy flirt unabashedly with him (he'd inadvertently stopped listening to her a few minutes earlier), he realized Emily was the only woman he genuinely cared about. She'd seen him at his worst and managed to remain patient and understanding through it all, no matter how ornery he became. She also managed to be cool and funny without being utterly self-absorbed. Her only problem was that her asshole-radar needed a serious tune-up.

At that moment, Hunter made up his mind he was going to do everything in his power to keep Emily away from Mitch. As soon as he could wrap things up with Stacy, he was going to give Emily a call. And this time he wouldn't take no for an answer. He had to make Emily see that getting back together with Mitch would be a huge mistake. He owed her that much. But that was only the first step. He and Emily were meant to be together, and he had no intention of letting her slip through his fingers again. As he gulped down the last of his coffee and tapped his watch to give Stacy the hint it was time to go, he made himself a promise. By the end of this day Emily would be done with Mitch once and for all.

The Sky Place

***

At one o'clock in the afternoon on New Year's Day, Emily decided to brave the Galleria for a long overdue shopping excursion. As she steered her SUV through the mall's maze-like underground parking lot, she realized she had a busy day ahead of her. She needed everything. Everything, that is, to look hot while staying cool on her tropical vacation.

After several hours at Saks, Emily was trying on her last batch of clothes. She tried two pairs of shorts in rapid succession, examining each one briefly in the mirror before returning them to their hangers. The third pair of shorts, distressed denim cutoffs, fit perfectly, and she lingered in front of the mirror to admire the way the back pockets highlighted the curves of her bottom.

Hunter would like these, she thought with a smile, recalling the last time she'd gone clothes shopping. It was almost six months ago, and Hunter had reluctantly agreed to join her, complaining as they drove that he was missing the Rangers game.

But once they'd arrived at the mall, his mood became lighter, more playful, and Emily had really enjoyed herself with him. He'd made it his mission that day to help her find a flattering pair of jeans. Emily's smile widened as she thought about how patient he'd been with her as she tried on pair after pair for him. *I must have tried on ten pairs at least*, she recalled. In that moment, she was deeply grateful for Hunter's friendship. Through the mess of the last two years, he was the one person she could always count on. She was sorry they'd fought, but his words had cut too deep for her to even think about forgiving him yet. She promised herself she wouldn't think about Hunter again until after she got back from Belize.

Returning her focus to her reflection in the mirror, Emily slid her hands into the pockets of the shorts and gave another half turn. As she turned, a sliver of blue fabric caught her attention. It was one of the cocktail dresses the sales associate had selected for her to try on. Emily slipped it off the hanger. The sapphire color was exquisite, and it was one of her favorite styles—a fitted bodice with a flared skirt—the kind that was perfect for an evening out, especially when dancing was on the agenda.

93

Her thoughts turned to Mitch. He always took her dancing when they went out together. He'd go out of his way to find the most charming, off-the-radar venues where they could spend time together and dance the night away. *He's a hopeless romantic*, she thought with a smile as she slipped the cocktail dress on and smiled at her reflection in the mirror.

Emily changed back into her clothes and took the shorts and the dress to the checkout counter. A few more hours finished the job, and she left the Galleria with five bulging shopping bags and a bit of reclaimed confidence. When she touched down in Belize, she would look damn good. As she drove home, she began mentally packing her bags, her excitement building all the while.

Thirty minutes later Emily entered her condo, pulled her phone from her purse, and checked her messages. She'd been so distracted after talking to Mitch that morning, she must have forgotten to turn the ringer back on before leaving for the Galleria. She opened her voicemail—two new messages. The first was from her father,

"Hi Emily, this is Dad. Just calling to wish you a Happy New Year. Sorry I missed your call on Christmas day. Jocelyn and I were in Breckenridge with the girls for Christmas, and you know how your stepmother is about vacations … always makes me switch off my technology. Anyway, I'm glad to hear you're working hard. Make sure you give it your all. Alright…. Well, I hope you had a merry Christmas. Love you. Bye now." Emily listened to the message again, and then pressed save when prompted by her machine.

The second message was from Hunter, "Hey Emily, it's Hunter. I really need to talk to you. Please call me at home when you get this message. I'll be waiting to hear from you."

Emily wasn't sure what to make of Hunter's message. His tone betrayed nothing, and she couldn't tell if he was calling to apologize. There was only one way to find out. She picked up the phone with the intention of dialing his home number, but quickly realized she didn't know it. She dialed his cell phone instead. What she found at the other end of the line was the last thing she expected.

CHAPTER 15 - MITCH AND MAGGIE

"**WHAT DID IXCHEL MEAN,**" Maggie asked, "when she said she'd been preparing for fourteen hundred years?"

"I don't know," Mitch lied. He had no intention of telling Maggie all the details of Ixchel's grand plan. It would only frighten her unnecessarily. And the last thing Mitch wanted to do was give Maggie one more thing to worry about. He'd already made up his mind to reveal only the tip of the iceberg when the time came to explain his debt to Ixchel. "You promised not to interrupt," he reminded her.

"Right," she said. "Sorry."

"No problem." He leaned forward and squeezed Maggie's shoulder gently before he continued.

"The first phase of our journey was to enter the underworld through an earthbound cave and make our way to the realm of the shapeshifters. At this point, we'd entered the mouth of the Cave of the Crystal Sepulcher and were heading toward a smaller opening within the cave itself. When we reached the opening, Ixchel took my hand and whispered, "Jump." We dropped like rocks at first, until Ixchel suspended us on a cushion of light, and we floated to the ground.

"We've arrived," she announced.

We were standing on the precipice of a great cliff. Below, the underworld stretch forth for miles, and we could see it all from our perch, as if we were looking down upon a three-dimensional map. The landscape below was separated into three distinct regions, the terrain of each producing a clear delineation of color, a triangle with corners of ocher, green, and brown. To the south was desert. The northwest held jungle terrain. The northeast, the seat of the lords of Xibalba, held marshlands. We were perched at the southernmost point within the underworld, its entrance. Immediately north of us, within the southern point of the triangle, twin canyons yawned amid the ocher desert. The towering walls of the canyons rose steep and narrow, forming one ragged abyss after the other. From the canyons ran four roads, each a different color and texture. Black tar. White limestone. Red clay. Green grass. Midway between the desert and the marshlands the roads merged and crossed, then veered away from each other. The green road curved northwest and the white road curved hard south. The black and red roads both ran northeast.

"Black Road leads to Xibalba," Ixchel said. "Green Road leads to the jungle and the realm of the shapeshifters. But we must first clear the canyons and the rapids...."

"The rapids?"

"Scorpion rapids, just beyond Gurgling Canyon." She pointed toward the second canyon, the one farthest from us. "You can't see the rapids from here, not with human eyes," she explained. "First of all, they are somewhat obscured by the twin canyons, Rustling Canyon and Gurgling Canyon. But more importantly, in the underworld, water is never as it seems, never as it should be. It is tainted with a dark enchantment, which gives it an elusive quality unless you are standing right in front of it. Even then, you cannot trust your eyes." She touched my arm to draw my attention away from the scenery below. We headed east along the ridge of the cliff. "From here until we reach Xibalba, we must travel as human souls," she said. "The eyes of the owls will be upon us before long, and if they catch the scent of magic, they'll raise the alarm, and we will lose the element of surprise. We will take the long road down, then head toward the jungle, where we will enter the realm of the shapeshifters.

"Remember this," she cautioned. "Xibalba is The Place of Fear, and the lords of Xibalba prey upon those who possess fear or weakness. You must steady your mind and summon your courage. There will be many tests along the way. If we fail even one, we will be defeated. We will either be cast out immediately, finding ourselves back upon this cliff, or, if the lords of Xibalba feel like trifling with us, we will find ourselves standing before them at the council table. Either way, our humiliation will be complete, and we will have no hope of prevailing."

The Sky Place

A few meters east, the cliff softened, the ridge breaking to reveal a small path, and we descended toward the desert and the canyons. The narrow path that wound down was steep and rocky, and we crawled and slid our way to the desert floor.

The canyons were less than half a mile away and we cleared the distance quickly and easily. We were then faced with an enormous wall of rock that appeared to be utterly insurmountable. It was the southern rise of Rustling Canyon.

"What now?" I asked apprehensively.

"We find the door," Ixchel replied. She walked briskly westward, stopped momentarily, then called for me to join her. Taking my hand, she led me into and out of all four walls of the twin canyons.

"You said you weren't going to use magic down here," I reminded her.

"This isn't my magic," she replied. "The seams in the canyons have always been here; you just have to know where to look."

The canyons were now behind us, and Scorpion Rapids ahead. I could hear rushing water in the distance, but I could see nothing in front of me but a growing cloud of black.

"Throng birds," Ixchel announced as the black cloud churned closer.

I could now make out the bodies of the birds, huge black crows, flying straight for us.

"Don't look at them!" Ixchel commanded. "Do not let them see your eyes. Shield your brow with your hands and look only at the ground. Stay close behind me. We must move quickly."

Ixchel covered her eyes and picked up the pace, jogging toward the birds. The sound of the crows' piercing cries and beating wings rose to a furious pitch as they swarmed overhead, and I felt as though I was running beneath the eye of a hurricane. I lost track of Ixchel but kept running straight forward. Within minutes, the birds were gone, and the sound of rushing water once again filled the air. I scanned the perimeter for Ixchel. She was standing near the bank of a raging river, but her eyes were focused on the sky.

Above, an enormous grey owl circled lazily in the clear sky. I squinted at it, asking, "Will it attack?"

"No. That is Macaw Owl. He's a messenger for One and Seven Death, and he's on a scouting mission. If we don't give him anything to see, he won't have anything to report." She paused. "We don't have to worry about him. It's Shooting Owl and Skull Owl we must look out for. They're nasty beasts, and they've been known to force a fight."

"Let's get out of here," I said. "How do we get across these rapids?"

"We walk across."

"What? How?"

"It isn't water," she replied. "To you, it appears to be water, but I can perceive its true nature. It's a nest of scorpions."

"I don't see how that's any better," I protested.

"It's a test. Most people try to swim across the widest part of the river, up there, where the current appears to be weakest. As soon as you submerge yourself in the water, the scorpions reveal themselves. You panic and try to scramble back to shore. Your fear causes the scorpions to turn back into water, and you are swept away by the rapids. But if you simply walk across without fear, you will not be harmed. We will cross here, at the narrowest point, where the water appears to rage and boil."

"How do I walk on water?" I asked as we approached the bank.

"Just follow me," she replied. "Put one foot in front of the other, and don't be afraid."

We were barely two paces into the riverbed when the water transformed into a seething nest of red and black scorpions. They emitted a screeching, unearthly cry that sent my heart to my throat and my stomach in the other direction. But I refused to panic. I just put one foot in front of the other until we reached the other side.

"We're almost there," Ixchel announced once we'd cleared the rapids. The entrance to the jungle is less than a mile ahead, just past the twin rivers."

We walked for a time in silence. Finally, in an attempt to make conversation, I asked, "I thought the underworld had nine layers. Am I missing something?"

She bristled, and I immediately wished I'd kept my mouth shut. "That was the work of the wretched Spaniards," she growled. "Dante's prose was ripe in their minds, and they wrote his stories into ours. In time, it became difficult to separate one from the other. Landa was nothing more than a well-read savage. He tortured my people in the name of Christ. If I could, I would have eaten his heart. But my husband did not want me to interfere.

At the time, I was still addled by the habit of submission. Fortunately, those days are centuries behind me. It took my husband almost one thousand years, but he has finally learned to accept our differences.

"Without a true companion it's easy to lose your way in this world," she added wistfully as her anger subsided. "I've been blessed with an extraordinary marriage, and I am thankful for it. Things have not always been easy between me and my husband. And our path to matrimony was filled with twists and turns. I had a choice to make back then. There were two men in my life, and they were as different as night and day. The choice between them was not an easy one to make, but I have never regretted my decision. My husband and I will celebrate our fourteen hundred and sixtieth wedding anniversary this year."

"Congratulations," I said.

"Thank you," she replied. "I have no idea what to get him. I've half a mind to capture a pair of throng birds on the way out. He has a soft spot for birds."

"They looked like ugly buggers to me," I offered. "Why don't you grab that big owl instead? He was something else. Those red feathers shone like a coat of rubies."

"Yes, Macaw Owl is the most handsome of the owls. But I'd have One and Seven Death on my tail for the rest of eternity. They love those owls like children. Besides, the throng birds are quite beautiful when they're not swarming like bees. You couldn't tell before, but some of them have wings of green and blue. Those are the ones I shall capture for my husband." She stopped. "We've reached the rivers."

I balked. Then blinked. She was right about the waterways in Xibalba. I'd been looking straight ahead as we walked, but I'd seen nothing but the jungle in the distance and the green road beneath my feet. Only now could I perceive the scent and sound of flowing water. The twin rivers glistened silver-blue to my left and right. I moved left, reaching for the surface of the one nearest me. Ixchel stopped me mid-stride.

"Do not drink from the rivers," she warned. "One is blood, and the other is pus. Only after you drink do you learn which is which. It is another test. Keep your eyes on the road, nothing here is as it seems."

We made our way past the twin rivers and into the jungle, where we planned to secure the aid of the shapeshifters. This was the only part of the plan that didn't scare the heck out of me.

I was alone when I entered the council place of the lords of Xibalba, an open, circular room with a plastered, painted roof supported by carved columns that ran the perimeter at three-foot intervals. It was dusk, and the lords were seated together at council. The lords were vile creatures, part human, part Halloween hideousness. I recognized each of them from Ixchel's description.

Scab Stripper and Blood Gatherer were the worst. The muscles and tendons of their limbs and torso lay open and exposed beneath cloaks of feathers and hide. Bone Scepter and Skull Scepter were likewise sans skin. But exposed bone is a lot easier to stomach than exposed sinew and tissue. The remaining six lords were equally unappealing. One and Seven Death looked downright regal by comparison. They appeared to be nothing more than a pair of mid-height, stocky men in capes of dyed leather and headdresses of oiled plumes.

Seven Death waved me over, and I approached the lords with as much confidence as I could muster. The perimeter of the council table reeked like rancid meat, and I struggled to deliver my practiced monologue without losing my composure and the contents of my stomach.

"Lords of Xibalba, I have defeated you," I declared loudly and drove my fists into the air. Most of the lords scrunched their faces at me in disbelief, others stared blankly. Bloody Teeth laughed, his red mouth causing me to shudder.

"It is true," I continued in the same commanding tone. "I have released your bats from Bat House. Go and see for yourself if you do not believe me. Look! There they go." I gestured to my left as half a dozen bats flapped and squeaked beyond the columns, then darted off into the gathering darkness.

"It cannot be!" One Death declared furiously. The lords rose in unison, and my bowls turned to water as they ran toward me. But they didn't stop. They ran from the council room and directly toward Bat House. I hurried after them.

One after the other, they piled into Bat House. And one by one they started screaming as the bats, still trapped inside, tore them apart. I watched as Ixchel jumped from an upper window carrying a small ball of light. She touched down lightly and placed the ball of light on the soft earth. It stretched and grew until it took the shape of a man, who I could only assume was Edward.

Ixchel was laughing to the point of tears as she walked over to me, Edward in tow. The sky had darkened with the fall of night, and six bats descended upon us from the purple-black haze above. As they approached, they shifted into human form and landed softly nearby. They were all laughing as riotously as Ixchel.

"How did you know they would all run inside the house like that?" I asked Ixchel, "Why didn't one of them just peek inside a window?"

"They're idiots!" Ixchel replied, still gasping with laughter. Finally, her laughter began to subside, and she grew serious. "We should get out of here," she said. "They will regenerate quickly, and they will want a rematch if we are still here."

At this, the shapeshifters transformed into various winged creatures—hawks, owls, vultures—and departed.

"Thank you!" Ixchel called after them.

"Anytime," the last to shift replied before taking the form of a falcon and flapping off.

"Come," Ixchel said to me. I walked over to her. Edward was still at her side. With a flash of white we were off. When the light faded, we were standing together at the base of Gurgling Canyon.

Ixchel sang out a wordless tune, and the throng birds appeared in the distance. She flew toward them, a stream of golden light forming in her wake. The birds engulfed her, churning in a knot of black. Suddenly the swirling knot seemed lit from within, and Ixchel emerged with a bird in each hand, flying toward us twice as fast as the swarm. She landed beside us, and we covered our eyes as the birds flew over and away. Smiling at her conquest, she lifted the birds upside down by their legs, their blue and green wings flapping wildly at her sides. "Aren't they lovely?" she asked.

The birds were larger than ordinary crows, with heads and beaks like polished ebony. At the base of their necks their feathers changed. One had feathers of midnight blue ornamenting its back and wings, the other, emerald green. "Yes," I agreed, "they're magnificent."

"Excuse me," Edward interjected. "Can someone please tell me what's going on here?"

Ixchel looked at him apologetically, but there was no time for an explanation. Without warning, the Demon of Filth spiraled down from above in a funnel cloud of dirt and smoke.

"You dare challenge the lords of Xibalba," he bellowed at Ixchel.

She shrugged. "I see no lords here, only a talking tower of dung."

"Wretched girl," he growled. "You have humiliated them. And they are too stupid to break the old traditions. They will not budge to avenge themselves. But I do not cower before archaic customs. I will have my revenge."

"You will have my sword up your ass," Ixchel replied nonchalantly. "I shall slay you where you stand." With that, she winked at me and thrust her arms forward. "Hold these," she said to me and Edward and handed us the birds.

Once confined to the hands of mere mortals, the birds flapped and pecked wildly. I struggled to subdue the blue bugger, while Edward wrestled with the green. Meanwhile, Ixchel and the Demon of Filth were circling each other in a menacing dance of I'm about to kick your ass.

From the swirling filth around him, the demon drew a double-edged spear. Ixchel answered in kind, conjuring a sword of light from thin air. The battle began in a flash and raged lightning fast. For every thrust and jab the demon offered, Ixchel defended and counter-struck until the demon was bleeding black from head to toe. In a desperate bid for victory, the demon lunged at the goddess with a two-handed thrust aimed straight for her heart. In a single fluid movement, she sidestepped his attack, severed both his hands at the wrists, and knocked him on his back. His spear disintegrated, and his hands fell to the ground between his splayed legs.

With the point of her sword notched under his chin, she demanded, "Where is Lord Water? Will he not face me, Sky Witness?"

"The Demon of Woe is no fool," Sky Witness answered. His breathe came in labored gasps and black blood oozed from his brown lips. "He knows what you intend for him. He will never face you."

"Then you shall bear the brunt of my rage!" she bellowed. With that, a second sword of light appeared in her free hand. She was as good as her word. Positioning her blade between his legs, she skewered him and decapitated him in short order.

The battle over, Ixchel's swords dissolved as quickly as they'd appeared. She came over to me and Edward and took the throng birds from our hands. By way of explanation, she offered, "That was Lord Sky Witness of Calakmul. He and Lord Water of Caracol destroyed my home and my family. They were villains in life, and they are demons in death. They now serve One and Seven Death as lords of Xibalba. They are now called Demon of Filth and Demon of Woe. One day I shall destroy them both completely. Today, I must be content with this small victory. Sky Witness will regenerate soon, and we have more important things to do today. Both of you, put your hands on my shoulders."

We flew straight to the upperworld, disembarking onto the verdant grass outside the fortress of Akna.

Ixazaluoh was waiting for us there amid the green. "Edward!" she waved gleefully. He ran to her.

"Are we set?" Ixchel called to Ixazaluoh.

"Yes, he's all yours," Ixazaluoh answered happily, wrapping Edward in a mist of red before disappearing.

Ixchel encased the throng birds in a cage of light, then turned to me, "Are you ready to go home?"

"Absolutely," I said. "Thank you for helping me."

"You're welcome." She grinned slyly. "Remember, you owe me."

"Of course," I replied. "But how can someone like me ever help someone like you?"

"You can't help me now, but when you return to me, you will join me in my quest to vanquish the Demon of Filth and the Demon of Woe."

"Don't take this the wrong way, but it seems like you're throwing good energy after bad. Those demons, they can't be destroyed, right? They just keep coming back."

"You're right. I cannot vanquish them, not in the underworld and not alone. Like all gods, my powers are specific. I cannot destroy another god, not completely. There is, however, someone who can. Kimi, the god of death. With his help, I would finally be able to vanquish them both. But

Kimi has not agreed to help me, not yet. I will need to secure his assistance. And I will need a way to lure the demons from the protection of the underworld. To this end, I could use all the help I can get."

"What about One and Seven Death? Aren't *they* death gods? Won't they try to kill *us*?" I asked.

"They will not bother," she said. "There are many versions of the same gods with similar powers. The upperworld gods, or sky gods, derive their powers from the ancient, supreme gods—Heart of Sky and Heart of Earth—the begetters of life, who existed before the beginning of time. Most of the old gods, including the old gods of the underworld like One and Seven Death, rarely stir from their palaces. Once they pass the mantel, they tend to idle in retirement, leaving the spiritual governance of middleworld to their younger counterparts. Only Heart of Sky remains vigilant. He likes to keep an eye on things, but he will not stir from his sky palace for the sake of two wretched demons."

I nodded silently for a moment as I processed this supernatural social hierarchy, then said, "I'll be happy to help you when I return. But I hope you don't mind waiting. I plan to live as long as I can."

She smiled. "I've waited fourteen hundred years, biding my time, gathering my allies. Another half century won't kill me."

Beneath me, the earth shuddered. Ixchel closed her eyes and opened her arms. "I will send you home now," she whispered.

I began to fall gently, as if buoyed on a pillow of air. The goddess did not follow me. I could see her standing above, her arms stretched open as if the force of her will was sending me back to the surface of the earth. I awoke to the glow of Manuel's lantern inside the chamber. My wound was healed."

Maggie looked as if she wanted to speak, but Mitch stopped her. "I'm not finished.... When we got the news about your prognosis two months ago, I wrote to Manuel, and I asked him to perform the ceremony on you."

Maggie's eyes grew wide, but she said nothing.

"I asked Manuel to tell me how he saved me. I wanted to know everything. In his letter, he explained it all to me, the history and the legend. He told me about the Sky Place, the tallest temple at Caracol. There, within the uppermost chamber, he repeated the incantations to call the goddess, and used the blood of the man he killed, my enemy, as an offering. All three of these things are required to save a life.

"Maggie, I want us to go to Belize," Mitch continued, his voice boiling with energy. "I want Manuel to perform the ceremony on you. I've arranged for Emily to meet us there, as your enemy. Obviously, she doesn't know the…."

"You can't kill anyone, Mitch!" Maggie blurted. "Not even her."

"No, of course not," he assured her, "I'm not going to kill anybody. Manuel has given me every detail surrounding the procedure. I wanted confirmation about everything, each requirement, before I proceeded. He responded just last week—I guess it was a day or two before Christmas. A blood offering is required. But only blood, not death. It won't be anything serious, just a small cut." He searched Maggie's face for any sign of her feelings, but her expression was ambiguous, offering nothing in return. "This will work," he insisted, gripping her hand in his. "Don't you understand? I should be dead. I'm a doctor, and I know I should be dead right now. But I'm sitting here on this chair talking to you. This. Will. Work."

Maggie shook her head. "I thought the neurologist determined that your injury was nothing more than a flesh wound. Maybe Manuel gave you something that made you hallucinate—some type of rainforest drugs or something."

Mitch straightened his back and looked his wife in the eyes. "I wasn't hallucinating," he insisted, his voice rising as he spoke. "And there is no way this was merely a flesh wound. I know it appears that way now. But that neurologist wasn't there in the heat of the fight. Trust me, Maggie. Everything I've told you is the absolute truth. I've already made all the arrangements. We leave for Belize tomorrow morning."

***

Maggie closed her eyes and tried to absorb the magnitude of Mitch's plan. The facts as Mitch saw them were before her, barefaced. There was nothing to question, nothing to clarify. The path Mitch wanted her to travel was in front of her. She needed only to take the first step. She needed only to believe.

She whispered to Mitch, "You know this is crazy, right? You know it is. I'm not saying I'm willing to accept my condition, but this plan of yours...."

"Well, I'm certainly not going to accept it," Mitch said. "Manuel saved my life that day, saved it with ancient magic and nothing else; and I'll be damned if I'm not going to do everything in my power to make him do it again. I am not going to lose you, not like this."

"This is madness," Maggie said, "it will never work." But she did not mean it. A small spark had ignited inside her when Mitch revealed his plan, and that spark was now a raging wildfire. Maggie had every faith in Mitch's ability to save her life. She was utterly amazed at how much she believed it, so much so that she could not even say it out loud yet. His idea, his grand scheme had somehow given her hope again, and she could feel the strength returning to her body already. She only prayed she could sustain that strength through what was to come.

Mitch and Maggie arrived in Belize City at eleven thirty the following morning and made their way to their hotel. Their reservations were for the honeymoon suite at The Radisson Fort George Hotel, which was located across the street from Emily's accommodations. After depositing their luggage, they made their way to the restaurant for a late lunch.

At three o'clock, the Hudsons returned to their room to unpack and await Emily's arrival. While Mitch wondered aloud whether Emily would keep her promise to meet him, Maggie released the gold tiebacks on the curtains, sending a shower of taupe fabric down against the louvered windows. She turned to face the sunless room and shook her head at him. "Of course, she'll be here," she said. "You're irresistible."

"I hope you're right," Mitch replied hesitantly.

"Where does she think you are right now, by the way?" Maggie asked. "How did you get out of sharing a room?"

"She thinks I'm waiting for her at a friend's hotel room. I told her that a former colleague of mine happened to be staying in the city, and I wanted to catch up with him." Mitch sat down on the bed, facing Maggie. With a sigh, he reclined onto the cotton comforter.

A mixture of pity and jealousy toyed with Maggie's heart. "This is hard on you, isn't it?"

"I don't care," Mitch asserted, but Maggie didn't believe him. As if to prove he was in earnest, he sat up and continued, "I only care about getting what we came here for. A second chance, for you."

"Good. Emily's not an innocent child," Maggie remarked coldly. "You don't have to feel guilty about hurting her feelings. She certainly doesn't care who *she* hurts, as long as she gets what *she* wants."

Mitch walked over to Maggie and put his arms around her. "I'm sorry about all this," he whispered. "I hate that she's back in our lives. The last thing I want to do is hurt you again."

"It's okay. It's just—you've already apologized to me and made things right. She never did. If I ever meet her face to face, I won't be accountable for my actions."

"I'll do my best to make sure that never happens."

CHAPTER 16 - HUNTER AND EMILY

AN HOUR AFTER EMILY DEPARTED for the airport, Hunter Marlow stood alone at the door to her apartment. After knocking without success, he walked to the business office of her complex for a pen and paper to leave a note on her closed door. Instead, he found himself staring at the bouquet of flowers he'd sent Emily that morning, a lavish arrangement of pink, red, and violet. The flowers were perched behind the front desk, the card still secured in front.

Hunter paced the floor as he waited to speak to the man behind the desk. The man was engaged in a heated conversation with one of the tenants, a young woman in a pink velour track suit with the words, "pretty little thing," embossed across her rear end. The man and the woman were shuffling through their opinions regarding the woman's overeager Chihuahua, and the exchange appeared to be going nowhere.

"Well, Julia," the man asserted curtly, "there have actually been several complaints."

"He's just friendly, is all. I really don't see why it's such a big deal." Julia pouted.

"You might want to think about getting him fixed. I'm sure it will help."

"He is fixed. I had it done last year. But I guess his little brain still remembers how it all works. I mean, he doesn't know he can't make puppies anymore. He's just doing what comes naturally."

"Maybe if you tried a shorter leash … then at least you'd have a little more control…."

Hunter's mind was assaulted by the image of a humping Chihuahua. He squeezed his eyes shut and drummed his fingers against his thighs in frustration. When he opened his eyes, the flowers behind the desk came into focus. He glared at them and wondered why they hadn't been delivered to Emily's apartment.

Maybe she refused to accept them, he thought miserably. *She probably thinks I do nothing but criticize. And maybe she's right. But she doesn't know why I criticize. I do it because she has so much more potential than she gives herself credit for. She's the best person I know, but she's wasting it.* He ran his fingers through his hair distractedly, cringing at the thought of the mess he made the day before. *I can't believe I made the whole situation that much worse,* he thought. *She might never forgive me.*

Hunter had made up his mind the day before at Starbucks that he needed to talk to Emily and explain himself. But he'd been so preoccupied with getting away from Stacy that he left his newspaper, with his cell phone tucked inside, sitting on the bistro table.

When Stacy returned his phone later that night, she cheerfully mentioned that Emily called, then casually remarked that Emily "seemed perturbed when I told her you forgot your phone with me after our date, but I would gladly give you a message the next time we got together."

Hunter called Emily back immediately, but her phone went straight to voicemail. The following morning, he arranged for delivery of a lavish bouquet of flowers. Still, he heard nothing from her. By that afternoon, he had grown tired of waiting, and decided to drive over to Emily's place and make his plea.

Now, as he paced inside the business office, it seemed there was little hope of reconciling with her at all.

Julia finally left the office and Hunter approached the desk. "Excuse me," he said, surprised that the man behind the desk was now sitting down, sifting through his inbox, and completely ignoring him. "Those flowers over there; why weren't they delivered?"

"Oh, Emily's on vacation until January 10th. She is – out - of - the - country," the man said, annunciating "out of the country" as if it were an odd thing to be.

"Do you know where she went or how I might contact her?"

"Yes, I do have her contact information. Are you a relative?"

"I'm an attorney. I work with Emily, and we have an important case going to trial in a few days. She has critical information regarding a bench brief for the judge, and I need to speak to her … urgently."

Hunter removed his Texas Bar Card from his wallet and slid it across the counter. He thought his lie had about a fifty-fifty shot of success, and he chided himself for not pretending to be a brother-in-law or a long-lost cousin. The man took Hunter's card and entered the information into the laptop on his desk. He then transcribed Emily's contact information onto a notecard. She was staying at The Great House, a hotel in Belize City, Belize.

Although Hunter dreaded what he might find on the other end of the line, he dialed the international number on the notecard as soon as he got home. All he wanted to hear was that Emily was staying alone in a single-occupancy room, and that Mitch Hudson was not a registered guest.

***

Emily caught the afternoon flight to Belize City out of Houston Intercontinental Airport. She smiled as she thought about her last conversation with Mitch. They'd spoken for almost thirty minutes, and she'd felt the connection between them grow as they discussed the details of their upcoming trip as well as their plans for their future life together. She'd told Mitch exactly what she wanted from him, and he agreed to everything without hesitation, which deepened her conviction that he was genuinely committed to their relationship this time.

As Emily made her way through the crowded terminal, the joy of reconciliation warmed her heart, and she thought happily about how much her luck had changed. Oblivious to the drudgery of security checkpoints and winding lines, she floated through the terminal as if she'd just walked into a fairytale, as if butterflies and nightingales might at any moment alight from the jetway and fill the boarding area at Gate E12.

With each passing minute, she felt better and better about her decision. Mitch was the one man in her life who always spoiled her, always made sure she was taken care of. When they were together before, not a week would pass without one extravagant display of affection or another. Expensive gifts were the norm. "Nothing's too good for my girl," Mitch used to say as he held Emily in his arms.

Emily sighed as she thought about how good it used to be with Mitch. Then her mind wandered a little farther down the road, and she sighed a second time. When their affair ended, she was devastated. She felt naked and raw, unprotected in a world that had suddenly grown treacherous. For months, she stumbled through the rooms of her condo, the halls of her office, like a child who'd lost her blankie. In fact, she never really recovered from the blow.

But now all was mended and soon she would have the life she'd always wanted. Soon her mother would be relieved, and her father would be proud.

Midway through her flight, Emily fished a guidebook from her shoulder bag. From the Belize Handbook she'd purchased that morning, she learned that Belize encompassed 8,866 square miles of territory—roughly the size of Massachusetts—and that the mainland was mostly flat, except for the Maya Mountains in the south and west, where the land rose to over 3,000 feet above sea level.

As the plane closed in on Belize City, the captain announced their final descent, and Emily peered through the window, hoping for a view of the landscape below. She stared in wonder. It appeared as if they were descending into a vast jungle. The Belize River, a yellow-green waterway skirting the Maya Mountains on its way to the sea, cut a rambling path through mangrove and swamp, while pockets of brackish water speckled densely packed foliage of deep green. There was almost no evidence of civilization. Here and there, a ribbon of ocher road wound through the wilderness, and occasionally the shimmer of tin rooftops could be distinguished among the endless miles of green. With each passing minute, Emily expected to see city sights—buildings, roads, cell towers—but nothing substantial appeared. Even to the last, there was nothing but jungle.

The plane touched down heavily. Although the runway had been extended to accommodate larger airliners, it was still short, and landings tended to be a little rough. Upon landing, the plane shuddered and barreled down the tarmac. The entire airport, a squat two-story building with a small tower rising from its midsection, flew past the window in three seconds.

Again, there was wilderness, but sparser, with yellow and brown mixed into the green. After a jagged turn, the pilot guided the plane back toward the terminal. A small tan-colored building with signage displaying the words BELIKIN BEER in large green letters stood alone just beyond the runway; and Emily smiled at the realization that, aside from the airport, the first sign of civilization should be an ad for beer. *I think I'm going to like this place*, she thought.

She peered through a window on the opposite side of the plane and caught a glimpse of a tall white hotel, the airport much shorter by comparison; the painted sign on the rooftop announced in black serif that "Jesus is Lord." The plane's progression now slowed drastically, and Emily shifted her gaze back to her window. The pilot steered the plane to a stop in front of the terminal, and a cluster of smaller airplanes housed inside an open bunker came into view. Emily could think only of the words "puddle jumper" as she pictured the small airplanes darting from point to point, froglike, almost smiling in giddy animation as they braved wilderness and weather.

With a crackle and hiss, the airplane's intercom came to life, and the pilot welcomed his passengers to Belize City. He then announced that there was no jetway available, and they would be exiting the aircraft directly onto the tarmac via a staircase secured to the plane.

Emily stepped from the airplane doorway onto a long flight of metal stairs. The staircase shuddered beneath her as she made her descent, and she gripped the handrail firmly. It was soft rubber and sagged beneath the weight of her palm. After a few downward steps, a hot breeze blew the hair back from her face. She paused, squinted against the sun, and made her way toward the customs office.

After clearing immigration and customs, Emily made her way outside. The warm air was laced with the fragrance of bougainvillea and hibiscus. Just outside the exit, taxi drivers sat languidly on polished wood benches. One of them, a stocky man with short dreadlocks that splayed at the ends, waved at Emily and asked, "Taxi M'am?"

Emily nodded and walked over to his cab, a gold station wagon with burgundy leather seats. The man drove lazily over double speed bumps on his way out of the airport then took off at breakneck speed as he wound his way through the little airport town and down the Northern Highway. Byron Lee played on the radio as the curve of the road brought the banks of the Belize River into sight.

The Sky Place

The river's flat surface was opaque green, the tangle of trees and brush that lined the bank forming a striking contrast with their rich shades of mint and emerald. After another turn, a bridge, barely wide enough to fit two cars, came into view. The muddy smell of the river floated in through an open window as the cab entered the city limits. Concrete bungalows, brightly painted, lined the roadside. Interspersed among the bungalows were two- and three-story wood and concrete buildings that housed shops and diners on the first floor, each announcing on chalk boards or hand-written signs the day's food specials—Rice and Beans with Stew Chicken; Conch Soup; Beef Burger with Fries.

When the cab arrived at the hotel, Emily could not believe her luck. The Great House, a large wooden home that had been converted to a guest house, was remarkably similar to her favorite law school retreat, the bed and breakfast in Richmond. It was the same shade of bright white with proud columns and two sweeping verandahs. Even the little portico that adorned the uppermost story was a near exact match. Emily stood at the open door of the taxi and stared, examining every detail—the bay windows, the graceful banisters, the French doors. *This is a good sign*, she thought.

A warm breeze rolled in from the ocean and shook the leaves of the tall palms that stood like a wall of giants at the perimeter of the parking lot. At the sound of the wind in the trees, Emily pressed her fingers against the cotton fabric of her sundress just in time to keep her skirt from billowing with the breeze. The rustle of the palms and the smell of the sea almost made her laugh out loud. Less than two weeks ago she'd been miserable. Now she was vacationing in paradise.

"Hey, lady! You coming?" The taxi driver had carried Emily's bags to the front desk on the second floor of the guest house and was calling down to Emily for her to come upstairs and check in.

"I'll be there in a minute," she shouted as she fished her phone from her shoulder bag. Except for the earlier missed calls from Hunter, she didn't have any new messages. Either her international phone plan wasn't working, or Hunter had finally given up trying to reach her. All she wanted to do was forget the past and focus on the future. This was her chance at a fresh start with Mitch, and she intended to make the most of it. The last thing she needed was another lecture from Hunter, especially now that he was dating Stacy and leaving the firm for greener pastures.

CHAPTER 17 - MANUEL

Caracol
Cayo District, Belize

APPROXIMATELY EIGHTY MILES SOUTHWEST of Belize City, in the foothills of the Maya Mountains, the night was as still as the stone temple that rose 43 meters from the jungle floor. It was Caana, the Sky Place, the tallest and grandest temple within the ancient kingdom of Caracol. Now a tourist attraction, the site offered a doorway to the past. It was once home to Lord Water, the king who allied with Lord Sky Witness of Calakmul, to overthrow Tikal.

Over fourteen hundred years had passed since Lord Water's death, but his body remained onsite, entombment beneath the temple. Between the time of his death and the demise of the Maya dynasty, Caana saw the rise and fall of 28 rulers. They were the Halach Winics or True Men, who each inherited absolute power and were revered by their people as holy god-kings.

Manuel Cocom had been Caracol's night watchman for the last five years. He'd always known he belonged here. The ancient city was in his blood, so said his grandmother and his great uncle. Manuel was raised on stories of the past; his ancestors fed them to him like sugarcane and he savored every word, even before he knew the truth and power behind them.

Manuel, a Yucatec Maya, was born and raised in the tiny village of San Eduardo, where he still lived with his wife and children. Although his village was less than half a mile from Caracol, Manuel kept a small hut onsite near the entrance, where he slept for brief intervals between his rounds. Tuesdays through Fridays, he stood watch over the site, while his wife, son, and daughter remained at home in San Eduardo.

Staring up from his cot at the thatch roof of his hut, Manuel listened as the macaws screeched in the jungle pines. On a makeshift table fashioned from two cinderblocks and a small plank of smooth wood, his kerosene lantern glowed dimly. A floor mat of braided cane stalks near the entrance was the only other furnishing in the room.

Manuel sat up slowly then stood. The cot squeaked with the release of his weight. Closing his hand around the thin metal strap of his lantern, he lifted it level with his face. As he walked toward the cotton sheet that hung in place of a door, the cane mat crackled beneath the soles of his shoes. Pulling the sheet aside, taking care not to bring the hot glass of the lantern too close to the cloth, he prepared for his nightly patrol of the site.

Seeking any sign of trouble, Manuel prowled the jungle paths as smoothly as a margay. When he arrived at the Sky Place, he stopped at the stone steps of the temple. Caracol's major temples had been freed from the clutches of the jungle decades earlier, and the stones of the structure before him glowed white as they caught the halo of light from his lantern.

Manuel bowed his head and whispered a prayer to his ancestors for the health and safety of his family. From the back pocket of his pants, he retrieved a small cotton pouch and spread an offering of maize at the foot of the temple. Setting his lantern on the ground, he squatted on the low steps of the temple, this time reaching into his shirt pocket for a folded letter. It contained a request for help from his old friend, Mitch Hudson.

Mitch had entered Manuel's life a year earlier when Manuel was still working weekends for the border patrol. It was the year Manuel's daughter, Sena, turned seven. Sena was born different; her upper lip was split open, distorting her face, and the Peace Corps nurse told Manuel and his wife that Sena had a medical condition known as a "cleft lip." But Manuel believed Sena had a fighting soul. He believed she'd dared to challenge the gods of the underworld during the time before her birth, and the gods marked her face to show their scorn.

Sena was scarred by the anger of the gods and saved by the hands of Dr. Mitch Hudson. It was the Peace Corps nurse who told Manuel about Mission Hope. She showed up at his door one sweltering Saturday with an apology on her lips. "I should have come sooner," she said. "Now, it might be too late."

The next day Manuel set out before dawn. Fifteen miles later he caught the bus on the Western Highway. Within four hours, he was trudging the dusty Ladyville road toward Phillip S.W. Goldson International Airport.

The doctors arrived in Belize City aboard a silver plane with the words, Mission Hope, stamped in blue along the side, the tail of the e whipping down the tail of the plane. Manuel would always remember the moment he saw that silver bird touch down on the tarmac. In that instant, his heart soared with hope for Sena.

He met the doctors in the airport parking lot and pleaded for help for his daughter. The crushing response came from a man in a grey suit. "If your daughter is not on our list, she will have to wait until another time. For now, we are only treating children we have previously assessed. I'm sorry, but it's not possible for us to help everyone."

The men broke away from him then, walking toward twin vans parked side by side. Manuel lowered his head and took a small roll of bills from his pocket. It was all the money he had. He clutched the money to his chest, raised his head, and stared at the backs of the men who were his daughter's only chance for a normal life. Each day was a struggle for Sena. It was a challenge for her just to eat or drink, and the children at school teased her until she ran home in tears, begging not to return.

Manuel hurried after the men as they began climbing into the vans. "Wait," he called, "I have money. I can pay." The doors of the vans slammed shut one after the other, and the sounds of the engines turning over muffled his broken voice. "Wait!" he cried. "I can pay…. Wait!" In desperation, he banged on the windows of one of the vans with both fists— one still tightly curled around the roll of money. "Wait!" He screamed and banged harder. He was frantic, almost blind with tears. Then, a door on the other side of the van opened briefly and slammed shut. Manuel wiped his eyes and ran his free hand over his shirt and pants. He was wearing his only good set of clothes. A man, all height and muscle, appeared from around the back of the van. He put a hand on Manuel's shoulder and asked him about his daughter.

Soon after, Mitch repaired Sena's damaged face. In Manuel's eyes, his daughter was transformed that day from a wounded bird to the beautiful little girl she was meant to be. Now he could think with joy about her future. And these days when Sena smiled, she showed her happiness to the world.

The week after Sena's surgery, Mitch planned to drive to Manuel's home to follow up on Sena's progress before his return to the States. Mitch had offered to make a house call so Manuel and Sena would not have to make the long journey to the nearest medical center in the village of San Antonio. That was the day of the attack; the day Manuel made a blood offering and summoned the goddess Ixchel to save the man who'd made his daughter smile again.

Manuel had hoped never to revisit those memories, but the folded letter in his pocket brought them to the forefront of his mind. Mitch was begging him to perform the ceremony again, and Manuel had already responded in the negative to Mitch's request. It had pained him to write that letter. Manuel wanted desperately to help Mitch, but it would be a grave transgression to perform the ceremony again. His old friend refused to give up, and Manuel had agreed to see him and Maggie again when they arrived in Belize. But the visit would surely be a miserable one.

Standing, Manuel turned and raised his eyes toward the sky. Caana was a towering mass before him, but by lowering his lantern, he made the top half of the temple disappear into the belly of the black night. He closed his eyes. The long history of Caracol ran through his mind like a song. There had been war. Lord Water and Lord Sky Witness had waged their notorious campaign. And after the siege, the victors had brought their captives here, to the Sky Place.

CHAPTER 18 - IXCHEL

Caracol
Maya Lowlands
Mesoamerica
A.D. 562

THE DAY OF THE CEREMONY HAD COME. It took four guards to subdue Itzamna and two more to drag Ixchel from his chambers. The guards deposited her at the entrance to the ceremonial plateau near the apex of the Sky Place. The massive temple was crowned by a triad of enclosed chambers of roughly equal size situated in a C formation upon the flat expanse of stone that formed the roof of the structure.

Inside the chambers, the daykeepers were preparing themselves for what was to come. Outside, along the northern perimeter, the captives were gathered, their hands and feet bound. Six fires burned upon the stone surface—one at each of the four corners of the temple and two at its center. Ajq'ij Dark Fox, adorned in jade and feathered finery, preached to the masses below, sharing tales of war and worship, sacrifice and bloodletting. At the base of the temple, the crowd cheered in anticipation of the spectacle that awaited them.

Ixchel stood quietly in the background. She studied the faces of those around her. Although none of them were known to her, the bond between them was eternal. These were her people, and their faces were the last glimpse she would have of her home. Ixchel gathered her strength. To be sacrificed to the gods ensured her a glorious rebirth into the afterlife, and she held onto the hope that by nightfall she would be in paradise with her family. They'd died with honor, and their places in paradise were secured that day. Soon she would win hers as well. But she would be sorry to leave the warmth and light of the jungle. She would miss the sounds that rang out from the trees outside her home when the moon was high and bright in the night sky. And she would miss the smell of the earth after the long, hard rains that came when the year was new. Her heart began to swell, and her throat burned with cries that would never pass her lips. Utterly miserable, but resigned to her fate, she shrank back into the shadows of the chamber.

Then, through the gloom, hope flashed. She heard his voice. He was walking quickly toward her from the northwest corner, calling to the guard stationed ahead of the captives. But the guard was distracted. The ceremony had begun, and he was being signaled by one of the daykeepers to lead the captives forward single file. Ixchel was nearly last in line. Suddenly, Itzamna was at her side, his arms around her. He cut the twine from her ankles and pulled her from the line.

They ran together down the long length of stairs behind the temple and disappeared into a residential chamber within the lower level. Quickly, Itzamna cut the twine from her wrists and cloaked her in a brown cotton cape. They emerged from the chamber and continued down the northern section of the stairs. To avoid the crowd gathered at the southern face of the temple, they traveled in a wide arc around the northeast corner and down toward the reservoir. The cheering crowd was entranced by the ceremony, and the fugitives were able to slip safely away.

Finally free of the temple and the crowd, they ran toward the market square. The square was all but empty, for the bulk of the city's inhabitants were being entertained by the raucous spectacle taking place at Caana. Itzamna found a nest of trees just beyond the clearing, and Ixchel hid herself among the webbed mass of roots and trunks. He entered the market square and quickly returned with clothes for them both.

Itzamna led Ixchel to the home of his friend, a merchant he'd known since childhood. "We can take refuge here," he said. "My friend is away, but we will be safe here."

The house was a simple structure of wood, thatch, and stacked stone resting on a low platform of white, hard-packed mud. The entire structure consisted of a single rectangular room with no windows, and a lone door facing east. A hammock hung between the walls on the right, and on the left, a raised surface of layered stone for cooking was fashioned tight against the wall.

Once inside, Itzamna helped Ixchel remove the adornments that had been fastened around her neck and ankles in preparation for the sacrificial ceremony. As he knelt to free her feet from the beaded anklets, she placed her hands upon his head and ran her fingers through his hair. For a moment, he stopped moving altogether. Then he sliced through the anklets, sending a shower of beads to the floor at her feet. With a careful hand, he placed the blade on the floor, but he did not rise. Instead, he moved his fingers to the hollows of her ankles then ran his hands gently along the curves of her calves. Ixchel trembled where she stood. Her breath quickened, keeping time with her pounding heart.

Itzamna rose to his feet and reached for her, wrapping his arms around her waist and pulling her close. She pressed her body against his and rested her head upon his shoulder. She could feel his chest heaving beneath her own. He released her ever so slightly, his fingers tracing the arc of her chin. He eased her face closer until she could feel his breath upon her skin. The moment was exhilarating, a wild shiver of anticipation, and she let it linger briefly before tilting her head upward and pressing her lips to his. From that moment on, they clung to each other, giddy and fumbling, taking advantage of the solitude inside their hideaway.

As the heat of the day gave way to the cool of night, the celebrations continued amid burning fires and beating drums. Ixchel and Itzamna lay curled inside the hammock, huddled together like birds in a nest.

"How long can we stay here?" she asked. The pounding of the drums was a fearsome noise, and she felt it growing louder and wilder, as if the noise itself was searching for her, as if it alone could pull her from the safety of Itzamna's arms and out into the raking claws of death.

"There is food and water here, enough for at least two days," he said. "I am certain that no one noticed our escape. They will not be looking for you, and I will not be missed. When my friend returns, I will ask him to help us escape to one of the western villages. He will know which place will be best." Itzamna pulled Ixchel closer, laced his fingers through hers. "It won't be easy," he whispered. "Our lives will be very different. Our home will be simple, like this one, and I will take up farming or trading. I would understand if you are ... hesitant ... to make that kind of change.

And if you don't want to live like this...." He lifted his hand, motioned to the dark interior of the room. "I can find a way to get you back home to Tikal."

Ixchel reached for Itzamna's hand and brought it back to rest against her heart. "No," she said. "I belong with you, and I am not afraid of living a simple life. It will be easy to live quietly and simply with someone who is dear to me. But you must choose as well. You would be giving up so much—your home, your family, your studies. I would not blame you, if you wanted to stay, and I would understand if you wanted me to go home."

Itzamna ran his fingers through her hair, kissed her cheek. "It is no choice at all," he said. "I have no desire to remain here without you. We will leave as soon as we can."

The night deepened and the drums beat on, but Ixchel was no longer afraid. She was safe, and she was loved, and that was all that mattered. They slept soundly that night, curled together in the dark, unaware that they'd been followed.

CHAPTER 19 - MITCH AND EMILY

Belize City, Belize
Present Day

AT FIVE FIFTEEN IN THE EVENING the phone rang in the honeymoon suite of The Radisson Fort George Hotel. Mitch moved instantly toward it and snapped the receiver to his ear. After a few quick words he hung up, sighing with relief.

"I told you she'd come," Maggie said as she closed the distance between them.

Mitch rubbed his palms together anxiously. "She's waiting in her room across the street. I'll be back in a few minutes."

"Don't linger," Maggie whispered and kissed his cheek.

Mitch crossed the street that separated the two hotels and climbed the stairs to the upper entryway. The sun would be setting soon, and everything—the parking lot, the towering coconut trees, the hotel lobby— was softened by the waning light of day.

Mitch stood at the open doors of the entryway, waiting for courage or heartlessness or both. The white glass-paned doors were thrown wide to the outer walls, and the hall glowed with the light of twin sconces and an overhead pendant. Standing in the warm glow of the entryway, knowing that Emily was only a few feet away, Mitch felt the gravity of the moment, and the weight of it made his pulse race and his shoulders slump. With some effort, he stiffened his spine and squared his shoulders as if to shrug off the mountain of worry that was pressing on him, but it was no use. He was about to do the hardest thing he'd ever had to do. He was about to try to convince Emily to remain in Belize for at least a few more days while

123

simultaneously informing her that Maggie was staying across the street with him.

Mitch shook his head. The whole thing was turning into a convoluted mess. Everything would have been so much easier if not for his troubles with Manuel. But, as it was, Mitch now found himself in the precarious position of having to bait Emily, and then keep her dangling, while he and Maggie made their way to Cayo to work on Manuel. If Manuel refused to help them, there would be no need for Emily, and Mitch would end the charade and send her home. But Mitch hoped it wouldn't come to that.

"Eyes on the prize," he whispered, "eyes on the prize." In three quick paces, he cleared the distance between the entryway and Emily's room. He took a deep breath and knocked on the whitewashed door. The door opened, and Emily's sweet, trusting face smiled back at him.

Where looks were concerned, Emily and Maggie were similar and different all at once, which was perhaps part of the initial attraction. Emily and Maggie had the same dark hair and alluring curves, but Emily was taller than Maggie, her proportions exaggerated. The most striking difference was their eyes. Emily's were bright and playful, Maggie's dark and vigilant.

Clasping Emily's hand, Mitch began, "You look beautiful. I've missed you so much." They hugged in the doorway. Emily nestled her face against Mitch's shoulder and lifted her head for a kiss. Mitch tried not to hesitate, but Emily's fierce happiness was more than he'd anticipated. He kissed her briefly.

Emily released Mitch and touched her fingers to her lips. "I missed you too," she said. "Come in. It's a beautiful room. I just love this hotel. Thanks for arranging everything for me."

"You're welcome," Mitch said. "I'm so glad you're here … that we're finally here together."

Emily pulled Mitch into the room and steered him toward a window-bench beneath a cove of bay windows. The bench curved along the perimeter of the windows, and a small bistro table stood at the center. The tabletop was glass, but beneath the glass a creamy floral tablecloth hung to the floor, a stitched ruffle at its hem.

"This little sitting area is so cute," Emily said, placing her palms on the smooth surface of the table. "I think I'll have my coffee here in the morning. Let's order room service for breakfast tomorrow." With a smile, she flopped onto the cushioned bench. "But I think it would be fun to go out somewhere for dinner tonight," she added. "We can ask the girl at the front desk if she knows any good restaurants, or we can go to the one downstairs. It looks romantic ... there's a little fountain in the courtyard. What do you think? I brought the cutest outfits for our vacation. I can't wait for you to see them all."

She stood, gave Mitch a quick kiss, and walked over to her suitcase. She threw it open to reveal a palette of bright colors. From the far corner, she retrieved a slip of sapphire blue fabric, which proved to be a short strapless dress. She lifted the dress to her chest and stretched the fabric across the front of her chest. "What do you think?"

"It's beautiful," Mitch said, "But you always look beautiful, darling." He was still standing near the bank of windows, his right arm braced against the ledge. His heart ached as he absorbed Emily's attention, witnessed her liveliness and energy. He wanted this for Maggie—vibrancy, life.

"Thanks," Emily said and placed the dress on the bed beside her suitcase. "Hey, where are your suitcases? Let's get settled so we can get ready for dinner." She moved toward the windows, tried to embrace Mitch, but he turned away and placed his palms on the tabletop as if trying to support himself. "What is it, Mitch? What's wrong?" she asked.

Mitch could hear the suspicion in her voice, and he couldn't risk losing her now, not when he was so close. He wrapped his arms around her, kissed her neck. Desperate and overwhelmed, he played his trump card right off the bat. "I love you, Emily, and I don't want to be away from you any longer," he said, his voice gaunt and raddled, "I want you to marry me. Say you will."

For a moment, Emily seemed unable to catch her breath. She nuzzled closer to Mitch. "Yes, I'll marry you," she whispered finally, looking up at him with bright, wet eyes.

"That's wonderful," he whispered. "You've made me so happy. There's a whole row of diamond shops just down the street at the tourism village, and we can go pick out a gorgeous ring, whatever you like." Emily was beaming, and Mitch figured it was safe to play his final card. "But there's something I've got to take care of first. Sit down so we can talk."

Emily sat, still beaming.

"Maggie's here," he said.

Emily's face transformed from joyful to indignant in an instant.

"Wait," he continued. "Let me explain. She's sick, really sick. She has terminal cancer, and she won't be able to hang on much longer. I can't put her through a divorce right now. When Maggie heard I was coming down here, she really wanted to come, and I couldn't tell her 'no.' Please say you understand."

Emily stood and paced the floor. "I don't understand Mitch, not at all. Are you saying you're waiting for her to die? I mean, what are you saying?" she shouted angrily.

"I'm saying that I love you, and I want to be with you. But things don't always work out exactly the way we planned. I just need you to be patient for me, please. When we get back to Houston, I'll work everything out. I promise."

Emily shook her head. "But what about now? I knew I shouldn't have come; this is ridiculous. I'm getting on the first plane out of here. I can't believe I was foolish enough to trust you again." She darted to the bathroom, grabbed her toothbrush and toothpaste, and flung them at her open suitcase. They landed in the center of her clothes. She stomped back over and closed her suitcase.

Taking her shoulders in his hands, Mitch tried to drag her away from her suitcase. She clamped a tiny lock onto the zipper pulls and wriggled from his grasp, but he caught hold of her arm as she turned to face him.

"Wait. Please." He begged. "Just hear me out. Maggie and I aren't together anymore—not like that. She's like a sister to me now. You're the one I love." He lowered his voice to a whisper, "But how could I refuse a dying woman's final wish? How could I say no when all she wanted was a few days to enjoy herself in the tropics? Please don't leave. You need to trust me, baby. I'll get everything straightened out soon, and in the meantime, there's so much here to enjoy. There's no reason for you to go."

Emily yanked her suitcase off the bed, but she didn't try to leave. Instead, she rubbed her temples with her fingertips and stared at Mitch.

"Look," Mitch slipped a little cheer into his voice and continued, "I've arranged for a top-notch guide to take you on a first-class tour of Belize starting bright and early tomorrow morning. You'll have a great time. I've made all the arrangements, spared no expense. Nothing's too good for my girl. My future wife." Mitch almost choked on those words, but they did the trick. Emily relented, and she didn't argue when he told her he couldn't stay long.

***

After Mitch was gone, Emily briefly questioned her decision to stay in Belize, but quickly determined that she'd made the right choice. She'd had an argument with the managing partner, Bill Walters, right before she'd left Houston, and she had no desire to see him again anytime soon.

Her decision to take time off from work had been met with acrimony, and she was still annoyed with Bill's comments. Emily hadn't even planned on speaking with Bill personally. She'd submitted her electronic request for time off, which Stacy had approved almost instantly. It was mere coincidence that Bill was in the office on Saturday morning when Emily stopped in to make the final preparations for her departure. When Bill saw that Emily was at work, he called her into his office with the stated purpose of discussing a client who had recently been granted a continuance, but Emily quickly realized that he was still angry about the blood drive. As it turned out, she and Don Eldridge had been the only holdouts.

Bill furrowed his brow and folded his arms across his chest. "I'm surprised Emily, surprised and disappointed," he scolded. "I thought you were a team player, but I guess I was mistaken. First the blood drive and now this sudden vacation. Actions speak louder than words. And I'm getting the message loud and clear. You are obviously not interested in the welfare of this firm."

Emily was stunned by his rebuke. "I know I'm leaving on very short notice, but I have all my files in order, and there are no deadlines, depositions, or hearings set between now and the date of my return. I have everything under control," she explained, a little miffed at having to do so. This was her first vacation in years, and she assumed that this fact—along with the fact that she was the highest billing associate at the firm—would count for something.

Apparently, it counted for nothing at all because Bill continued to frown at her, and, during the course of their contentious discussion, he went so far as to question Emily's commitment to the legal profession and wonder out loud if she was partnership material after all. Eventually, he gave his grudging consent to Emily's taking time off "if she thought she could leave in good conscience."

Livid, Emily simply replied, "Yes, I can leave in good conscience."

That had ended the discussion, and Emily had darted out the door while Bill drew his face into a pinched scowl.

As Emily recalled the bizarre details of her conversation with Bill, a small pressure began to grow in her chest, a rising sense of dread. *What have I done? If this is a mistake, it's unfixable now,* she thought. But soon another thought began to creep through the doubt. The thought was weak, but it would prove to be resilient. *My life is beginning.*

Emily finally understood what Hunter had been trying to say to her all along. Work is work and life is life. The two should not be confused. Because no matter how much you stretch and knead your work, it will never fill your life. *Well, Hunter, I guess you've decided to fill your life with a nice helping of Stacy Goodwyn,* Emily thought wryly. *That's why she approved my vacation request ASAP. She couldn't wait to have you all to herself.*

Emily really didn't want to go back to Houston yet, and she certainly didn't want to admit that she'd made a huge mistake by coming on this vacation, especially after her battles with Bill and Hunter. She decided to give Mitch the benefit of the doubt. *We're getting married,* she told herself, *he's obviously in love with me.*

That evening, she ordered room service and ate alone at the little table near the window. She tried her best to savor the shrimp cocktail, conch ceviche and tortilla chips arranged in front of her, but her heart kept fluttering in and out of excitement and despair. Her situation with Mitch was elating and infuriating. Here she was, engaged, and she couldn't even spend the night with the man she loved. And to top it all off, her argument with Hunter kept nagging at her. Each time she thought about him and Stacy, her heart flinched. She tried to pretend that his opinion of her didn't matter, and she succeeded in fooling herself on the surface. But deep down, she hated the idea of him walking out of her life and thinking badly of her.

Focus on the positive, Emily. Your life is beginning. She lifted her drink. "I'm engaged," she whispered into her Mojito, crushing the mint leaves with her straw in jittery excitement. She spoke the words again. "I'm engaged." They sounded fantastic. A smile spread across her face and stayed put until she fell asleep that night.

***

Across the street at dinner that night—room service on the balcony with a view of the Caribbean Sea—Mitch told Maggie about a tour guide he'd hired just in case Manuel didn't come through. "It'll be easier to get into the site after dark if we have a licensed guide," he said, "otherwise we'll have to enter during the day, and then stay hidden until nightfall. If Manuel backs out on us, this guy's the backup plan."

"How can Manuel back out on us when he's already said no?" Maggie asked flatly.

Mitch shook his head ruefully.

"Sorry," Maggie whispered. "What's the tour guide's name?"

Mitch folded his napkin and placed it on the table. "Jay Kinnder. He'll also be babysitting Emily for a few days. And don't worry about Manuel. I will convince him to help us. We're driving down there tomorrow, and I'm going to have a long talk with him. There isn't much that a little—or a lot—of money can't solve. He's got two kids, and the kind of offer I'm going to make him.... Well, I don't see how he can refuse."

"Okay, we drive down there tomorrow and talk to Manuel," Maggie said. "Then what? When do we go to the temple?"

"The day after tomorrow," he replied. "Jay is going to bring Emily to the site in the evening, and I'll take it from there. If all goes according to plan, we'll fly back to Houston on Wednesday."

"And what if everything doesn't go according to plan?" she asked softly.

"Don't worry," he said with more conviction than he felt. "It will."

CHAPTER 20 - EMILY

EMILY AWOKE THE FOLLOWING MORNING at eight and dressed quickly. The morning sun broke through the windows of her hotel room with bright promise and the air beckoned fresh and light. Although she hadn't expected it, she was looking forward to the tour and the prospect of a little adventure. She hurried out of the hotel and searched the street for a taxi to take her to meet her tour guide, a Mr. Jay Kinnder.

As the cab pulled out of the parking lot and onto the street, Emily glanced at the neighboring hotel. Her mood fell. She hoped that Mitch's wife knew nothing about their affair, especially now that she was critically ill. Emily didn't want to build her happiness upon someone else's misery. But she didn't want Mitch to be miserable either. If he was in love with her, then he didn't belong with his wife. Quickly, before she could think too much about it, she reminded herself that Mitch had promised to take care of everything once they got back to Houston. And she trusted that he could do it in a way that was minimally injurious to his wife. Emily decided that the best course of action was to put the whole unpleasant situation out of her mind and enjoy herself until Sunday.

After a short drive, Emily's cab pulled into the parking lot at The Coral Hotel, the designated meeting place for the start of the day's excursion. The exterior of the hotel was flamingo pink and flaming orange. But upon entry, the garishness of the exterior was replaced by sky blue walls and abundant tropical plants. Emily made her way through the hotel lobby and toward the rear door that led to the seaside bar and docks. As she pushed through the door, a gush of warm breeze sent her hair flying, and she stopped in the doorway to shoulder her tote and rake her fingers through her hair before stepping out onto the weathered deck that overlooked the ocean. The deck was lined with umbrella tables and chairs, and the bar was tucked into the far corner.

When Jay Kinnder contacted Emily the night before, he told her to look out for a white boat with blue lettering. She shielded her eyes against the sun and peered out at the ocean. The dock was empty. But the hotel bar was open. Emily stowed her tote and duffle at the nearest table and walked to the bar. Briefly she toyed with the idea of ordering a Margarita, but since it wasn't even nine o'clock yet, she asked for an iced coffee instead. The best they could do was a Coke Light.

Beverage in hand, Emily settled into a seat beneath a neon orange umbrella. She closed her eyes and reveled in the feel of the wind on her face, the sun on her shoulders. Through her reverie, she caught the sound of a boat engine in the distance. She opened her eyes. The surface of the ocean glittered like faceted crystal, and she squinted to make out the lettering on the approaching white boat.

Emily watched as Jay docked his boat, the Mariana, alongside the crawl. With graceful ease, he maneuvered her into place, set the bumpers, and tied off each end, bow then stern. Jay gave Emily a nonchalant wave then jumped from the boat to the dock. Before he was halfway down the dock, she could tell he was flirting with her. She knew the type— tall, dark, and handsome with a great smile and a few jokes thrown in for good measure. A guy like that was as predictable as a Sunday sermon. Emily leaned back in her chair and pulled her drink a little closer.

As Jay approached Emily's table, he grabbed one of the nearby metal chairs, brought it over, and placed it next to hers. He sat down languidly then called to the bartender for a Coke. Emily folded her arms in front of her and hunched over her drink.

Leaning in, Jay smiled slowly. "Aren't you enjoying yourself? This is paradise after all."

She replied with a curt, "Yes, of course; I'm just fine." Something had begun to gnaw at her, something undefined. But she assumed it was just her current predicament with Mitch. She forced a smile and scolded herself into a better mood.

"We'll be leaving the boat here," Jay said, "and visiting the inland wonders of Belize. I've got a great two-day trip lined up for you. If you're ready, my jeep's parked in the back lot, and we can get this adventure underway." Jay paid for his bottle of Coke, grabbed Emily's duffle bag, and together they made their way over to the parking lot. Jay's jeep, an older model Grand Cherokee, all but sparkled in the early morning sun; even the tires shone softly. Above the shimmering black body of the vehicle, a copper-colored canoe glinted from the roof rack like a shining metal Mohawk.

As Emily walked toward the pristine spectacle before her, she began to question the competence of her tour guide. Surely any tour guide worth his salt would have a little more dirt beneath his fingernails or at least at little road wear on his SUV. She pulled the passenger door open, and, glancing down, she was somewhat relieved to notice tiny mud clumps and a few stray pebbles wedged between the treads of the front tire. With one quick movement, she hoisted herself into the jeep and plunked down into the passenger seat. Her hip slid straight into the gearshift. Large quantities of Armor All® had colluded with her momentum to send her flying across the leather seat. Emily adjusted her butt in the seat and slid her hands beneath her shorts to ensure there wasn't any excess oil being mopped up by her new denim cutoffs. Her fingers came back clean, so she shrugged, clicked her seatbelt into place, and stashed her shades in the side pocket of the door.

Jay turned the ignition and slid the jeep into reverse. "All set?" he asked as he turned around to guide the jeep out of the parking spot.

"Absolutely," Emily replied with forced enthusiasm. "By the way, when was the last time you took this beauty out into the jungle? It looks a little too pristine. Are you sure you know what you're doing?"

"Hey, I'm a professional," Jay said politely, "and my services are worth every penny. Part of the deal is a clean ride and cold A/C. Now, if you'd rather spend the day in a raggedy-ass van with six other people, all coughing because the windows are sucking in dust, I can arrange that for you; but there'll be a cancellation charge."

"Sorry, I was only messing with you." Emily shook her head and smiled. Jay was beginning to grow on her. She decided to give him a break and enjoy herself.

"And by the way," Jay continued, also smiling, "I just made a run down to the caves two days ago, but I got her all cleaned up in time for my rendezvous with you."

"Well, I appreciate it … thank you."

They drove in silence through the city toward the Western Highway, Emily watching from the window as pedestrians, bicycles, and vehicles maneuvered in, out, and around each other on the narrow streets. Every passing moment brought a fresh instance of alarm as each moving part within the mechanism of the city only narrowly avoided impact with every other moving part. "It's like every two seconds there's almost an accident," Emily noted.

"Welcome to Belize City," Jay laughed.

Less than ten minutes later, they'd cleared the city limits, made their way past Yarborough Cemetery and out onto the Western Highway. "What are our plans for the day? Where are we heading?" Emily asked as she reached into her tote for her copy of the Belize Handbook.

"We'll be heading west to Cayo District, the interior of Belize. The drive should take about an hour and a half. Our first stop will be a river tour through Barton Creek Cave. We'll have lunch along the bank of the river, then we'll head over to the town of San Ignacio where we'll explore the Maya site at Cahal Pech…. I'm not sure if your guidebook says anything about Maya ruins, but nowadays we refer to them as sites."

"Hmm," Emily flipped through her guidebook, "No, it says site in here."

"Good," Jay replied, "must be a recent edition."

She held it up so he could see the cover.

"I'm not familiar with it," he said and returned his eyes to the road. "Is it any good?"

"It's okay," she said, "I like it because it's small and it fits in my purse. But I wish it had more pictures."

Jay chuckled. "Why don't you put the book down and look out the window? It's all right in front of you."

Emily was stunned by how quickly the city had transformed into rambling wilderness. At ground level, a flourish of wild grasses lapped the bank of the road in waves. From there, a tangle of muddy underbrush rose toward the broad shoulders of evergreen pines and hearty palms, the wide leaves of the palms spilling a tawny shower onto the dark green of the crested pines. Emily put her guidebook in her purse. "It's beautiful here," she said.

"Well, there's a lot more to see. If you think this is nice, wait until we get to Cahal Pech. The views there are something else."

"Oh, that's right," Emily said, "you were telling me about our plans. Please continue."

"Right. After we finish up at Cahal Pech, we're going just up the road to San Ignacio Resort Hotel, which is where we'll be staying tonight and tomorrow night. It's a beautiful resort with a great restaurant. We should arrive in plenty of time for a nice, relaxing dinner before the night tour begins. They have a medicine trail tour that starts at eight o'clock, and I signed us up. Tomorrow, we'll have lunch at the hotel before heading over to Caracol. It's a long drive, and we should try to get on the road by one o'clock, two at the latest."

"That all sounds great. I know Mitch is excited about meeting us at Caracol, but what's so special about it? I mean, how's it any different from Cahal Pech? Isn't one Maya site as good as another?"

Jay responded with what Emily recognized as practiced tour guide verbosity, "Caracol, which is the Spanish word for snail, is the grandest Maya site in Belize with the tallest manmade structure in the country. From the temple at Caana, which is also known as the Sky Place or Sky Palace, you can see all the way to Guatemala. During the classic period, Caracol supported a population of over 140,000 people, and it was a thriving nation. In fact, Caracol once defeated the city-state of Tikal. But you'll hear more about that when we get there. Two of their greatest conquests, Tikal, and later, Naranjo, are documented on huge stone stelae at the site.

"I think you're really going to like Caracol," Jay continued. It's definitely worth the drive. Cahal Pech is much smaller by comparison, but it's still a cool site. There are two ball courts, and some interesting figurines at the little museum on the property. Plus, the view from Cahal Pech Tavern is amazing. And you can grab a cocktail for the road when we get there. You're on vacation after all."

"That sounds like a plan. I can't wait. How long's the drive?"

"We've got about an hour or so to go. I have a sampling of local music if you're interested, and I've also got satellite radio; I can play pretty much anything you want to hear."

"No, it's fine. I'd rather talk. And I would love to know how you ended up working as a tour guide?"

"What do you mean *ended up*?" he asked, a note of wounded pride in his voice.

"I didn't mean anything negative," Emily replied, "It seems like a fantastic job, at least ten times more interesting than mine, anyway. I think it's fascinating when people find their way to interesting careers, and I would love to know your story."

"It's actually not much of a story."

"Well, I promise not to nod off or anything," she encouraged.

Jay squinted at the road; the curve of his brow gathered in thought. He ran his palms up and down the circumference of the leather steering wheel before responding. "I've got to say that I haven't really thought about it in a while. I guess I've been here almost five years now. And I haven't looked back once."

Jay paused as if his abbreviated response was all he was planning to say on the matter, which only heightened Emily's interest. "So…." she urged.

"I was born in Belize City, but after college, I ended up living in Cabo," he began. "My mom was born in Mexico, and I have dual citizenship. I went to college in Merida, then started working as a mechanic for a big dealership in Cabo. I liked the work just fine, don't get me wrong. I always liked working on cars, and the job wasn't bad. But one day it occurred to me that I didn't own a single one of my possessions. My condo, my car, even the mattress I was sleeping on belonged to someone else because I'd bought it all with loans or credit cards. I was fed up with everyone else owning a piece of my life. I cashed out my savings, sold everything, and moved back here. I bought my boat and my jeep, and now I'm a free man. I run my own show. And, I've got to tell you, this is the life. I wouldn't change a thing."

"But what made you decide to come back to Belize instead of starting over in a big city in Mexico with more opportunities?"

"I'd been back and forth to see my girlfriend over the years, and I figured she could get me set up, maybe show me the ropes."

"Okay, so you're here with your girlfriend. That makes sense."

"Well, by the time I decided to make the move, she'd become my ex-girlfriend."

"Your ex-girlfriend helped you start your business here?" Emily asked. "That's surprising."

"Hey, this is Belize. It's a small country. If I ignored every woman I ever slept with, I wouldn't have anyone to talk to, would I?" Jay threw a goofy wink at Emily and laughed at his own joke.

She couldn't help but laugh.

He continued, "So I moved back here, found a little dump to live in, and started running tours. Monique, my ex, works at The Coral Hotel, so I get regular references from there, and I'm registered as a licensed tour guide for all the Maya sites, so I pick up some trips that way. But what I really want is to expand beyond the city. I have a guy who works with me part time. He'll be picking up my boat at The Coral and running a few tourists out to San Pedro while I'm on the road. There's so much opportunity here to branch out. What I need is to get a couple hotels in Cayo under my belt and get regular references from them. Then I can hire my guy full time to work the city and the islands, and I can move out to Cayo and focus on the jungle and the caves. I mean, look at this place, I love it here." Jay scanned the horizon, and Emily could tell he was enjoying every minute of his life.

"I guess you're really living the life down here," she said.

"Now, don't get the wrong impression," Jay added quickly. "It hasn't been easy, not by a long shot. You've got to be vigilant to survive in a place like Belize. Nature is always scheming against you and threatening to take away any little progress you make. It's funny, people in the states sit in their air-conditioned living rooms and worry about global warming and the fate of the environment. They worry that there's a war going on between human beings and nature, and that people are destroying the earth. And, technically, they're right. But those people never tried to live and work in a third-world country. They don't know what it's like to be at the mercy of the heat, the salt, the flooding rains. Every time you manage to carve out an inch, some damn thing happens to set you back a mile, like saltwater corroding your hull and engine because you can't afford a boat lift, or potholes the size of canyons blowing out two of your tires at a time. And that's just the tip of the iceberg. It's a battle alright, but from where I sit, it sure as hell doesn't feel like I'm the one who's winning."

"So why on earth would you stay here?"

"Because this is where the action is. This is life," Jay said. He reached over and shook her shoulder as if trying to wake her from a dream. "Everyone else is just playing at it."

136

"Maybe you're just addicted to drama," she teased. Jay smiled and shook his head, and Emily couldn't help but admire his perseverance.

"What's your deal?" he asked. "What do you do for money?"

"I'm … an attorney." For some reason it always took her a second to decide whether she would say attorney or lawyer when someone asked her this question. She usually went with attorney. The vague memory of an old joke about lawyers and liars always swung the vote in favor of attorney.

"Well, that's something," Jay replied. "What's it like when you're picking the jury? What are you secretly thinking about them? I bet you see a lot of nut jobs."

"I've actually never had the chance to pick a jury. I've never had a case of mine go to trial. We usually just file a bunch of motions, take a bunch of depositions, and settle at mediation…. Hey, do you think you could put on some music now, please? Something relaxing would be nice. I didn't sleep well last night, and the sun coming through the window is making me want to close my eyes. I think I'll just try to take a nap if that's okay."

"Sure thing," Jay said. "I'll wake you when we get there."

As Emily nestled into her seat, she thought about Jay's life and how it compared to hers. He obviously loved his job, and he was excited about his future. She hadn't felt that kind of excitement in years, not since law school, not since her romanticized notions about the practice of law had hardened into reality. The real difference was that Jay was completely in charge of his own destiny. There was no one holding him back or keeping him down. But there was no one to write him a steady paycheck either. He had to fend for himself.

At quarter past ten that morning, Jay turned from the highway onto the Barton Creek cutoff. The side road, a thin white tail whipping through green, was unpaved, and as they traveled the length of it, the tires of the jeep kicked up a cloud of fine limestone dust. By the time they covered the distance between the highway and the cave, Jay's black jeep was powder white. Emily climbed from the jeep and examined the exterior. She immediately felt guilty about teasing him earlier. He'd obviously put a lot of effort into getting ready for her tour.

Jay grabbed a backpack from the rear of the jeep and walked over to her. "I'm going to need your help with the canoe," he said, "but don't worry; it isn't heavy." Together they released the canoe from the roof rack and carried it overhead toward the river, Jay in front, Emily behind. The canoe was remarkably light, and Emily was happy to have a little cover from the heat of the sun.

As they neared the river, the jungle thickened around them. Emily felt the ground beneath her feet begin to soften, and soon she could smell the mossy aroma of the riverbank.

"There's a bit of an incline here, and then a sloping curve," Jay called back to Emily, "so watch your footing as we go down along the path here."

Emily eyed the soft, dark path below, a winding ribbon of pebbled soil and moss, and stepped carefully to avoid the slick faces of the larger rocks that speckled the trail. At the foot of the incline, the ground cover changed from jungle floor to stony riverbank, and she could feel Jay lifting the canoe above them. Together they turned it on its spine and placed it near the edge of the river.

Emily stared at the sight before her. Because the canoe had obscured her view of everything but her feet, she felt as though she'd been led blindfolded into the middle of a wonderful surprise. The gently flowing river was opaque green, except near the edges where the water adopted the variegated earthen tones of the river stones below. To her right, the cave's entrance was bordered by a massive wall of pale limestone, covered with hanging vines and clinging foliage.

Once inside the cave, Emily found more to admire. The walls shimmered beneath the glow of Jay's broad-beam flashlight as though painted with crushed diamonds. Stalactites hung like enormous iridescent icicles from the roof of the cave, clustered so tightly in places that the channel became narrow, only a few inches wider than shoulder width. As they paddled, Jay told Emily the history of the cave and its place within the fabric of Maya lore.

"This cave is an ancient Maya waterway," he began. "The Maya believed that caves were openings to the underworld. The underworld is a little hard to describe, but you can think of it as a great basin beneath the earth where souls and demons roam. It's considered to be the home of some of your more gruesome gods. More than a thousand years ago, the Maya used this cave as a staging ground for worship, ritual bloodletting, and sacrifice. In a few minutes, you'll be able to see a collection of ancient pots that have become calcified within the cave. These pots have remained perfectly preserved for over a thousand years, and they would have held maize, food items, and possibly blood offerings for the gods. The pots would have been brought into the cave as part of a ritual ceremony."

Jay scanned the walls of the cave with his flashlight. On a wide ledge, the ancient pots lay clustered together, some round and whole with smooth rims, others cracked and broken. Emily stared intently at the broken pots until she realized she was trying to distinguish stains of blood on the clay. She quickly turned her eyes toward the water. Although she could not separate the dark surface of the water from the blackness around her, she could hear the rush of it as it cut through the walls of the cave and gushed over bedrock and stone.

On the other side of the cave, the river widened. Jay and Emily paddled slowly out of the dark, cool interior and into the bright, hot galley of the riverside jungle. As they meandered along the river, Jay pointed out the indigenous plants and animals loitering along the banks. First up was a pair of sunbathing iguanas perched on neighboring branches. The larger of the two was orange and black with a fat body and a short, thick tail. Its smaller companion was thin and green with a long, slender tail that dangled from the branch like a frisky fishing line.

Jay went on to explain some of the medicinal properties of the local plants, and after providing a brief history of the logwood industry in Belize, he listed off the more popular of the local hardwood trees, Billy Webb, Santa Maria, and Mahogany.

As the day progressed, Emily grew increasingly interested in everything around her. Each new tidbit of information came at her like compatible conversation on a first date. It all just seemed to fit.

The middle of the day found Jay and Emily halfway through their river trek and making camp on a rocky stretch alongside a slow-running portion of the river. Jay spread a small patchwork cloth on the ground and took four sandwiches, two snack packs of potato chips, and a large thermos from his pack. He set the thermos in the middle of the cloth and spread the food out around it.

Emily watched as he retrieved the final items from his backpack—two molded plastic cups and two small cloth napkins. As Jay carefully arranged his makeshift table, Emily couldn't help but be reminded of Hunter and the exquisite dinner he'd prepared for her on New Year's Eve. And there was something else. Jay's passion for his job reminded her of Hunter's new-found energy. All the best parts of Hunter were beginning to shine through, and Emily was afraid she would miss out on seeing him transform into the person he was always meant to be. They'd never fought like this before, and she hated the idea of their friendship being over forever. The thought of losing Hunter's friendship brought Emily to the verge of tears. She turned away from the picnic and walked toward the river, feigning interest in the smooth river stones that littered the bank.

Fortunately, Jay was distracted; he was on his cell phone. Emily hadn't heard it ring, and she wondered how he was even picking up a signal. At present, her phone was nothing more than a paperweight. The international plan she'd purchased before leaving Houston wasn't working, and when she'd tried to call Mitch earlier that morning, she'd realized her phone was useless.

She continued to meander along the riverbank, relieved that Jay was caught up in his conversation. Her relief lasted only moments because before long Jay was standing next to her, pushing the phone into her hands. "It's Mitch Hudson," Jay said. "He wants to talk to you."

Emily took the phone, and the sound of Mitch's voice instantly improved her mood. "Hi," he said. "Are you having a good time?"

"Yes," she replied, a smile spreading across her face, "I'm having a great time. So far this has been the perfect day, except I wish you were here."

"I miss you too. But we'll see each other tomorrow, and I'll be thinking about you every minute until then."

"I'm thinking about you too, Mitch, and I have so much to tell you. The river tour was amazing; Jay pointed out some interesting plants, and we saw two iguanas. They were just incredible and...."

"Well, I want to hear all about it, but Jay mentioned that you guys are getting ready to have lunch, and I don't want to hold you up. I know you have a full schedule today. I'll call you tonight, okay? I love you."

"I love you too," Emily replied. It was the first time she'd said those words since they'd gotten back together, and she felt flustered as soon as they were out.

After she hung up with Mitch, Emily sat down to lunch. She hadn't realized how hungry she was until she swallowed the first bite of her ham sandwich. She ate quickly, polishing off both sandwiches and the snack pack of chips within minutes. Jay turned to retrieve a pair of brownies from his backpack as Emily crumpled the snack pouch and two sandwich baggies into a ball for the trash. "Where should I throw this," she asked, thrusting her fist of balled-up plastic toward Jay.

He took the ball of plastic from her hand, removed the snack pouch, and began to smooth the sandwich baggies out against his thigh. "I don't throw these away," he said. "I try to recycle and reuse whatever I can. Every penny counts."

"I'm sorry. I didn't realize."

"No worries," he replied as he held the slightly less wrinkled baggies up for her to see. "Good as new."

When lunch was over, Jay and Emily made their way back to their starting point by cutting through a side trail that circumvented the cave and wound back toward the parking lot. After they lashed the canoe to the roof rack, Jay maneuvered his jeep slowly down the dusty side road and back onto the highway. Their drive to San Ignacio would be quick, and Emily stared out the window to take in the new and changing landscape.

The roadside foliage just before the river cutoff had been mostly low and wild, a tangle of scrub palms and ferns. But now the road was cutting through an expanse of rough-cleared land with short palm trees gathered like platoons of soldiers guarding the perimeter of overgrown mounds. Again, the landscape changed, this time rising into a web of lean brush and clinging underbrush. All the while, the January sky remained a perfect shade of blue as fluffy white clouds lolled overhead.

Emily was mesmerized by the changing scenery. Before long, the landscape opened into a meadow of cleared fields filled with cattle grazing on knots of grass growing in thick, bushy clumps. Trees of a kind she had never seen before stood tall among the grassy fields. Their mottled bark was mostly white, and their spreading branches grew horizontally beginning far up their wide, smooth trunks. A crown of shimmering yellow-green leaves fluttered atop the white. Emily asked Jay to tell her the name of the trees and attempted to point one out, but they appeared only at intervals, like lonely sentries standing straight and proud; and she had to wait a few moments to learn they were ceiba trees.

"The ancient Maya believed that a massive ceiba tree, the World Tree, ran through the center of the world," Jay said. "They believed it connected the earth with the upperworld and the underworld."

The landscape grew more beautiful by degrees, and Emily sat and stared in wonder. "I'm beginning to understand why you want to move out here from the city," she said, turning her gaze from the window momentarily to glance at Jay.

"It's something else, isn't it?" he asked.

Emily had never given much thought to nature and the outdoors before. But now that she'd gotten a taste of it, she began to regret that she would very soon be without it again. Natural beauty was not one of the many charms of Houston. "Yes, it's beautiful," she replied. "But don't you ever miss the big city life in Mexico?"

"No, never. In my mind, home is where things feel right. I think some people are just born in the wrong place. When I lived in Cabo, I was always thinking about getting away. But now that I'm here, I never think about leaving. Sometimes I forget about Mexico altogether. Then someone will say one thing or another, and I'll remember that there's a whole world out there. But I'm just fine right here."

The view from Cahal Pech Tavern was everything Jay promised—a lush expanse of rolling green rising and climbing up and away from the blacktop. Tucked into the green, like jewels on a lavish gown of emerald velvet, were brightly colored cottages and bungalows with rooftops of shimmering silver or deep terracotta.

After enjoying a pair of Margaritas at the bar, Jay and Emily began meandering through the trails at Cahal Pech. Perched high on a hilltop, the site at Cahal Pech contained 34 structures nestled within less than one square mile of space. When the ancient Maya sought to expand the residences at Cahal Pech they did so by building upward, as there was no space to expand outward along the hilltop. This gave some of their buildings the appearance of a layered cake with newer rooms atop older ones and stairways floating in between.

Jay guided Emily through the central plaza and up into the first of the elite residential structures, explaining that Cahal Pech was once a ceremonial site complete with an altar, which they would visit shortly.

As Jay and Emily explored the corbelled archways and narrow rooms of the residential structure, he told her more about the history of the Maya people—how they were known as "philosophers of time," and how they viewed time as cycles within cycles, each independent, but all overlapping. "The Tzolk'in 260-day calendar or short cycle," he said, "and the Ja'ab 360-day solar cycle are sequenced together to form the Calendar Round, a sacred cycle that governed daily life. The first cycle of the Calendar Round, the Tzolk'in cycle, consists of a sequence of days roughly equivalent to the nine months of pregnancy, and those who followed this cycle came to be known as daykeepers. The second cycle, the Ja'ab, tracks the sun's journey from equinox to equinox, and is referred to as the Solar Year. Within both the Tzolk'in and Ja'ab cycles exist two separate cycles. The first of each consists of twenty days, the second, nine and eighteen months respectively. Inter-connected and perpetually cycling through eternity, the Tzolk'in and Ja'ab cycles come together to create a larger cycle of fifty-two years, which is known as the Calendar Round."

Emily tried to absorb Jay's explanation of Maya timekeeping, but she was more interested in the lives of the ancient people who once walked the creeping staircases. She brushed her fingertips against the stone walls of the structure that was once home to a family with hopes, dreams and fears, and she tried to imagine what it might have been like to live in such a place at such a time.

CHAPTER 21 - JAY

"I KNOW A GREAT STORY ABOUT THIS PLACE," Jay said to Emily as they walked across the courtyard at Cahal Pech. "A Maya prince and princess lived here in secret over fourteen hundred years ago."

"Really?" Emily asked eagerly. "Why were they living in secret?"

"They were hiding from the prince's brother," Jay answered. "Legend has it that a princess of Tikal named Lady Ixchel was captured in battle and brought to Caracol where she was destined to be sacrificed by Lord Water, the victorious king of Caracol. But the king's younger brother Lord Itzamna fell in love with her, and they ran away together on the day of the Festival of Conquest.

"One of Lord Water's royal guards followed them when they made their escape and lurked outside their hideaway. He hoped to curry favor with the king by recapturing the princess. The pair remained hidden for two days until the celebrations ended. The guard waited until Itzamna left the house to replenish their drinking water. He didn't want to risk an encounter with the king's younger brother, knowing Lord Water would be furious if his brother was injured for the sake of a single captive.

When Itzamna was gone, the guard snuck into the house. It was a one-room structure with a hammock for sleeping at one end and a hearth for cooking at the other. The morning sun was rising, but Ixchel was still asleep in the hammock. The guard grabbed her by the wrists and yanked her to the floor. Startled and confused, she scrambled back toward the wall. The guard came at her again, but she was ready for him.

Having regained her bearings, she had no intention of going easily. She lunged at his legs, wrapped her arms around his thighs, and slammed his

144

back against the floor. He grunted as the breath went out of him. Ixchel darted over him and headed for the door, but he caught her by the ankle as she ran. Her forward momentum cut short, she crashed face-first into the bamboo door. Within seconds, the guard had her by the wrists again. Ixchel went limp and sank to the floor, forcing the guard to wrangle with a hundred pounds of dead weight as he struggled to open the door. It was more than he could handle. He released one of her wrists and tried to wedge the door open behind her. She bit down hard on the hand still clamped around her, sinking her teeth into the pad of soft flesh at the base of his thumb. As he howled in pain, she bolted for the hearth.

The guard, his eyes slits of fury, pulled a flint blade from a scabbard at his hip and bore down on Ixchel. Within the hearth, a dwindling fire winked red. Taking a shallow clay bowl from the fireside, Ixchel scooped a mound of hot embers up and out. She tossed them, bowl and all, at the guard. Through the burning cloud of ash, he attacked, slashing wildly with his blade. Ixchel screamed in agony as the blade ripped through her abdomen again and again.

Itzamna was on his way back. Hearing Ixchel's screams, he flew toward the house, desperate to save the woman he loved. When he entered the house, he found the guard standing over her, his knife dripping with her blood. Ixchel was on the floor, dying.

Itzamna descended upon the guard, burying his own blade in the back of the wretched man. The guard turned and railed against Itzamna, but the guard was near blind from the hot ash. Itzamna slammed his fist into the pocket of flesh beneath the guard's shoulder, sending the man whirling. Wrenching his knife from the guard's back, Itzamna took him by the hair and slit his throat. The guard crumbled at Itzamna's feet.

The battle over, Itzamna let his blade thud softly to the earthen floor. Ixchel lay dead at the mouth of the hearth, and he felt as if all the air had been sucked from the room. He was suffocating with despair.

Just then, Itzamna's friend, Seven Turtle, walked through his front door. Shocked by the carnage, he asked, "What has happened, my friend?" Cradling Ixchel in his arms, Itzamna told Seven Turtle everything.

"She died bravely, she will awake in the upperworld," Seven Turtle offered in sympathy. Itzamna nodded, but he had no intention of letting her go. He had learned the secrets of Heart of Sky from his first master, the oldest and wisest of the daykeepers, Ajq'ij Dark Fox, and he was determined to bring Ixchel back to life. He collected a blood offering from the body of the guard, and he and Seven Turtle carried Ixchel to the Sky Place.

For decades, Ajq'ij Dark Fox had tried in vain to call forth the sky god. Ajq'ij Dark Fox never discovered that his renegade former pupil succeeded where he failed. As far as Ajq'ij Dark Fox and Lord Water were concerned, Itzamna ran off during the Festival of Conquest and his female consort died with all the rest. Maya sacrificial ceremonies are drug-induced spectacles of madness. It's impossible to keep the body count straight.

Itzamna was able to use Ajq'ij Dark Fox's incantations to summon Heart of Sky because he knew the one thing Ajq'ij Dark Fox did not. The sky god was a champion of justice. Itzamna begged Heart of Sky to right the wrong that had been done to Ixchel, and before long he received an answer.

When Heart of Sky alighted inside the Sky Place, Ixchel was with him. Her soul had flown to the upperworld early that morning, and, by sheer coincidence, she'd been claimed by Heart of Sky. The sky god promised to resurrect Ixchel under one condition. Itzamna and Ixchel must choose to serve him thereafter, just as the first celestial beings once served him. Eventually, they would become gods themselves. Itzamna and Ixchel agreed. Moments later, Ixchel awoke inside her body, her injuries healed.

Itzamna and Ixchel traveled northward until they found a small village where they could settle. They made their home here at Cahal Pech. It is said that on the day of their wedding, Ixchel wore a red hibiscus in her hair and bid farewell to her old life. They both abandoned their noble heritage and lived amid the merchant class, dedicating their lives to helping and healing all who came to them for aid.

"Wow," Emily exclaimed when Jay finished his tale. "Where did you hear that story? Is it a well-known legend here?"

"Not really," Jay replied. "It isn't well known. I heard it from a friend of mine. His name's Manuel Cocom, and he's got the best stories about the ancient Maya." Jay chuckled. "He claims he's a direct descendant of Maya nobility. He's the caretaker of Caracol. Nobility or not, he's got a million stories up his sleeve, but that one is my favorite."

"It's a good one."

Jay smiled and shook his head. "You know, Manuel's convinced that Lady Ixchel and Lord Itzamna are both gods now, a goddess of war and a god of agriculture, or something like that. If it's true, then we are walking in the footsteps of gods."

"I would love to meet a Maya god," Emily said.

Jay laughed. "Be careful what you wish for."

CHAPTER 22 - MAGGIE AND MITCH

THE AFTERNOON FOLLOWING their arrival in Belize, Mitch and Maggie set out in their rented Ford Explorer for Manuel's home on the outskirts of Caracol. Their journey would take four and a half hours, the final portion over unpaved roads.

"If I wasn't driving, I'd be drinking," Mitch said to Maggie with a heavy sigh as they weaved in and out of traffic on Princess Margaret Drive. Maggie threw a worried look at him and he immediately tried to laugh away the tension in the air. "He'll help us," Mitch soothed. "I know he will."

Maggie wasn't quite so certain, but she didn't want to dwell on it. She was tired and wanted to rest. But during the last two months seatbelts had become her nemesis. The lap belt pressed painfully against her sore abdomen, and she squirmed uncomfortably beneath it. In anticipation of their long drive, she'd brought a little pillow with her from home to prop under the seatbelt near the buckle, which helped to alleviate some of the pressure. She reclined her seat and maneuvered the pillow into place.

Mitch reached his hand across the gearbox and touched her thigh gently. "Do you want some music?" he asked.

"Sure," she replied, absently twirling her wedding band on her finger, "something relaxing would be nice." Mitch searched the satellite radio, finally settling on classic instrumental. As Maggie listened to Fur Elize, she thought about her life—about what she'd accomplished and what she hadn't—and she wondered what it took to make a life whole. Hers, certainly, was incomplete. She'd felt the swinging pendulum of her biological clock tick-tocking long before her illness. *But was the secret to life really that simple—good health and a loving family?*

Maggie recalled a story Mitch once told her about a surgeon he'd met during his residency. While traveling through South America, the man had been kidnapped and held for ransom for almost a year. After he was rescued, the man never had another bad day at work. Whenever Mitch would complain about his workload or lack of sleep, the man would simply ask, "When you got up this morning were you able to open your door and walk outside?"

Maybe it's all just anamorphic art, Maggie thought, *most people can't see the image behind the distortion. But for some, the ones who are forced to stand still and stare at what's been lost, it all becomes crystal clear.*

It was late in the day when Mitch and Maggie arrived at the home of Manuel Cocom. At the sound of the approaching vehicle, Sena ran eagerly from the house to greet Dr. Mitch and his wife. Mitch parked the Explorer near the low fence that surrounded the Cocoms' bungalow. By the time he'd helped Maggie down from the passenger side, Sena was standing at the front of the vehicle, waiting for them.

"Hello, princess," Mitch said to Sena as she smiled up at him.

"Hi, Dr. Mitch," Sena replied, running over for a hug. Mitch lifted Sena in a bear hug, and then placed her bare feet gently back on the ground.

"This is my wife, Ms. Maggie," Mitch said, as Maggie negotiated the narrow space that remained between the fence, the vehicle, and Mitch.

"Hi, sweetie." Maggie bent down to greet Sena, offering the child her hand.

"Hi, Ms. Maggie," Sena replied. "I'm in Standard Three now," she added as she shook Maggie's hand gleefully.

"Wow," Maggie said. "You certainly are a big girl."

"I'm nine years old," replied Sena. "And Ms. Perez says I'm the best in the class at reading and spelling."

Mitch and Maggie responded in chorus, Mitch's "That's great" somewhat overpowering Maggie's "How wonderful."

"Sena," called her mother from the front door, "please show our guests into the house. It isn't polite to keep them outside."

"Yes, mamma," Sena answered, and, gesturing toward the open gate, she asked, "Would you like to come inside now?"

"That would be lovely, thank you," Maggie replied.

Mitch took Maggie's hand and together they followed Sena into the house that held all their hopes for the future.

The entryway to the Cocoms' home opened into a one-room living and dining area behind which stood a semi-enclosed kitchen. To the left of the modest great room were three doors of darkly varnished wood. A mixture of photos and handmade embellishments adorned the walls. The eyes of St. Vincent stared out of a gold-foil frame from beyond the dining table, and three hand-woven tapestries flanked the far wall to the right.

Manuel and his son, Evan, were in the backyard, manning the grill, and the smell of food and spices filled the house through the open windows. Sena's mother, Marisol, asked Mitch and Maggie to wait with Sena in the living room, while she prepared refreshments and fetched her husband. Manuel greeted the Hudsons warmly and Maggie could tell that Manuel was genuinely happy to see them.

Dinner was excellent—a feast of grilled pork, rice and beans, stewed carrots, cassava bread, and fried plantains. During the meal, conversation was light and easy. The two families talked first about the weather, which had been dry and mild for over a week, with warm, sunny days and cool, comfortable nights. Manuel mentioned that a wet cold front was expected within a day or two, and Marisol, glancing at the photo of St. Vincent, added that, although she wasn't looking forward to the cold, they could use a little rain.

Next, they discussed the children. Sena had made excellent progress since her surgery, and Evan, who was currently home on Christmas break, was doing exceptionally well at St. John's College in Belize City. Evan remarked that he'd recently decided to major in Hotel Management. His plan was to return to Cayo and apply for a job at one of the resorts in the area. Marisol smiled as Evan discussed his plans, and Mitch and Maggie were told that Evan had previously been toying with the idea of remaining in the city long term, but his parents were happy he'd changed his mind and decided to return to Cayo instead, where they would be able to see him more often.

At this point, the conversation stalled. It was Maggie who finally broke the silence. To Marisol, she said, "The tapestries on the far wall are beautiful, did you stitch them yourself?"

Marisol laughed. "Oh, no. I'm not that talented. They are very old, actually, and have been in Manuel's family for generations."

Manuel took his wife's cue and added, "They were loomed by my great-grandmother, and together they depict the three forms of Heart of Sky." With pride, Manuel explained that his great-grandmother loomed the tapestries as a gift to commemorate the wedding day of her eldest daughter; and they'd been passed down to each firstborn daughter thereafter. He'd gotten them by default as he had no sisters and was the eldest son.

Manuel explained that the god Heart of Sky can take three forms, Hurricane, Lightning, and Thunderbolt. "He can manifest into all three forms at once," Manuel said, "which allows him to magnify his power by degrees. He is one of the creator gods, the most esteemed of all the gods."

Maggie looked at the tapestries; she was so nervous that she'd failed to notice their exquisite details when she entered the house. The first tapestry showed Heart of Sky incarnated as the god Hurricane. The ornamented face of the god, his mouth a crooked beak, was encircled by swirling black clouds and orange flames. In the second tapestry, Lightning, the god's full body was outlined, his torso and arms those of a man, his legs, twin snapping serpents. On his wrists were thick jade bracelets and, in his hands, knives with blades of fire. His head was a crested monstrosity, spewing fire and daggers. The third tapestry depicted the god Thunderbolt as a dancing, tattooed being, his elaborately plumed head gazing off into the distance, a jade and onyx necklace falling against his chest.

After dinner, Mitch and Manuel went to the living room, while Marisol steered Maggie to the flower garden in the backyard.

***

As soon as the two men were seated, Mitch began, "You know why I'm here Manuel, and you know how serious Maggie's situation has become. I wouldn't ask you to help us if our circumstances were anything less than desperate."

Manuel rubbed his brow. "I wish I could help you, Mitch. I wish I could save your wife for you, but there is nothing I can do. I've explained why I can't perform the ceremony again, and I told you in my letter that I don't believe the ritual would work for her, even if I did choose to ignore the code and call the goddess a second time. Your wife is dying from a natural illness. It is her time. I don't believe there is anything that can be done for her."

"But you're not absolutely certain, are you?" Mitch asked, standing. He'd known about Manuel's doubts, but he'd ignored them and refused to let them shake his resolve. He'd been determined to remain unflappable for Maggie's sake, and he'd done everything he could to prevent the seeds of doubt from sprouting in his mind as well as hers.

"Nothing is ever certain," Manuel replied.

"Then help us. Give us a chance. Please."

"I have already told you...."

"Yes, you've told me, but I don't understand. Why can't you do this simple thing for us? This simple act could...."

"It is forbidden," Manuel interrupted, "to take too much from the earth, to ask too much of the gods. This thing you are asking me to do is not *simple*. It is a sacred ritual, and I made a blood offering once before on your behalf. I bargained for your soul to be returned to earth. It is permissible to perform this ritual once in a lifetime, for a loved one, or for someone who has given you something precious in this life. But, to do so again would be a grave transgression, and I cannot risk the wrath of the gods coming down upon me and my family."

"Please," was all Mitch could think to say.

Manuel did not respond, instead he put his face in his hands and shook his head.

"I can pay you a great deal of money," Mitch offered finally, "money you can use for Evan and Sena, for school, for their future. Please Manuel. I am begging you to help us, and I am offering to pay."

"You cannot buy my soul, Mitch Hudson," Manuel said, standing to face his friend. "If I could do this for you, I would. Money would not be a greater inducement than your friendship and the kindness you have shown my daughter and my family."

"I'm sorry, but I had to try," Mitch said, slumping into his chair. He felt weak and heavy, like a crumpled vehicle on the losing end of a crash. For a moment, all he could do was sit and suffocate beneath the weight of hopelessness.

***

Outside, Maggie watched as Sena came cantering around the side of the house and hurried toward the garden. The child clutched her mother's hand as soon as she reached her side. "Mamma, where's Evan?" she asked, tugging on her mother's wrist. "I need to find him."

Marisol turned to Maggie and apologized for Sena's interruption. In turn, Sena also offered a mumbled apology, but kept her eyes glued to her mother's face.

"He's down the road, baby," Marisol answered, "at Tony's house."

Without another word, Sena ran from her mother's side and disappeared around the back of the house.

"She gets so excited sometimes," Marisol said to Maggie after Sena was gone. "But it is wonderful to see her personality coming out after all these years. She used to be so quiet and shy, but now she is a lively little spirit, just like any other girl."

"I'm so glad," Maggie said. "You must be very proud of both your children."

"Yes, I have been blessed with a wonderful family," Marisol replied.

Maggie's heart skipped in her chest. She was hardly less eager than Mitch for a positive response from Manuel, and it was all she could do to keep her hands from fidgeting and her feet from tapping out the fierce energy that had risen inside her with each day of mounting hope. She tried to think of something to say, anything to fill the silence, but nothing came to mind. She smiled awkwardly and folder her arms across her chest.

"I know why you're here," Marisol said softly.

Maggie nodded.

"Manuel and I were sorry to hear about your illness. We are praying for your recovery."

"Thank you," Maggie said.

Marisol's eyes scanned the garden as though she was searching the leaves on the trees, the petals on the flowers, for something to say.

Maggie was used to these kinds of hesitant conversations, the ones that always transpired whenever her illness became the focus. She was about to break the silence with a question about Marisol's family background when Mitch appeared at the back door. As Mitch walked toward her,

Maggie could tell from the look on his face that they would be leaving empty-handed. She suddenly felt hollow, and as she spoke her goodbyes to Marisol and Manuel, her voice echoed inside her chest.

Together Mitch and Maggie moved through the garden and out to the front yard, each supporting the other, unaware of the motion of their bodies, the falling of their feet upon the soft soil.

They had played their hand and lost. There was nothing left to try, no ace up a sleeve. And now, they had no choice but to return home and negotiate the few bittersweet months that remained. As they walked toward their vehicle, the sound of the gate creaking behind them seemed to announce the end of hope, and Maggie felt disconnected from the world, set apart from everything but Mitch.

When they reached the vehicle, Maggie stopped and held onto Mitch, wanting to postpone for a moment the long, bleak drive that lay ahead. But the sound of distant voices forced her to focus her attention on a pair of figures calling out to them and running forward from the road beyond the house. Sena and Evan came bounding toward them.

Maggie braced herself for contact and prepared to offer a set of composed goodbyes. But Sena had something else in mind. Winded and hyper, Sena blurted her words out as soon as she reached Mitch and Maggie.

"I can help you, Dr. Mitch," she said, her voice trembling with excitement. "Evan was there before ... he knows the words to call the gods ... he will tell me what to say." She came to a stop in front of them. "I can help you," she said, "because of all you have done for me."

Relief caught in Maggie's throat like a rolling wave, and she suddenly found it impossible to speak. She watched mutely as Mitch put his hand on Sena's shoulder and gave the little angel a squeeze.

"Thank you," Maggie whispered finally. Sena, smiling ear to ear, was all but hyperventilating in front of her. Tears warmed the corners of Maggie's eyes, and she pressed her cheek against Mitch's shoulder as she wiped them away.

Sena, Evan, Mitch, and Maggie made arrangements to meet at Caracol the following evening, which was a Tuesday—Manuel's first workday for the week—and because Sena did not want to tell her father what she and Evan were up to, the children would have to sneak into the site and then avoid detection by their father while Sena performed the ritual for Maggie at the Sky Place.

Maggie hoped everything would go according to plan. Mitch made it sound so easy, too easy. She had the nagging feeling there was something he wasn't telling her, but she was already one hundred percent committed, and she'd rather go in blind than go in terrified.

CHAPTER 23 - EMILY AND JAY

EMILY AND JAY COMPLETED their tour of Cahal Pech at three thirty in the afternoon. Moments later, they were back in Jay's jeep winding their way toward the San Ignacio Resort Hotel. They arrived at the resort within thirty minutes and by the time they'd checked in at the front desk it was quarter past four.

As the porter led Jay and Emily to their rooms (Emily's was first along the corridor), Jay said, "Let's meet for dinner at six. That should give us plenty of time to eat before the night walk begins at eight."

"Sounds good," Emily replied as she stepped inside her room. Emily's garden room was a divine mixture of rustic ambiance and modern luxury. The semi-enclosed porch looked out onto a lush garden of tropical trees and plants, and a hammock stretched across the porch's length, bracketed by a pair of dark wood chairs. The door panels, window frames, and furnishings were all constructed of the same glossy, heavy wood as the chairs, and the room's light blue walls were decorated with original paintings of parrots and tropical flowers by a local artist.

It took Emily less than an hour to unpack, shower, and change, which gave her a full thirty minutes to relax before dinner. Having finished Persuasion on the plane, she searched inside her bag for her backup book (Wuthering Heights). Book in hand, she made her way onto the patio and settled into the first of a pair of chairs that welcomed her. But before she could so much as open Wuthering Heights she was struck by the view from her patio. Setting her book on the arm of the chair, she approached the side railing to get a better look. From her perch above the trails, she saw layer upon layer of nuanced green. In the distance, the brown-green expanse of the jungle canopy rolled like the swell of a wave, rising to greet the golden-blue of the evening sky. Closer in, a shower of sapodilla leaves and bushy cabbage palms fell in amber-green spurts over the perimeter of the garden. And, in the vicinity of her own room, almost close enough to touch, the emerald-green leaves of screw palms bowed and waved with each passing gust of warm wind.

Forgetting her book entirely, Emily felt compelled to explore the landscape in the time remaining before daylight was relegated to dusk. As she meandered along the close-in trails, she found herself enveloped by rich vegetation. Above her, a shimmering curtain of foliage danced lazily in the lingering light. Everything was fresh and green—it even smelled green—like pine needles and cut grass. In that instant, Emily felt as though she'd never known the earth before.

Mindful of the time, Emily let herself explore the grounds only a few moments longer before returning to her room to put away her book and collect her purse. She met Jay outside the dining room at six o'clock sharp. The dining area was an open-air verandah overlooking the pool and surrounding jungle. The tables were each covered with either a peach or white cloth, and the verandah was illuminated by candles burning at the center of each table and within sconces fastened to the surrounding support poles.

Within moments of their arrival, Jay and Emily were greeted by the hostess, who seated them in a quiet corner. Their table was shielded from the front portion of the restaurant by a wall, and, as she took her seat, Emily wished the setting was a little less romantic.

It would be wonderful to be here with Mitch, she thought as she nonchalantly toyed with the silverware. She turned her attention to the people around her, the couples and the families, the groups and the lone travelers. *They probably think Jay and I are together*, she mused, and she wondered whether she would seem different to them if Mitch was with her instead. Mitch was ten years her senior, and he had a certain presence to him, a way of drawing every eye in the room toward him. Jay was easily as handsome as Mitch, but Mitch was always impeccably dressed, no matter what the occasion or the venue. Jay was utterly casual, which wasn't any better or worse, just different. And Emily was certain that beneath Jay's friendly exterior beat the heart of a dyed-in-the-wool player.

She watched as Jay rested his napkin on his lap and eased himself into a semi-reclining position in his chair. Suddenly, Emily pictured Hunter in Jay's place, his eyes flashing the way they did on New Year's Eve, his hand reaching out for hers. The memory hit her like a hammer, and she could feel the expression on her face sink from happy to sad. She scrambled to think of something else, something light and cheerful, but what she ended up with was the memory of her and Hunter's first—and only—kiss.

It happened a few weeks after her breakup with Mitch. Emily was still shaken and woeful, and although Hunter had hated the guy and told her he was happy to have him gone, he didn't scold her, and did his best to lift her spirits during that time. It was a cold Saturday night in February, and they were having dinner at Shade—their favorite Heights restaurant—with three of their friends. After several hours of food, wine, and conversation, their friends decided to head over to Midtown for music and dancing. Emily declined the invitation to join them, insisting that she wasn't in the mood for dancing. Hunter begged off as well, insisting that he wasn't in the mood to let Emily get behind the wheel after the amount of wine she'd polished off that night.

After Hunter drove Emily home, she invited him upstairs. Drunk and slightly incoherent, she flopped onto the sofa and motioned for Hunter to join her. He did. Emily straightened herself up, grabbed the remote control, and began chattering about her favorite TV show. Apparently, this wasn't what Hunter had expected. He took the remote from her hand, placed it on the coffee table, and laced his fingers through hers. She stared at the remote control for a moment then down at her fingers entwined with his. Turning to face him, she met his gaze. His eyes were soft and inviting, and she wanted to collapse against his chest and fall asleep cradled in his arms. But her head was spinning from the wine, and she seemed to have forgotten how to speak without slurring. Suddenly, Hunter was kissing her. She'd wrapped her arms around his neck and kissed him back. Her heart fluttered and the skin on the small of her back tingled from his touch. She closed her eyes, which was a huge mistake. Her stomach lurched and she pulled away quickly.

"What's wrong?" Hunter asked.

"I don't feel good," she replied and darted from the sofa toward the bathroom. But she only made it as far as the kitchen.

Hunter followed her into the kitchen. "Are you okay?" he asked seconds before she began vomiting into the trashcan.

"Oh, Jeez," he said. "That is so disgusting. I'm sorry; I know this is much worse for you than it is for me, but I really hate vomit."

Emily had mumbled an apology into the trashcan, but Hunter was out of earshot. He was standing in the hall, eyeing the kitchen doorway with a pained expression on his face.

He'd stayed with her long enough to help her get cleaned up and into bed. At work the following Monday, things between them had been awkward and uncomfortable. Emily was utterly embarrassed, and she was certain that Hunter regretted ever laying his hands on her. They never talked about what happened that night, and, eventually, things between them had gotten back to normal.

While Jay chatted about the restaurant and the chef, Emily tried to make her way back to the moment, but it was a struggle. Fortunately, she was soon sufficiently distracted by the arrival of their waitress, a pretty, young woman who greeted them with a bright smile on her heart-shaped face.

"Good evening," the woman began, "I'll be your waitress tonight, would you prefer ice water or bottled?"

"Ice water is fine," Jay replied with a glance in Emily's direction.

Emily made no objection, and the waitress proceeded to inform them of the daily specials, which were located on a separate menu. "Here we have the Chef's daily four course connoisseur menu," she said as she handed each of them a printed sheet of beige paper.

"That's a mouthful already," Jay joked. To Emily's amusement, he winked at the waitress who smiled shyly back at him.

Emily lowered her eyes and fought a smile. The waitress proceeded to offer a detailed description of the courses on the daily menu, all made fresh with local produce and spices. As Jay and Emily examined the newly acquired menus, the waitress requested their drink orders.

"Do you have frozen Margaritas?" Emily asked.

"Yes, we make them to order, in the blender."

"Hmm," Emily hesitated, "Can you do a Mojito?"

"Yes, of course," the waitress replied.

159

"Do you make it with fresh mint leaves or crushed?"

"We use fresh leaves."

"That sounds good...." Emily said thoughtfully. "Actually, I'll have a Margarita after all ... but on the rocks, please ... with salt."

"Certainly. And for you, sir?"

"I'll stick with water for now, but I'd like a Belikin with the appetizers."

"And do you know which appetizers you'll be having?" the waitress asked politely.

"Uh," Jay stammered and scanned the menu.

"I'll have the soup ... from the daily menu" Emily interjected.

"Yeah," said Jay. "I'll have the soup as well."

"Excellent choice," asserted the waitress. "I'll be right back with your beverages."

Jay watched the waitress as she walked away, and then turned to Emily. "So how do you like your room?"

"It's amazing, and the view from my patio is incredible."

"Yeah, I love this place," he said. "I'm glad your friend agreed to let us stay here."

"What do you mean?" she asked. "I thought this whole get-away was his idea."

"Well," Jay hedged, "he called and asked me to give him a list of five-star hotels in the city, as well as here in Cayo. I gave him the names of the places I liked best, and I quoted him the prices. He was really cool about the whole thing and agreed to everything I suggested. He said that nothing was too good for Ms. Stillman, and he also said that I should 'spare no expense and endeavor to treat you like royalty for the duration of our time together.'"

"Are you serious?" Emily asked, her cheeks flushing as she struggled to minimize her smile.

"Yes," Jay replied. "Those were his exact words because I certainly don't talk like that if I can help it."

The waitress returned to deliver their drinks and collect their dinner orders. Jay managed to place his order for the main course with minimal flirting, and, after Emily placed hers, she relaxed into her chair, sipped her Margarita, and allowed herself to savor the moment.

As she watched the flames of the candles on the surrounding tables flicker, she felt the warm glow of contentment spreading through her chest. It was *really nice* to be a priority in someone's life, and her heart hummed with happiness as she thought about Mitch.

Across the table, Jay began to fidget in his seat. Emily gave him a quizzical look, but he was too busy fishing his phone out of his pocket to notice.

"Speak of the devil," he said as he looked at his phone. "Hello, Dr. Hudson," Jay said with a glance in Emily's direction. "Yes, we're doing just fine.... As a matter of fact, she's right here.... We're having dinner.... Yes, of course.... Well, here she is...."

Emily took the phone from Jay and pointed toward the front of the restaurant. She maneuvered around the wall and walked toward a small alcove that housed the doors to the restrooms to take her call.

"Hi, Mitch," she said. "How's everything going?"

"Hi, gorgeous," Mitch replied. "To be honest, this hasn't been an easy time for me, but just knowing you're here makes all the difference in the world. I'm so glad you came, and I can't wait to see you tomorrow."

"I can't wait to see you too."

"How's everything going? How do you like your hotel? How's Mr. Kinnder treating you?"

"The hotel is amazing. I love it here. And Jay has been great. Everything has been perfect so far, except that you're not here with me."

"I know, and I'm sorry about that, but remember that this is only a temporary setback. All the kinks will be worked out soon. I promise."

"I know. I'm just anxious to see you."

"Me too, Emily, me too. Well, I'll let you get back to your dinner now, and I'll see you tomorrow."

"See you tomorrow."

Emily hung up the phone and walked back toward the dining area. As she approached the rear wall, the sound of Jay in conversation with their waitress made her stop and listen. From her hiding place behind the wall, she could hear Jay making his move.

"Where are you from?" Jay asked.

"I live in Santa Elena. I'm a Cayo girl," the waitress replied.

"All the most beautiful girls are in Cayo," Jay said sweetly, and from his tone Emily could all but see the playfulness in his eyes and the charm in his smile. She hated to cramp Jay's style, but she was eager to get back to her Margarita, and she didn't want the whole restaurant to misinterpret the situation and think that her boyfriend was flirting with the waitress right under her nose. After a few forceful coughs, she walked out from behind the wall and returned to her seat.

Emily and Jay finished eating at quarter past seven and Emily decided to return to her room to relax before the start of the night walk at eight o'clock. Jay said he would remain at the bar for now and meet her down at the trails when it was time.

For most of the day, Emily had eagerly anticipated the start of the night walk, so much so that when she finally found herself walking along behind her guide with her headlamp ablaze, she was somewhat disappointed. The January night was cool and clear, and Emily had her lamp full-on above her face. But rainforest darkness is dense and permeating, and it seemed to be eating back at the light, consuming a little more of the granulated beam each time she turned her head to glance a tree frog or wayward fruit bat.

The natural beauty she'd glimpsed earlier in the day was thoroughly diminished by the darkness, like a black curtain thrown across a lively stage in the middle of the first act. Only the lingering scent of foliage remained, but as they moved deeper into the rainforest, the scent seemed to rise away from her, pushed up by the muddy, mossy smell of earth and bark.

As the group meandered along the rainforest floor, one behind the other, like miners plodding the channel of an excavated cave, their guide highlighted the more interesting varieties of local plants and animals. Emily strained her eyes to see the strangler fig, and then the give-and-take palm, whose bark-borne thorns contained a powerful toxin, the pain of which could only be relieved by its own milky sap. She walked gingerly past the thorny tree, careful to avoid the small spikes that covered the entire length of its tall, narrow trunk.

For Emily, the most appealing feature of the night walk was the symphony of songs and calls that rose from creatures secreted near and far. The chatter of the cicadas mingled with the trill of the owls, and above it all, consuming it all, were the resonant cries of the howler monkeys. It was a fearsome noise, and it grew to fill the space above and around her. Emily found it impossible to believe that such a violent cry could come from something as small as a monkey, something not grotesque and bloodthirsty.

At the end of the night walk Emily found herself exhausted from her adventures, and, graciously declining Jay's offer to walk her to her room, she made her way back alone for a nice, long rest.

But less than five minutes after she'd settled into bed, she heard the whoosh of an animal as it bounded through her open patio door, followed by the gentle thump, thump of its front and back paws making contact with the floor only a few feet away. Surprised and panicked, she snapped on the bedside lamp, half expecting to see a jaguarondi or ocelot creeping across the hardwoods. Instead, her eyes fell upon the figure of a wiry, gray cat that immediately let out a plaintive meow in response to the sudden flood of light.

Relief washed over Emily like a shower of rain, and she flopped back against her pillow. The cat, satisfied that he, likewise, was in no danger, made his way toward a cushioned chair in the corner of the room. He sprang up to the chair and kneaded the cushions briefly with his paws before curling up and settling in. A few seconds later he lifted his head and looked at Emily.

"Oh," she said. "Shall I get the light?"

The cat placed his head affirmatively upon his paws, and Emily clicked off the lamp.

When Emily awoke the next morning, Houston seemed ages away. She felt as though nothing else existed beyond the perimeter of the jungle. The coolness of night still lingered in the air, and the rustle, caws, and croaks of the nighttime creatures had given way to whispered conversations from the pathways below and the occasional hum of a vehicle negotiating the steep entryway.

Emily snuggled her face into her pillow and pulled the crisp sheets closer. After a few drowsy minutes, she raised her head to check the time. Six thirty.

***

By six thirty that morning, Jay had been awake for over an hour. Breakfast on the patio was followed by a run along the medicine trail, then a long shower. Ordinarily, Jay did not linger in the shower, but each bathroom came fully stocked with luxurious soaps and shampoo. It all smelled delicious. The bathroom at his rental was absolutely depressing by comparison. With its cracked tiles, flickering lights, and cold water, it was not somewhere Jay cared to spend any more time than necessary. But this shower stall was a different story altogether. River stones covered the entire stall, floor to ceiling, and the smooth curves of the stones felt great against his bare feet. The bathroom was situated on the eastern corner of the room, and the morning light fell through the skylight above the shower in warm waves. The fixtures sparkled as the water bounced and flowed off the chrome surfaces.

The water even tastes better out here, Jay thought with a smile. Then he thought about the pretty young waitress he'd romanced the night before and smiled again.

After he'd gotten absolutely nowhere with Emily (not even so much as a walk back to her room), which he'd pretty much expected (engaged women generally being much harder to seduce than married women); he'd headed back to the bar and waited for the dining room to close for the night. Then he'd made his move. The waitress, Lily (or Laura or maybe Leah), had refused to come back to his room, but they'd had some fun under a mango tree behind the laundry room, and Jay hoped to seal the deal before the end of his stay.

By the time Jay stepped from the shower, the bathroom was practically bulging with steam. He toweled off and checked the time. Seven o'clock.

***

At seven o'clock, Emily urged herself out of bed. She was eager to start her day. Today she would see Mitch again at last; he would join her later that afternoon at Caracol.

She slid her legs from beneath the sheet and placed them on the wood floor. The chill of the morning air caught her bare legs, and she briefly considered diving back into bed. Instead, she retrieved a long, thick robe from the bathroom and set the coffee pot on the counter to brew a single cup of local coffee.

While she waited for her coffee to brew, Emily made her way onto the patio. Although it was a chilly morning, she could feel the humidity resting upon her skin like a layer of gauze. Her sleeping companion, the gray cat, was gone, as was yesterday's glorious view. In its place was a cloaking white mist, which gave her the distinct sensation of being tucked inside a cloud. The mist permeated every crevice beyond the immediate perimeter of her patio, and it was so thick and heavy that when she reached her hand beyond the railing she half expected her fingers to return with a bundle of cotton-white something or other.

After breakfast, a morning hike, and a quick lunch, Jay and Emily began their three-hour drive toward Caracol at one o'clock in the afternoon.

"We're getting an early start," Jay said. "Mitch asked me to arrive at five thirty and take you to the South Acropolis on the outskirts of the site, but I see no harm in getting there an hour and a half early. That way, I can give you a tour of the primary features of the site myself."

"Sounds good to me." Emily said as she pulled her guidebook from her tote and began flipping through the pages to find the information about Caracol.

The rough-hewn road to Caracol once offered a scenic route that rivaled any other in the country, but the surrounding jungle had lately been ravaged by an insidious parasite. Emily was shocked by the miles and miles of stripped, mottled trees that stood bare and stark beyond the road.

"What happened to all these trees?" she asked Jay.

"Bark beetles came through here and killed them all," he replied. "It's really a shame. This use to be a nice piece of country out here."

"Ugh," she cried, "I can't believe that beetles caused all this damage. How is that possible?"

"I don't really know," he said. "I've never seen them in action, but that's why they make you fill out that little form on the airplane, promising that you aren't harboring any foul insects or disagreeable organisms. I mean, those suckers are worse than a forest fire. After they ran through here, I heard they made their way over to Guatemala and then down to Mexico."

"What a mess," Emily sighed. "What a waste."

Emily spent the remainder of the drive glued to her book, determined not to so much as glimpse another ravaged tree. When she grew bored with her book, she allowed her heart to float with anticipation at the prospect of seeing Mitch again. They'd been apart for so long and had spent so little time together lately that she felt she hardly knew him anymore. She tried to picture the little things, the sweet details, that made Mitch so special to her, but they eluded her, scurrying off before taking shape, impossible to grasp. Still, the one thing she could always hold onto was the bigger picture, and she let herself get lost in thoughts of the future. Again, she imagined the wedding day that she and Mitch would cherish always, the new home they would soon share, and the children they would nurture with pride.

CHAPTER 24 - EMILY AND MITCH

JAY CUT THE ENGINE and checked his watch. It was four o'clock. They'd made good time, arriving a full hour and a half early.

"Do you think Mitch is here already," Emily asked Jay. "Why don't you give him a call and find out?"

"I'd rather not," Jay answered. "He's footing the bill, and he was pretty specific about when and where he wanted us to meet him. I'm sure he won't mind if we take a look around, but I don't want to bother him before five thirty."

After a quick stop at the restrooms just off the parking lot, Emily followed Jay up the hillside trail that led toward the entrance to the site. The layout of Caracol was such that the location of the primary buildings roughly formed the shape of a waning crescent moon. From the bottom up, the structures began with the South Acropolis at the lowest point, then A-Reservoir, A-Ball court, and A-Plaza. The Central Acropolis was situated at the midpoint, followed by B-Reservoir, B-Plaza, and Caana, a broad and towering structure that rose from the ground in great layers.

Emily and Jay made their way through the site at a rapid pace and within thirty minutes they were standing in front of the tallest Maya structure in Belize—Caana, the Sky Place.

"Hey," Jay said as Emily snapped a few pictures. Emily turned and watched as he rifled through is backpack.

"What is it?" she asked.

"I left the water bottles in the jeep," he replied. "I'll be right back."

Emily nodded and Jay jogged off in the direction of the parking lot.

After snapping a couple more pictures of the Sky Place, Emily turned to go, but what she saw in the distance stopped her cold. Mitch and his wife were seated together just a few meters away, resting on the shallow steps of a small structure within B-Plaza. Emily hadn't given a moment's thought to what Mitch might do with Maggie while he spent time with her, but this certainly wasn't what she expected. Instinctively, Emily searched for cover and quickly concealed herself among a large group of tourists who were loosely clustered together, listening to their guide, and staring upward at the temple.

Emily held her breath and stared. Maggie was smiling down at her husband as he tended to her feet. Mitch removed Maggie's shoes and carefully rubbed her ankles and the soles of her feet before replacing her sneakers and retying the laces. He slid his fingertip beneath the brim of each shoe to make sure he hadn't laced them too tightly. He untied and retied the right shoe and checked again. Mitch helped Maggie to her feet and supported her as they descended the stairs. As she watched the couple interact, it became clear to Emily that Maggie was not the third wheel in this love triangle. She was.

Emily exhaled and then began to hyperventilate.

As the group around her thinned, she readjusted her position, but her eyes remained glued to the scene that was unfolding before her. There was nothing romantic happening between Mitch and his wife, no hugs or kisses. But Emily was amazed to see how careful he was with her, and how clearly responsive he was to her smiles and comments. Mitch was staring at Maggie with a look she'd never seen before, not on Mitch's face anyway. She'd caught it once or twice in Hunter's eyes, but it had always been so fleeting, so easy to ignore.

As Mitch helped Maggie to a drink of water, Emily's focus shifted to Maggie's face. Maggie looked utterly devoted. In that instant, Emily was overcome by the sensation of waking from a dream. Her perception of Mitch transformed before her eyes—the picture in her mind going from Sepia to Technicolor to High Definition, every flaw and blemish now magnified. The bar fight at The Marquee (yes, a bar fight!) was no longer justified as "his passion for living." His inability to recall the simplest details of her life was no longer explained away by "his unflinching devotion to work." And his inability to commit or plan ahead was no longer dismissed as "his desire to live life in the moment."

The spell was broken. Emily finally saw Mitch for the man he was, and she did not love him. Resolute and self-reproaching, she turned her gaze inward. Mitch was not the first man to disappoint her. She'd painted a picture in her mind of what she thought she needed in her life. But in that painting, there was nothing original, nothing of her own. This painful truth was enough to crack the foundation of willful blindness she'd built her life upon. She didn't need her father's approval to make her happy. She didn't need anyone's approval. And she certainly didn't need Mitch.

"Hunter," she whispered. Hunter had been right all along about Mitch. He'd tried to warn her, and all he'd gotten for his effort was a mountain of insults from her.

I need talk to him, she thought anxiously. Her heart raced. She needed to hear Hunter's voice, but her cell phone was nothing more than dead weight in her purse. Panicked and desperate, she bolted around the temple stairs to look for Jay. At least he had a phone that worked.

***

Mitch caught sight of Emily as she ran across the grassy expanse in front of him. "Shit! Emily's here!" He grabbed his pack and darted after Emily, leaving Maggie behind on the temple stairs.

Emily was almost sprinting, but Mitch met her pace easily, his mind clutching at any possible excuse he could use to subdue her obvious anger. At last, he realized there was nothing he could say to her. She'd clearly seen him with Maggie, and now there was nothing that would stop her from running as far away from him as possible. The ruse was over, and he had to act fast.

***

The gravel path beneath Emily's feet meandered along shrub-lined outcroppings then through clusters of tall trees with spreading roots before disappearing altogether. When she realized she was lost, she stopped running and looked around to get her bearings.

Mitch was standing less than two feet in front of her. Surprised and confused, she gasped and stumbled back. With startling speed, Mitch caught hold of her arm at the elbow and raked the blade of a scalpel across the outside of her upper arm. Emily stared at Mitch in wonder, too shocked to scream. Her skin, still damp with sweat from running, bristled cold with fear.

Mitch moved with clinical precision. Within seconds, he'd discarded the blade and produced a clean rag. Averting his eyes from Emily's face, he pressed the rag to the wound he'd opened on her arm and squeezed hard. The pain snapped Emily to attention. She screamed as she watched the rag turn from white to red. Emily struggled to free her arm from Mitch's grasp, but he held firm.

"I'm sorry," Mitch whispered seconds before Jay punched him in the side of the ribs. Mitch twisted in pain and turned to face Jay, the rag falling to the ground. Emily stepped back and sank down against the trunk of a pine tree. She whimpered as she pulled the bottom of her T-shirt up and pressed it over her wound, hugging her arm close against her chest.

Emily stared in disbelief as Mitch and Jay went at it. Mitch landed a right to the jaw that sent Jay spiraling to the dirt. But Jay recovered quickly, scrambling to his feet, and tackling Mitch at the waist. They both went down. Then Mitch pulled Jay up toward him by the shoulder and performed the craziest superhuman maneuver Emily had ever seen. Still on his back, Mitch sort of bench-pressed Jay's entire body above his head, and then tossed Jay into a nearby shrub. This put Jay out of commission long enough for Mitch to grab the bloody rag and take off.

Fortunately, Jay wasn't hurt badly. After he regained his footing and his composure, he helped Emily to her feet, tore the bottom of his shirt into a bandage for her arm, and led her back toward the trail. As Jay and Emily walked through the site toward the parking lot, the events of the last week swirled in Emily's brain. She recalled every interaction between her and Mitch, every word, every look. But now it was all so different cast against the stark background of the truth. In her mind's eye, she saw nothing but memories changing their character. It was one thing to be jilted by a lover; it was something else entirely to be thoroughly duped and then attacked by another human being. Her head began to ache.

How could I be so stupid? she thought despairingly. Mountains of lies rose violently around her, and she felt her strength slip away. Her shaking fingers lost their grip on her wound. Her legs weakened, and she had three seconds of peace as she fainted to the ground.

The jungle floor, matted with foliage, was soft and damp, and she regained consciousness almost as quickly as she'd lost it. When she opened her eyes, Jay was kneeling next to her, holding her shoulders and head off the ground.

"Are you okay?" he asked, a frown of deep concern on his face.

Emily struggled to right herself. "I'm fine," she insisted, clasping her hand gently around her bandaged arm. "It's just that my arm hurts." In a hurry to prove her point, she stood too quickly, and her shaking legs forced her to the ground again. She began to cry.

"What the hell just happened?" she asked.

"I don't know," Jay replied. "That was completely insane."

When they reached the jeep, Jay lifted the hatchback and cleared a space for Emily to sit down to his left. He retrieved a first aid kit from his box of supplies and unpacked it next to her. After rubbing his hands down with sanitizer, he cleaned and dressed her wound.

"It's really not that bad," he said when he finished securing the bandage.

"Yeah, I know. I can't believe there was so much blood. The cut's a lot smaller than I expected." Emily gently cupped her arm with her palm. The pain had tapered off now that her arm was bandaged, and all that remained was a dull stinging sensation.

Jay nodded. "Less than an inch long for sure, and it's not that deep, but I think we should swing by the medical center in San Ignacio just to be on the safe side. You might need a couple stitches."

"Do you think I should call the cops?"

"Not unless you want to spend the rest of your vacation knee-deep in bureaucracy. I mean, it's just like the States. You'll have to file a report, and then wait for them to bring him in. And they might request that you remain in the country until the case is resolved, considering you're both non-nationals."

"Never mind; I can't do that. I have to get back to work."

Jay packed up the first aid kit and snapped the lid shut. He placed his palms on top of the kit, and then looked at Emily. "Do you have any idea why he did this to you?"

Emily stared out into the parking lot and searched her mind for the smallest scrap of an idea, but nothing came. "No, I don't," she said finally. "This is by far the craziest thing that has ever happened to me. And I have no idea what brought it on." She placed her palms on the edge of the tailgate and eased her feet onto the ground. As she stood blinking into the sun, a vague notion crossed her mind. "Maybe he was trying to prove something to his wife," she said and began to walk toward the front of the jeep.

"What the hell? He's got a wife?"

"I'll explain later. Can we get out of here, please?"

"Sure thing," Jay responded, but Emily could see anger gathering in his eyes. They climbed into the jeep in silence, and within moments they were heading back to San Ignacio.

CHAPTER 25 - MITCH

AFTER HIS ATTACK ON EMILY, Mitch ran for cover, stopping only momentarily to slip the rag into a nylon pouch and place it inside his backpack. As he folded the rag (the final piece of the puzzle) and slipped it into the pouch, Mitch felt an electric buzz beneath his skin. He was charged with energy and ready to make the final push toward the climax of his plan.

But first he had to hurry up and wait. He'd just committed a crime, and it would be foolhardy to brave the crowded areas within the boundaries of the site before nightfall. Fortunately, Mitch had anticipated this kind of complication, and he and Maggie had arranged to meet just after dark in a concealed area near B-Reservoir. Sena and Evan would join him there as well. The site would be closed to tourists by that time and their only worry would be avoiding Manuel as he made his rounds.

Although Mitch didn't believe that Manuel would have any objection to Sena performing the ceremony, he didn't want to run the risk of having his plans collapse before his eyes, not when he was so close. And Sena didn't want to risk upsetting her father. She had asked for secrecy, and Mitch intended to honor her request. It was the least he could do.

CHAPTER 26 - EMILY

BY THE TIME JAY AND EMILY entered San Ignacio city limits and made their way to the clinic, the sun was long gone. The clinic was small but clean, and Emily didn't have to wait long for assistance.

Once inside the examining room, she fed the nurse a line about a broken bathroom mirror. The nurse cleaned Emily's wound and secured a blood-pressure band to the upper portion of her good arm, pumping the rubber reservoir to fill the band with air. Emily sat quietly as the nurse tended to her while Jay scowled on a metal chair in the corner of the room. After a few perfunctory tests and a couple questions, the nurse jotted down some notes and promised to return in a few minutes with a doctor to handle the stitches.

"All right," Jay said when the nurse was gone, "What's the deal with you and Mitch Hudson?"

"I honestly don't know."

"Well," Jay said in a tone of aggravation. "There's more to this story than you're letting on, and I would like to know what the hell I've gotten myself involved with here."

"Don't get mad at *me*," Emily snapped. "I didn't attack anybody."

"I'm sorry," he said, his tone softening. "But can you at least tell me a little bit about your history with the guy? Shit like this doesn't just come out of nowhere. And now you're telling me he's got a wife. I thought you two were engaged."

"I had an affair with him," Emily said flatly. As soon as the words left her mouth, she realized that simple sentence now summed up the whole of her history with the man whose shoulders she'd lately rested all her hopes and dreams upon. She was utterly ashamed of herself, and she grudgingly acknowledged that Mitch wasn't the problem, not really. He was the solution she'd clung to when there were no others to be had, a wild distraction she'd used to fill the blank space that was her life. She'd been swimming in self-pity, and when Mitch came along with something bright and shiny, she'd swallowed it, hook and all.

And now I'm choking on it, Emily thought bleakly. She shifted her weight on the examining table and checked her watch, but her mind failed to register the time. Her heart chafed with self-reproach, and she continued to chide herself even as the doctor—a petite woman with a gentle voice— entered the room, numbed her arm, and placed the first of three neat stitches across her wound.

CHAPTER 27 - MITCH AND MANUEL

THE SUN SET OVER CARACOL at five thirty amidst a tumult of burnt orange and crimson, but Mitch would have none of it. He was anxious for darkness, anxious to be moving forward with his plan. As the grainy light of dusk crept across the site, first Maggie, then Sena and Evan appeared from the shadows surrounding B-Reservoir, and together the small group made their way toward the Sky Place.

They moved quickly beneath a violet-gray sky deepening into black. Their feet made only muffled sounds as their shoes sank softly into the spongy surface soil, which was netted together by creeping grass and wandering roots.

Before long, the temple appeared in the distance, and the group quickened their pace in unison like a flight of birds arcing toward a beckoning perch. Forgoing the main staircase, they approached the temple from the far side at the northern corner. This angle of access meant a hard climb because the stairs were broad and rough along the outer sections of the temple. But they all agreed that the greater promise of concealment outweighed the trouble of the climb. It was slow-going all the way. Sena's short legs and Maggie's weakened condition made constant assistance from Evan and Mitch a necessity. But once they cleared the upper rise of the structure and made their way inside the sacred chamber, they moved quickly, each making their own preparations for the ceremony.

From a small bag he'd brought with him, Evan removed a shallow clay bowl. The surface of the red-orange bowl was peppered with black inscriptions, and its four feet were shaped like jaguar paws, the pads and nails stained black. Mitch retrieved his hard-won rag and placed it gently into the bowl.

Evan guided Sena toward a corner of the room and in a hushed voice conveyed his final instructions. As brother and sister huddled together, Mitch spread two towels on the floor, a large one for Maggie and a smaller one just above the first.

Maggie reclined upon the larger towel and tried to make herself comfortable, while Mitch placed a compact medical kit upon the smaller towel above her head. From the kit, he extracted a slender syringe and a small glass bottle of clear liquid.

"I'm going to give you a little something to help you sleep," he said to Maggie. "It's a mild sedative, but it'll work fast. You'll be out in no time."

"Okay," she said softly. Taking Mitch's hand, she added, "Don't worry, I know this is going to work. I trust you."

"I love you," Mitch whispered. He kissed his wife, then slid the syringe into the upper contour of her arm.

"I love you too..." Maggie mumbled and drifted off to sleep.

As soon as Maggie was asleep, Evan ushered Mitch from the chamber. Sena knelt beside Maggie and began.

As he stood, tense and nervous, against the outer wall of the chamber, Mitch listened keenly to Sena as she chanted. The sound was unsettling at first (a halting dialect with guttural undertones rising from the voice of a child), but as Sena's chanting continued, her words flowed together like link upon link in an infinite chain, and Mitch was taken back to the day of his own rebirth. His body growing limp, his mind spiraling through time, he slid gently to the floor and began to dream.

Evan woke Mitch just before midnight. Mitch's eyes snapped open, and, as his dream fell to memory, so went with it all remnants of peace. The instant he came to his senses, he bolted into the chamber and collected Maggie in his arms. He stroked her cheek tenderly and called her name, but she was sleeping more deeply than he'd expected.

As Mitch struggled to revive Maggie, Evan and Sena collected the few items in the center of the room, then joined Mitch at Maggie's side. By this time, Mitch had soaked the small towel he'd brought with him in cool water and was applying the compress to Maggie's forehead. She began to stir.

"Maggie," Mitch said, "Are you okay? Tell me what happened? Did you see anything? Anything at all?"

"I saw….," Maggie mumbled, still groggy from the meds, drifting in and out. "I saw ... I died ... I ate tree bark.... and I died...."

Mitch's brow creased with worry. "Maybe the meds are making her confused," he said to Evan and Sena, cradling Maggie in his arms. Mitch darted a pained look at Evan and began to rock Maggie gently.

"It's different for everyone," Evan offered.

Mitch nodded uncertainly.

A few minutes later, Mitch was able to rouse Maggie enough to lead her slowly down the steps of the temple with Evan's help. But, because Maggie could just barely put one foot in front of the other and certainly couldn't manage any heavy climbing, the group was forced to descend straight down the main staircase.

***

From the periphery, Manuel watched his children and his friends negotiate the steps of the ancient temple. He waited until they all safely reached the ground before slipping back into the darkness.

CHAPTER 28 - MITCH

WITH MAGGIE ASLEEP AT HIS SIDE, Mitch began the long drive back to Belize City. As he traveled the desolate road, he did his best to smoothly navigate the uneven surface, but the world beyond his high beams was an ocean of black, and he found it difficult to keep the vehicle from yawing on the worn and weathered road.

The night was filled with the kind of darkness that can only be achieved by underdevelopment, and the isolation quickened the blood in Mitch's veins and set his senses on high alert. He was all that stood between Maggie and the lonely black night—him and the integrity of their rented vehicle. The last thing they needed right now was to be stranded in the dark in the middle of nowhere. Mitch balled his fists around the steering wheel and whispered a prayer into the windshield. He asked the gods (any and all of them) to save Maggie's life. Tomorrow he would pray for other things.

Mitch was aiming to be back at their new hotel on the outskirts of the city by one o'clock in the morning at the latest. For the time being, his primary concern was getting Maggie quickly and safely out of the country. In all likelihood, Emily had already gone to the police, and the last thing he wanted was for Maggie to be stuck someplace where it would be virtually impossible to determine the current status of her medical condition, let alone manage her disease.

Earlier that afternoon, he'd called the airline to lock down their open-ended tickets for departure the following morning. And, out of an abundance of caution, he'd also switched hotels when they'd left Belize City the previous day. He'd checked them out of their hotel near the coastline and moved them inland to a hotel near the airport where he'd registered under an assumed name.

As he drove, Mitch felt like a tension wire about to snap. His mind was a tumbling spiral, the same three words snaking their way around and around. *Did it work?*

The night droned on. The drive seemed endless. And the solitude began to wear on Mitch's mind. His insides were a tangle of wild emotions. He felt raw and restless, like the way he used to feel when he was a teenager, bristling for a fight.

A dirty, bloody fight. That was what Mitch had gotten a year earlier when Manuel saved his life. In his mind, he fought that fight again and again. And each time he did, he felt like he was right back where it all started—his cheek in the dirt, his eyes wide as he writhed in pain and stared in disbelief at the pool of blood forming beneath his skull.

Forget it, he told himself, *let it go*.

Beside him, Maggie began snoring softly, and Mitch reached his hand across the divide to touch her face. He needed her to live. She was the one person who saw him for who he really was. Just a man. Not a prince or a paycheck. She was the exact opposite of Emily. Where Emily was soft-hearted and hopelessly romantic, Maggie was decisive and hopelessly pragmatic.

Fifteen months earlier, Mitch had started his affair with Emily because he'd somehow turned into the kind of man he'd always hated—a self-assured, arrogant ass—and Emily was more than willing to feed his new-found addiction to fawning adoration. Like many of the surgeons he was friends with at the time, he'd developed a minor god complex. Turns out, meeting actual gods and goddesses will cure you of that affliction almost instantly. As he fought for his life in the underworld, Mitch remembered all the reasons why he loved Maggie more than any other woman on earth. And later, with her help, he was able to find his way back to himself.

What he wanted most now was to talk to Maggie. He was dying to know what she'd seen and heard while she was unconscious. And he was keen to find out if she'd made any life-altering promises during her other-worldly journey. But he would have to wait. Maggie was sleeping as soundly as he'd ever seen her, even with the turbulence of the vehicle. For the next four and a half hours, Mitch did nothing but drive, and hope.

CHAPTER 29 - EMILY

ALTHOUGH EMILY SLEPT until ten o'clock in the morning, she felt drained and weary as she carried her bag down the hotel corridor to the lobby. She was sorry to leave. Despite all that had happened, or maybe because of it, she felt a connection to this place and its rustic grandeur. With eyes that wanted only to linger, she scanned the hallway and sighed as she took one last look at the amber walls with their brightly colored paintings.

As she was turning to go, Emily shook her head at the thought of her own bad judgment. She had chased a fantasy straight into the snapping jaws of a bad dream. She thought about Hunter, which conjured a mixture of joy and anguish. The early months of their friendship had been clouded by Emily's failed romance with Mitch, and she'd been too busy sulking to notice what was right in front of her face. But Hunter had been a true friend to her through it all. She cringed at the thought of anybody else (maybe Stacy—maybe right that moment) enjoying Hunter's easy smile and warm laughter. But for now, there was nothing that could be done. All Emily could do was wallow in regret, and hope that it wasn't too late to repair the damage she had lately done to their relationship.

Emily made her way to the lobby to meet Jay. She found him leaning casually against the front desk and chatting with a young woman. Emily recognized the young woman as the waitress Jay flirted with at dinner two nights before.

"Did anyone call for me?" Emily asked as soon as Jay was within earshot.

Her question caught Jay in mid-flirt—he was in the process of admiring the young woman's necklace by running his finger along the edge of the pendant as it lay against her skin.

"Ah … no, sorry, no phone calls," he replied, quickly opening a sliver of space between himself and the young woman.

Emily raised an eyebrow at him. "Are you ready?" she asked.

"Yes. We're all set," he said. "I was just finishing up with the bill and getting everything squared away with the trip to Actun Tunichil Muknal that you wanted to cancel."

Emily glanced at the young woman who was now staring down at her shoes, then returned her attention to Jay. "Thanks. I'm just not up for a long hike through a cave today."

Jay nodded.

"Well then, I'm ready to go," she added when Jay made no movement toward the exit.

"Right." He rubbed his palms together and eyed the young woman before retrieving Emily's bag and heading for the door. Emily followed Jay through the door and out to his jeep.

"Why didn't you introduce me to your friend?" she asked as Jay raised the hatchback and loaded their bags.

"She's not my friend, exactly … more like an acquaintance." With a shrug, he added, "And I forgot her name."

Emily shook her head and climbed inside the jeep.

They drove in silence as Jay negotiated the narrow sideroad that led away from the property. As they approached the highway, Jay turned to Emily. "How's your arm?"

"Fine actually. It doesn't hurt that much," she said as she subconsciously fingered the trim of the cardigan she'd put on that morning to cover the bandage.

"Good to hear it," he said and scrolled through the offerings on the satellite radio. "That was something else yesterday. I still can't believe it. Have you given any more thought to…?"

"Jay?" Emily interrupted. She was determined to give as little thought as possible to the prior day's events and was intent on changing the subject immediately.

"What's up?"

"What was it like to go from being a mechanic to a tour guide? I mean, wasn't it hard to make such a drastic transition?"

"Not really. Why? Are you considering a career change?"

"No, not seriously anyway. I was just wondering…. I mean, for a while I thought it would be cool to own a little bed and breakfast or something like that, but I wouldn't even know where to begin."

"Here's the deal," Jay said, "I believe that most people think too much. They think and worry, worry and think, and then they die. Personally, I try not to think if I can help it. And that's the secret to my success."

"That's really deep; you should write a book or something."

"I've been thinking that myself."

"Doesn't that go against your whole philosophy there, Plato?"

"What?" Jay asked, turning his attention to the satellite radio, which had started pulling down nothing but static.

"Never mind," Emily said. "Ugh—not jazz, anything but jazz," she added as Jay scrolled through the channels.

Jay finally settled on classic rock. "How's this?"

"Fine, can I borrow your phone again?"

"Sure," he said as he lowered the volume and fished his phone from his pocket. "But you've left the guy five messages already. I think he gets the picture."

"I've only left three messages, and if it goes to voicemail this time, I'll hang up."

Jay sighed and handed her the phone, "Don't forget the 00."

Emily dialed the numbers and waited through the silence that seemed de rigueur for each call. She held her breath as the first ring crackled through the silence. The phone rang again then gave way to the sound of Hunter's voice saying, "Hello, you've reached Hunter Marlow, please…."

Emily hung up the phone and held it in her lap. "Why isn't he answering? It's not like he knows it's me; it's your phone after all."

"He probably got your three messages and figured it out."

"Thanks."

"I'm sorry, but if the guy's avoiding you, there's nothing you can do about it. And calling him over and over like a maniac never helps, trust me. What is it with you and what's-his-name anyway?"

"Hunter. His name's Hunter."

"Okay. What's the deal?"

"He told me he was interested in me as more than a friend, and I rejected him." Emily stared down at the phone and blinked back tears. "I'm such an idiot."

"If the guy likes you, he likes you," Jay said. "He'll come around."

"Do you really think so?"

"Yes. Trust me."

Emily decided that she would, in fact, trust Jay, and she made up her mind to consider her situation in the best possible light. Maybe Hunter just needed a little time to cool off.

It was almost noon on Wednesday when they crossed the Macal River. The Western Highway as it wound through San Ignacio toward Santa Elena was bustling with activity. People had pulled their vehicles, bicycles, and horses up to the roadside shops—their shelves and counters laden with papaya, mawmee, mangoes, and Creole bread and bun—to purchase food for lunch.

As they neared Santa Elena, the smell of chicken stewing on an open grill made Emily's stomach growl. In the near distance, she could see a man tending a large metal grill covered with chicken, tortillas, and plantains. She watched as the man plated the meal, a local favorite known as "Dinner", for a waiting customer—first the chicken and plantains, then a ladle of rice and beans from a nearby pressure cooker; the plate was then topped off with a hot tortilla and the whole thing wrapped in foil for easy transport.

"Can we stop for some food?" Emily asked as the jeep approached the grilling station. "I didn't have any breakfast this morning, and now I'm really hungry."

"Me too," Jay replied. "There's a restaurant I've been meaning to try a few miles up ahead, just after Santa Elena. We can stop there."

"But what about that chicken right there? It smells really good." She nodded toward the man with his grill as the jeep sped past him.

"That's takeaway. They don't have any tables. We'd have to pull off the road and eat out of the jeep. I think it would be better to head over to the restaurant."

"Sure," Emily agreed, "I guess I didn't consider the table situation. Will they have local food at this restaurant? Can I order a plate of "Dinner" for lunch?"

"Yes," Jay chuckled. "I'm sure you can."

As they cleared another curve in the road, the flat grassy land to the right rose upward to form a wide tree-topped hill. The boughs of the trees were full and round, a parade of tall green mushrooms ascending the expanse of the hill. Nestled among the trees were brightly colored bungalows of various shapes and sizes, their red rooftops glowing warm against the green. Before the view was relegated to memory, Emily made Jay pull to a stop at the side of the road so she could take a picture.

"Here we are," Jay announced a few minutes later, "the restaurant at Travelers' Lodge." He cut the engine and stepped out onto the pebbled parking lot. Emily raised her eyes to examine the place, but Jay had parked too close to the building for her to get anything more than a narrow view of a bright yellow wall. She left the jeep and walked back a bit to get a better look. The exterior walls of the bar and restaurant were concrete, but the portion that enclosed three quarters of the structure was only shoulder high. Above the walls, wood beams supported an expansive thatch roof. The remainder of the structure, presumably the kitchen, was fully enclosed and topped with a red shingled roof.

"Was there a particular reason why you chose this place?" she asked Jay as she moved toward the entrance.

"Not really," he replied, pulling a flyer from a box affixed to a metal stake sprouting from the pebbled surface near the doorway. "But it's for sale, and I wanted to sample the cuisine before someone buys the place and changes the menu."

As Jay and Emily walked inside, a waiter greeted them at the door and led them to a table near the front of the room. The dining area was a large rectangular space with a glazed concrete floor and pine rafters. The restaurant's furnishings were casual, consisting of tables with brightly colored tablecloths surrounded by molded plastic chairs. Each table had at its center a decorative clay pot with black edging and scrollwork. All in all, the space was open and inviting, and Emily liked it immediately.

After they placed their drink order, Emily opened the menu and scanned the pages for rice and beans with stewed chicken, while Jay reviewed the flyer he'd brought with him from the entrance.

From the flyer they learned that the property for sale included the structure that housed the restaurant, bar, and kitchen; six guest cottages; a two-story loft home designated as the owners' residence; and a rental bungalow, all contained within an acre of land complete with mature vegetation.

"This price is a bargain," Jay said.

"How long has it been on the market?" Emily asked.

"Not long, a few months at the most. A place like this probably makes decent money. I wonder why they're selling."

"I think those are the owners over there," she said, "I'm sure they'd tell you if you ask them." She nodded toward an older couple seated at the rear of the restaurant. The husband appeared to be sorting through chits and receipts, and the wife appeared to be providing instructions to one of the waiters, who stood at attention in front of her.

After their meal, Jay and Emily made their way across the room and struck up a conversation about the property with the couple, who invited them to the bar for a drink. Apparently, the bar at Travelers' Lodge was famous for its Caribbean rum punch, and the bartender had just made a fresh batch.

After the drinks arrived, Jay began asking more specific questions about the business. He asked first about laundry services for the guests (full services available on site) then about utilities, whether they were pulling water from the city or collecting their own. The husband responded generously to each of Jay's questions.

The husband, whose accent was heavily British, spoke in a manner that was rather elegant for a Wednesday afternoon, with tumbling phrases and dawdling subjects. "And in the cisterns with metal casings, beyond the banks of palm trees, two deep, with iron grates above the inlets to catch the larger debris, water collects for the cottages and the kitchen." Emily worked to hold the cisterns, the palm trees, and the iron grates in her mind while she waited for the water to arrive. It was more than she wanted to contend with just then, and she let Jay keep up the conversation with the husband, while she transferred her attention to the wife.

The Sky Place

"Janine," she began, "it is Janine, right?" The wife nodded and Emily continued, "What made you decide to purchase a hotel in Belize?"

"Well, Mark and I always knew we wanted our retirement years to be something of an adventure. Mark had a friend who'd been down this way once and just kept coming back. He raved about the people here and the great business opportunities. We came down—I guess it was twelve years ago—and had a look around, and we really liked the country. As soon as we were able to, we purchased this little place.

"In retrospect, I don't know what we were thinking. It really was so hard to get the place going. There were so many difficulties and disappointments, first with the concessions, then the contracts. The kids thought we'd blown it for sure. Oh, I remember when I used to call Sally in London (Sally's my daughter) and ask her to ring me back because we couldn't afford the phone bill.

"It was hard in the beginning," Janine continued, "But now we have a steady stream of business, even in the low season. We get catering jobs, and we host weekend dances and business conferences. Whoever purchases the place now wouldn't have it nearly as hard as we did. And we have an absolutely wonderful staff here at Travelers' Lodge. It took some time, but I think the group we have now is just brilliant. It's been well worth the trouble. But it's too much to manage at our age. We're meant to be tromping about with the grandkids, and they're back in London. We haven't had a peek at them yet. And I'm not sure how much longer I can hold out. I can't wait to get back there and spend time with them."

Emily's conversation was interrupted by a waiter who urgently needed assistance in the kitchen, and Janine apologized as she excused herself to arrange the lunch specials for the following day. Jay was still in conversation with the husband, and Emily could hear him making a pitch for his tour services, so she snuck away to explore the courtyard behind the restaurant.

The courtyard was roughly circular. Interlocking flagstone pavers formed a looped walkway in the center of the yard in the shape of an enormous O with six smaller walkways breaking away toward six cottages, three on either side, arranged in semicircles on the right and left. Each cottage wore a different coat of paint, their colors bold and crisp, like the colors in modern art. The flagstone portions at the top and bottom of the O were longer and wider, forming two small patios. Within the belly of the O, the land was flat and grassy, and Emily was struck by the starkness of it. In contrast, the section of land beyond the cottages, directly back, was a towering cluster of rich vegetation that seemed to consume the entire rear of the property. This lush expanse of foliage rose from the ankles of the far patio and was prefaced by a pair of whitewashed wood benches.

Emily made her way toward the benches, and she soon found herself seated amid a bright and perfumed flourish of trees, shrubs, and flowering plants. The trees held deep green leaves, and the shape and structure of each different variety entwined to form an unparalleled picture. Toward the back, mango trees grew up two stories, the tops emerging into full round boughs thick with hanging fruit. Near the front, a quartet of stocky banana trees stood with clusters of smooth green leaves fanning up to the sky. And in between, there was such a great gathering of different plants—breadfruit, mawmee, soursop—that it made the space feel like a primordial place, secreted away from the rest of the world.

With such a picture before her, Emily could not help but settle into tranquility. She felt the weight of the previous day shift from her shoulders as she savored the scents and scenery around her. A warm breeze rustled the leaves above and toyed with the edges of her hair. She closed her eyes and let the wind wash over her face.

Within this quiet pocket of seclusion, Emily's mind cleared. She flipped through the pages of her past that led her to this point in her life. For most of the recent past, she had seen the world as countless circles of people that only ever thinly overlapped, layer upon layer of them. She was a small person in a small circle—a group of litigation attorneys in Houston. And there were countless others—real estate agents in Dallas, accountants in Chicago, poets in New York. Each circle was an independent entity with its own birth, growth, and death, and each felt the weight of its own importance and influence on the portion of society within its spill area. But lately Emily had become certain that she was not truly a part of her circle; that she, in fact, was meant for something else.

She thought about Hunter's new life and was instantly jealous. He was moving on, chasing his dreams, and leaving her behind to muddle through the status quo alone. Emily sighed. She was sorry she had to leave Belize so soon, and she regretted that it would probably be a long time before Walters would consent to another vacation. Still, in one respect, she was desperate to get back to Houston. She was determined to make things right with Hunter, and since he wasn't answering her calls, her only option was to make her plea in person.

She walked inside the restaurant and found Jay waiting alone at the bar. "Sorry," she called and quickened her pace.

"No worries. This is your vacation after all." Jay waited for Emily to reach him then walked with her to the Jeep.

"You should buy that place," Jay said to Emily when they got on the road, as if the lodge was a bracelet or a new bikini. "Then we could write up a contract for my services, and I could rent the little bungalow in the back. Yup, that would be the life."

"I can't buy a hotel," she said with a laugh. "Besides, I thought wood buildings were a lot of maintenance. Those cottages behind the restaurant are all made of wood."

"Yeah, but that's pressure-treated lumber they've got back there. That stuff will last you a hundred years, probably more. All you need to do is slap a fresh coat of paint on it now and then."

"That's good to know, but I still can't buy a hotel," she said. After a moment, she added, "What did the husband say about working out a deal with you? I overheard you making your pitch."

"At first, I thought he was interested, but then he said he would have to think about it, and that he didn't want to get locked into something right now while he's trying to sell the place. I told him it could be a selling point, having a dedicated tour guide kicking back a nice percentage on every tour. Then I hinted at him that he's losing out on a lot of money by not offering tour packages to his guests. After that, I told him he's missing a great opportunity to market his place as an ecotourism destination. I mean, I gave the guy the full pitch, and he still didn't bite."

"That sucks. I'm sorry."

"Thanks."

For a few minutes they sat in silence, Jay fiddling with the radio again, Emily studying the landscape beyond the glass.

"Tell me more about your guy, Hunter," he said suddenly. "I hope you used better judgment with him than you did with Mitch Hudson."

"A little salt for my wound. Thank you, Jay."

"Don't mention it."

"First of all, Hunter's not my guy, not yet. Second, I'm going to have to ask you not to place Hunter and Mitch in the same category ever again. Mitch was a stupid mistake I made, twice, unfortunately. And Hunter's been my friend, my best friend really, for a long time now. But he never told me that he wanted anything more until a few nights ago. By that time, I was already tangled up with Mitch again, like an idiot girl who can't bite an apple without choking on it, can't run down a flight of stairs without losing a damn shoe."

"Look on the bright side. At least you've got everything figured out now. I've learned from experience that ninety-nine percent of the battle is figuring out what you want."

"Thanks," Emily muttered. "Too bad it took the business end of a scalpel to help me see the light." But she knew that was a lie. It wasn't a cut that did (or undid) the damage. It was a look. It was something unmistakable behind the eyes of Maggie Hudson, a woman Emily had always hated, always considered to be her nemesis. It was love. And Emily was hungry for it, more now than ever before, because this time the thing she craved was real.

CHAPTER 30 - MAGGIE

MAGGIE KNEW MITCH WAS EXPECTING TROUBLE at the airport, but there was none. He and Maggie breezed through check-in and found themselves seated comfortably aboard the plane without the slightest setback.

Perhaps it was the medicine, but Maggie's memories of the night before had been spotty when she awoke that morning, pulsing in and out of her consciousness like static breaking through a radio transmission. She could recall the sensation of movement—movement of a kind she'd never experienced before, a weightless kind of movement. But beyond that, she didn't remember much initially.

As the hours passed, however, she began to remember more and more details. It all came flooding back to her over the course of a few hours, and by the time she and Mitch were seated in the departure lounge, Maggie remembered everything. It took her another hour to digest it all. It wasn't until midway through their flight that she turned to Mitch and said, "I remember what happened in the temple.

"I was standing next to my own sleeping body in the sacred chamber holding the bloody cloth in my hand when a woman emerged from a doorway of bright light.

"The youngest of my kin has called upon me," she said with a nod in Sena's direction as the light dimmed around her. "I am Ixchel."

"Hello," I replied, "I'm Maggie."

She smiled warmly. "You look as though you are not surprised to see me."

"No," I replied. "You helped my husband, Mitch Hudson, once before."

"Yes, I remember your husband. I have heard his prayers these five months past. I was expecting you." She took the cloth from my grasp. "You have brought me something," she said. "We will find the soul who has been conquered in your name, and bargain with the lords of Xibalba for your release. I will call Kimi."

An instant later, a man with dark eyes, skull tattoos, and a loincloth appeared in a swirl of black smoke. Ixchel introduced him as Kimi, death god of the upperworld.

Kimi put the rag in his mouth, closed his eyes, and began to tremble. "A woman," he purred lasciviously.

"Where is she?" Ixchel asked him.

"Upon the sky-earth," Kimi replied.

"I'm sure that's where her body is, but where is her soul?"

"Inside her body."

"What?" Ixchel asked, exasperated.

"Emily isn't dead," I interjected.

"If she isn't dead," Ixchel said. "There can be no exchange."

"This soul called Emily appeals to me," Kimi insisted. "I will take her now and make the exchange." He conjured a swirling mist of black around himself and began to fade from sight, but Ixchel lurched after him and grabbed him out of the mist. As soon as he was solid again, she shook him roughly.

"Snap out of it, Kimi!" she ordered. "You cannot rip a soul from a living body without cause. Heart of Sky would be upon you like a cat on a cockroach."

Kimi frowned but grunted in agreement.

"You can go now," Ixchel said to him. "Neither one of them is dead yet."

Kimi stayed put.

"And you're a god of death," Ixchel added, "so I guess I'll see you later."

"But I want the one called Emily," Kimi grumbled.

"You're just going to have to wait," Ixchel replied firmly.

Kimi was obviously unaccustomed to waiting. He fumed where he stood. An angry death god is a sight to behold. Tendrils of smoke spewed from his neck and back, and his skull glowed orange beneath his olive skin.

"I will help you," he growled, "if you promise me this soul will be mine when she meets her end."

"If she flies to the upperworld, then you have my word, she is yours. But if she falls below, we will have to seek her there, and free her."

"Agreed," Kimi said with a smile, his skin and skull returning to normal.

"I want something else," Ixchel added nonchalantly.

"Name it," Kimi replied.

"I want the Demon of Woe and the Demon of Filth. If I vanquish them, will you promise to take their souls."

"One and Seven Death will not be pleased."

"Do you fear them, Kimi?" Ixchel asked sweetly.

Kimi laughed. "Why do you tease me woman? You know the lords of Xibalba are nothing to me. If you were not so beautiful, I would not be so patient. But honestly, you are always getting me into trouble. I don't know why I keep company with you."

Ixchel grinned. "Because Ixazaluoh is no fun at all, and Cizin is still mad at you for the Cape Cotoche massacre."

"He has been holding that grudge for five hundred years!" Kimi shook his head. "I had every right to step in. He was too tangled in Maria's bedsheets to do his duty."

"In his defense," Ixchel put in, "Maria's beauty is legendary. In Latin America, they call her La Llorona. She's quite famous."

"I don't care," Kimi said flatly. "A death god must be prompt if nothing else. Nobody was dying. One of Corbodo's men was running around with twelve darts in him. Three men had lost their heads and found them again!"

"Ah, the good old days." Ixchel smiled nostalgically. "But we digress," she added quickly. "Maggie needs our help, and there is only one thing to be done."

Ixchel turned to me, a frown of concern on her brow. "You must die," she said. "And it must be done by your own hand. Once your soul flies to the upperworld, the goddess Ixtab will claim you. Kimi will arrange an exchange with her. I'm sure a warrior's soul (or two) will suffice. After she releases you to Kimi, I will send you back to your husband."

"Why don't you give Ixtab one of yours?" Kimi asked gruffly.

"You have more souls than all the other upperworld gods combined, and you said you wanted to help." Ixchel chided.

"Fine," he grumbled and disappeared in a swirl of black smoke.

Ixchel closed her eyes and raised her arms. Suddenly the room was suffused with soft white light. I was back in my body and Sena and Evan were asleep. Ixchel took my hand in hers and helped me sit up. "Are you ready?" she asked.

"Yes," I answered, but my heart was beating through my chest. The thought of dying right then and there was terrifying. Ixchel released my hand and cupped hers in front of her. They glowed white, as though she was holding a small ball of light in her palms. The light transformed into a small clay bowl.

"This is widow's bark," she said as she handed me the bowl. "I've mixed it with a bit of cashew wine to cut the bitterness. Drink every drop."

I took the bowl immediately. Afraid that if I hesitated, I would lose my courage altogether. I drank every drop. Suddenly, I was standing on the ground beneath the shelter of a massive tree amid a festival of feasting, dancing, and drumming. A middle-aged woman smiled down at me. She was wearing a blue dress hemmed and belted with lengths of bleached rope. She wore a section of white rope around her neck, like a noose.

"I am the goddess Ixtab," she said. "Welcome to paradise. Although I'm afraid you won't be staying long."

The scent of smoldering ash told me Kimi was already there. He walked over and offered me his hand. "Come," he said with a smile. "It is done."

He pulled me to him and wrapped an arm around my waist. He was almost charming. An instant later, we were flying within a stream of black smoke. It was like nothing I'd ever experienced before. We were falling and flying all at once. And the smoke wasn't hot or choking. It was more like the idea of smoke than smoke itself.

When we arrived at the Sky Place temple, Ixchel was waiting for us. "How do you feel?" she asked me.

"I don't feel any different," I replied. I was outside my body again, and I could see myself on the bare stone floor. "Did it work?" I asked anxiously.

"Yes," Ixchel said. "Your soul will heal your body."

"What if it doesn't?" I asked.

"Then you will return to me sooner than we planned," she answered. "But I don't believe that will happen. I believe you and your husband will live a long, happy life together. Now brace yourself. I'm sending your soul back home."

"Wait!" I cried. "Can't you heal me now?"

"I could," Ixchel said gently. "But your body is sick with disease. If I simply healed your body, the disease could return at any time and reclaim you. This whole process—you belong to me now, and I have enchanted your soul, the same way I did your husband's. You are children of the upperworld, but you walk upon the sky-earth. Part of my magic lives in each of you. Once you are healed, you will always be healed. You will be bound to me forever, just as your husband is, and I shall call upon you when the time is right."

"I see ... thank you," I whispered.

"Are you ready to rejoin your body?" she asked.

"Yes," I replied. "I'm ready."

"I awoke inside the chamber," Maggie said to Mitch, "you were at my side."

"How are you feeling?" Mitch asked immediately. "Can you feel any kind of change at all?"

Maggie wished she could tell Mitch exactly what he wanted to hear, but the truth was she didn't feel much different. A little less pain maybe, a bit less pressure beneath the seatbelt slung across her hips. But she was still using her little pillow to prop up the strap, still wearing one of the billowing dresses that cinched nothing in the vicinity of her torso.

She was feeling a little better, but there was no drastic improvement. "I hope Ixchel is right," Maggie said. "I hope my soul heals my body and I live long enough for her to call upon me in the future, whatever that means, but I don't feel like I'm healing yet."

The truth seemed to crush Mitch's hopes, and Maggie could tell he was fighting back tears.

"I'm sure you just need a little more time," he said, his voice cracking. He pressed his eyes shut, allowing the tears to escape down his cheeks.

Maggie took his hand. "Yes," she said, "I'm sure you're right."

CHAPTER 31 - EMILY

WHEN JAY PARKED HIS JEEP in front of The Great House, Emily was half asleep. "I'll get your bag," he said as he threw the door open and stepped out into the warmth of the afternoon sun. Emily grabbed her tote and met Jay behind the jeep.

"Do you want me to take this up to your room for you?" he asked as he lifted her duffle bag from the rear of the vehicle.

"Would you mind leaving it at the front desk?" she asked, "I want to run next door to the coffee shop and grab a cappuccino—I can't seem to keep my eyes open."

"Sure thing," he replied, and with her bag in hand, he turned to go.

"Hey, wait a minute. Aren't you going to say goodbye?"

Jay smiled. "I was going to meet you at the coffee shop. I could use a little pick me up myself."

"Alright, I'll see you over there," she said and trudged across the parking lot.

Inside the coffee shop, Emily placed her order and found a seat next to a bank of windows with a view of the courtyard. Jay entered a few moments later, placed his order, and took a seat across from Emily. She squinted at him over the rim of her coffee cup. "Can I borrow your phone again?"

He sighed and handed it over. Two minutes later she handed it back in disappointment. As Jay pocketed the phone, the barista placed his coffee on the table. He thanked the young lady then turned to Emily. "Just give it time," he said.

She nodded grimly and sipped her cappuccino.

When they'd both drained the last of the coffee from their cups, Jay and Emily said goodbye to each other.

After a quick hug, Jay said, "I wish I could stick around, but I've got to run. I'm taking a couple of newlyweds into Pine Ridge tomorrow, and I need to get my jeep cleaned and fueled. I also need to check in with Javier and make sure he got my boat to the dock in one piece."

"Sure, I understand," she said. As Jay left the coffee shop, Emily returned to the counter and purchased a side salad and a small loaf of Creole bread for supper.

Jay was pulling out of the parking lot just as Emily was walking into it, and she waved goodbye as she watched him drive away. When he was gone, she turned around and stared out at the ocean. She felt utterly alone, and she had no idea what to do with the four days that remained of her vacation. With tears in her eyes, she began walking slowly back toward the hotel.

"Emily! Emily!" The sound of someone calling her name stopped her in her tracks. She looked around. Hunter was standing on the verandah of The Great House waving down at her.

She hurried across the parking lot as Hunter descended the stairs and met her at the lower landing.

"What are you doing here?" she asked.

"Oh, you know, I had a little time to kill before the semester starts on Monday, so I thought I'd treat myself to a vacation," he joked.

"I've been calling and calling. Have you been here the whole time? I mean, seriously Hunter, what are you doing here?" she asked, giving his shoulder a squeeze.

Hunter's smile caved. "I wanted to apologize for the things I said that night at my apartment. I never should have spoken to you that way. I hope you understand why I said what I did. I wasn't trying to hurt you. I just want you to be happy, Emily. I want you to make the most of everything you've got."

"It's okay," Emily said. She could see that Hunter was upset, and she wanted to put him at ease. "I know you were angry, and I'm sorry too. Did you really travel all the way here just to apologize?"

"Yes. And no. I'm not giving up on us, and I had no intention of waiting out the week without trying to make you see that we belong together."

Emily was stunned. She reached for Hunter's hand and laced her fingers through his.

Hunter smiled. "When the concierge at your condo told me you were here," he explained, "I called the hotel and asked if you were here alone. I was so happy to hear that you were on your own, without that jackass, Mitch. Right then, I knew I had to come. I would have called you when I arrived at the airport, but my phone died on the airplane, and I forgot to pack a charger."

"I'm thrilled you're here," Emily said, shocked and delighted that the one person she'd been wishing for had just materialized before her eyes. She knew she'd have to come clean about Mitch sooner or later, but that could wait. For now, she just wanted to be with Hunter.

Hunter carried his bags into Emily's room, while she made space in the chest of drawers and on the bathroom counter for him. She folded her bath towel in half, slid it over on the hanging bar, and placed a fresh towel next to hers. As she fluffed the matching white towels, she felt the nervous energy that had been building for the last nine days fall away.

From the moment Mitch walked back into her life, Emily had felt displaced. She'd mistaken apprehension for anticipation, and until Hunter's appearance that day she hadn't known what it was like to feel right with the world. For the first time in her life, she was exactly where she belonged.

Hunter made short work of his bags; he'd packed in a hurry and hadn't brought much with him. His things unpacked, he moved toward Emily, who was now sitting on the edge of the bed. He'd kissed her once before, but it seemed a lifetime had passed since then.

Emily's heart flip-flopped in her chest as Hunter pulled her close and put his lips to hers. She wrapped her arms around his waist and pressed her weight against him, savoring every second of their embrace. He ran his palms along the sides of her face then down her back. He held her for a long moment, and Emily knew this was the beginning of happiness.

A chill settled on the city that afternoon with the arrival of a cold front that pushed the temperature down into the low 60's. Emily and Hunter dined early in the hotel restaurant at a little table near the fountain. Less than an hour earlier, as she showered and changed for dinner, Emily realized exactly what she needed to tell Hunter about what happened to her in Belize. And she knew that words alone would not be enough.

The appetizers had been ordered. The drinks were on the table. Now was the time. Emily began, "Hunter, there's something I want to talk to you about, but not here, not now. I think it would be better if I showed you in person. Because you need to see it for yourself … to understand."

Hunter eyed her quizzically.

When are you heading back to Houston?" Emily asked.

"On Sunday."

"Me too. That means we have plenty of time."

After dinner, they returned to their room. Once inside, Hunter crossed the floor to the bay windows, drew the curtains, and turned toward Emily. She was leaning against the bed, unfastening the small buckles on her sandals. As he closed the distance between them, he mused, "You realize this is our first night together?"

"Actually," Emily replied, "we spent the night together at work that weekend when you first started at the firm, working on that Motion for Summary Judgment, remember?"

"How could I forget?" he replied with a groan as he walked over to her and ran his fingers through her hair. He cradled her face in his hands and tilted her head for a kiss.

Emily placed her hands on Hunter's chest, then began to undo the buttons on his blue cotton shirt.

He glanced at her hands as she undid his buttons. "You keep this up and I might just let you have your way with me."

"I'm counting on it," she replied, slipping his shirt from his shoulders. The shirt fluttered to the floor.

Hunter lifted Emily and placed her on the bed. Within moments, Emily's yellow sundress joined Hunter's blue shirt on the hardwood floor.

CHAPTER 32 - EMILY

Houston, Texas

IT'S NOT EASY to come to terms with the realization that you've wasted time pursuing the wrong thing, be that a career or a lover. It is, however, a little easier to stomach such a realization if it comes after you have already moved on to something better as opposed to when you are still knee-deep in your last wasted effort. Emily was lucky in that she now fell into the former category.

One week after returning to Houston, Emily Stillman broke the lease on her apartment, sold her furniture, and started packing. One way or the other, she was moving out and moving on. There was only one crimp in her plan. She wasn't exactly certain about her new address yet. There was a small possibility that she wouldn't be moving any farther than Houston Heights, but, if everything went according to plan, she'd be moving south, way down south.

It was mid-morning, and she was in the process of sorting her clothes into three piles: keep, toss, and donate, when the doorbell rang. When she reached the front door and looked through the peephole, she saw a man in a navy suit, manila envelope in hand, standing in her hallway.

"Who is it?" she asked.

"Jim Thompson. I'm an attorney with Boon Skeen. I have some paperwork for you."

She opened the door.

"Good morning," Jim said immediately. "May I come in?"

"Sure. May I ask what this is regarding?"

"Ms. Stillman?"

"Yes. Sorry. Emily Stillman. Nice to meet you." She extended her hand.

Jim shook Emily's hand then opened the envelope he'd brought with him. "I'm here on behalf of Dr. Mitch Hudson."

She titled her head, too stunned to speak.

Jim continued, "Dr. Hudson has asked me to deliver this check to you personally. The amount is…." Jim pulled a check from the envelope and glanced at it. "Yes, the amount is one hundred thousand dollars." He thrust the check toward Emily.

She folded her arms across her chest and glared at him. "I don't want Dr. Hudson's money," she hissed. "You can tell him to go to hell."

"Ms. Stillman," Jim said. "I understand that this is an awkward situation for you. But I'm here to assure you that Dr. Hudson is deeply sorry for what happened, and he hopes this will bring some small measure of closure."

His wife is dead, Emily thought, *and now he's trying to make amends.* Although she would never forgive him, in that moment, she felt sorry for him, and sorry for the woman who was gone. After struggling for days to make sense of his actions, she'd come to the conclusion that he'd gone crazy after learning his wife was dying. There really was no other explanation.

"Closure?" she questioned. "You mean closure for him because I'm doing fine. Well, he doesn't get to have closure, and he does not have my forgiveness. Please make that clear."

"Very well," Jim said, slipping the check back into its envelope. "Here's my card if you change your mind."

Emily grudgingly took the card from his outstretched hand. "Goodbye, Mr. Thompson. Have a nice day."

With that, Jim Thompson said goodbye and left her apartment.

Emily shook her head. "Unbelievable," she muttered.

Except for her piles of clothes and a silver-tone telephone in the corner, the floor of her living room was barren. She picked her way through the clothes and sat cross-legged on the floor next to the phone. Lifting the receiver to her ear, she dialed Hunter's number.

"Hi," she said, and she realized she was grinning like a schoolgirl. "Care to grab a cup of coffee with your girlfriend?"

Emily met Hunter at the Starbucks on the corner of Gray and Shepherd, the one with the outside seating. "Was this the site of your infamous date with Stacy?" Emily teased as they settled into a table with their lattes and scones.

"It wasn't a date," Hunter protested. "Just a friendly meet-up kind of thing."

"Sure," she replied with a smirk.

"It's not like I ran off with her to Belize or anything," he countered with a wry grin of his own.

Emily squirmed. "I should have lied through my teeth, damn it!" she joked.

With a laugh, Hunter said, "I'm glad you told me the truth about Mitch, even if it was hard to swallow at first."

"Oh—speak of the devil—you'll never believe who just came to see me." Emily fished Jim Thompson's business card from her pocket and slapped it onto the table. "Mitch's attorney! He tried to buy my forgiveness with a check for a hundred thousand dollars. I told him to shove it."

Hunter picked up the card. "Uh, let's not be so hasty."

"What?" Emily's eyes narrowed incredulously.

"Don't look at me like that." Hunter reached across the table and took her hand. "We could use that money. That way we won't have to tap our retirement plans."

"But then Mitch would have the satisfaction of ... whatever kind of satisfaction you get when you slice someone's arm open and then give them money," Emily countered with a frown.

Hunter shrugged. "Who cares what Mitch thinks? Just take the money. We'll be able to wrap up this deal that much sooner. By combining Mitch's check with the cash we pulled from our savings, we'll be set. Please take the money. I gave up my spot at the Culinary Institute; I'm all in. But I'm tired of hemming and hawing on this deal. I just want to get back to Belize and sign on the dotted line. Besides, aren't you dying to give Bill Walters your resignation? We can cash the check today, and you'll be able to quit tomorrow afternoon."

"All right," Emily relented, shaking her head. "But I'm only doing this because I love you." Retrieving her phone from her satchel, she dialed Jim Thompson's number.

"Thank you," Hunter whispered as Emily told Jim to bring the check to her at Starbucks.

Hunter proposed to Emily two days later. Within a month, he and Emily closed on their purchase of Travelers' Lodge and settled permanently in Belize. They didn't change much about the lodge after moving in. Hunter took over as head chef, and they worked on adding a few personal touches to the décor and the menu.

Hunter instituted taco Tuesdays, complete with handmade tortillas and buckets of beer. Emily's big project was planting a spreading tropical garden within the barren center of the courtyard behind the restaurant. She started with white hibiscus, red ginger, and yellow-orange birds of paradise at the very center then worked outward adding pink flamingo lilies, purple tropical orchids, and a border of green bird's nest ferns. The garden took four weeks to bloom. Two months later, Emily and Hunter celebrated their wedding day.

Their wedding was everything Emily never knew she always wanted—a quiet ceremony just off the courtyard. There was no pomp and circumstance, no exploding guest list. In the end, they decided to include only each other, their new staff, and Jay, who was renting the guest bungalow on their property.

Emily's one luxury was her lace wedding dress, a slim, strapless silhouette finished with a row of Swarovski crystals beneath the bust. It was much too extravagant for the occasion, but she wore it anyway.

At the start of the ceremony, as Emily waited for the music to start, she realized that every disappointment, every agony had been worth it. Her life was beginning, and this time it was real. When the first notes of Pachelbel's Canon floated through the air, she fixed her eyes on Hunter and walked herself down the aisle.

CHAPTER 33 - MAGGIE

Santa Elena, Cayo District
Six months later

"CAN WE STOP SOON?" Maggie asked, "I have to pee again."

"Sure," Mitch replied. "But we'll be at San Ignacio Hotel in about half an hour. Can you hold it?"

"Nope."

"I'm not sure we're going to hit anything soon. You might need to cop a squat in the bush like last time."

"Okay. If we don't see anything in the next five minutes, just pull over next to some friendly looking shrubbery."

Mitch hit the gas. "Sounds like a plan."

Maggie angled her body toward Mitch, trying to alleviate some of the pressure from her bladder. With a smile, he took his palm from the steering wheel and rested it on her belly. She was only four months pregnant, but her belly was already protruding noticeably from her petite frame. Mitch had told her more than once that he considered this to be a very good sign, and she knew he was hoping for a boy—a baby boy who would grow into a towering young man capable of mowing down every player on the Longhorns' defensive line.

"Shit," Mitch said. "I forgot to call Manuel before we left the city. That means he'll be about four hours behind us instead of three."

"Oh, it'll be fine," Maggie said. "It's not even ten o'clock yet. We can do a little exploring in town and then have a nice lunch."

"Can you hand me my phone? It's in the glove box." She handed over the phone and Mitch made the call. As he was talking to Manuel, Maggie poked him in the shoulder and pointed toward the side of the road. A sign affixed to a mahogany tree announced that Travelers' Lodge was half a mile away. Mitch nodded and Maggie relaxed back into her seat, thankful she wouldn't be copping a squat in the bush again.

She fixed her eyes on the road ahead, but her thoughts were pleasantly elsewhere. Her Level 2 ultrasound was scheduled for the week following their return to Houston, and she couldn't wait to have a picture of their baby to carry with her and send around to family and friends. These days all she wanted to do was celebrate. Her pregnancy was month upon month of happiness, and she awoke each morning eager to savor each minute of every day. As she stared happily ahead, a second small sign caught her eye.

"The lodge is coming up," she said.

Mitch eased up on the gas. Within minutes, a yellow building came into view. Mitch pulled off the road and into the parking lot. As the vehicle rolled to a stop near the entrance, Maggie threw open the passenger door and sprang from her seat.

"I'll meet you inside," Mitch called after her as she darted for the entrance.

Fortunately, the restrooms were located at the front of the restaurant, immediately left after the entrance. Maggie hurried gratefully into a stall. It wasn't until she was washing her hands that she realized she'd forgotten her purse in the vehicle. She'd wanted to freshen up her makeup before they hit the road again. Maggie studied her face in the bathroom mirror. She wasn't sure if it was her new lease on life or her pregnancy glow, but she was sure she looked better than she had in her twenties. Undoubtedly, she felt better than she ever had in her life, even being four months pregnant. She hadn't experienced the slightest bit of morning sickness or fatigue.

"Maggie, I'm heading to the bar to get some bottled water," Mitch called from the doorway.

"I'll be right there," Maggie replied.

When Maggie reached the bar, she froze with shock. It took her several minutes to be certain that she wasn't suffering from auditory and visual hallucinations.

Kimi, the god of death, was seated at the bar wearing a Dive Belize t-shirt over his leather loincloth. He was trying to convince Mitch to kill Emily, who was standing behind the bar, glaring at them both. Apparently, Kimi still wanted Emily's soul quite badly.

"Just ignore him," a handsome young man seated at the bar said to Mitch. "He asks everyone to kill her; it's just part of his charm."

"Thanks, Jay," Mitch replied. "But it doesn't sound charming to me."

"Don't insult my customers," Emily snapped. "What the hell are you doing here?"

"I just want two bottles of water. What are *you* doing here?"

"My husband and I own this lodge," Emily replied. "We live here."

"I didn't realize you were married," Mitch said. "Congratulations."

"Tell this woman," Kimi put in, "to leave her mortal matchmate and take her place at my side for eternity. I can offer her the riches of the upperworld and life everlasting."

Before anyone could respond to Kimi, a man walked into the restaurant from the kitchen. When he saw Mitch, his face went cold with anger. "Get the hell out of here!" he shouted.

"Hunter," Emily soothed. "It's fine. He's just here to buy water. Look, his wife is here too." Emily pointed at Maggie, which caused every head to turn in unison toward her.

Kimi spoke first. "Beautiful lady! You are alive. This gives me great pleasure, and I shall tell Ixchel when next I see her."

"I already know," said a familiar voice near the entrance. Everyone else was now gaping at whoever was behind her, and Maggie turned quickly to see who had spoken.

Ixchel smiled. "I'm glad you're all here. My plans have changed. It's time to return to the underworld."

EPILOGUE - EMILY

"WE'RE NOT GOING BACK to the underworld! Maggie's pregnant."
Mitch shouted as Maggie cradled her belly. Mitch clearly had his hackles
up, but the woman who'd introduced herself as the goddess Ixchel
appeared unfazed.

The goddess offered Mitch a sweetly menacing smile and replied,
"Maggie is bound to me, just as you are. This isn't open to debate. The
price for your lives was clear, and now you both must pay me what you
owe. We will return to Xibalba together and vanquish the Demon of Filth
and the Demon of Woe."

"You told me the demons could never be completely destroyed," Mitch
countered. "I watched you annihilate one of them, only to have him
regenerate shortly thereafter. What is the point of taking a pregnant woman
to the underworld only to repeat what you've already done countless times
before?"

"That was different," the goddess said. "We didn't have Kimi last
time."

"You don't have him now," Kimi grunted. "I didn't get what you
promised me."

"How many times do I have to tell you, Kimi?" the goddess scolded.
"You can't rip a soul from a living body. When she dies, she will be yours.
I promise you."

Kimi glanced at Emily and smiled.

"Absolutely not!" Emily was livid, and her patience with the god of
death had finally run out. "Stop this now! I am sick of this nonsense. I will
never be yours! The sooner you get that through your head, the better."

Kimi frowned. "See what I mean?"

207

"Don't worry about that now," Ixchel said. "You made a promise to me, and you must keep it. I will uphold my end of the bargain when the time comes. A soul cannot control where it ends up."

Emily had no intention of ending up with Kimi, even if he was rather charming for a death god. "If I take Maggie's place and go with you now to the underworld … to … help you with whatever you're doing, will you release me from this ridiculous bargain that I never agreed to in the first place?"

"Have you gone mad?" Hunter asked Emily.

"No," Emily insisted. "I need to untangle this mess once and for all. We've had a death god loitering on our property for months asking people to kill me. Our customers find it unsettling."

"It's part of the ambiance," Hunter countered. "Our customers love it."

"You can't help us anyway," Ixchel cut in. "I haven't imbued you with my spirit. You are merely mortal."

"Imbue away," Emily said. "There's no time like the present."

"Emily!" Hunter said. "You can't go with them. Aside from this being the most insane thing you've ever contemplated. Stacy's arriving tomorrow, and you can't leave me here alone with her."

Emily scowled. "I don't know why you agreed to let her come in the first place."

"Because she's our friend," Hunter replied.

"She's *your* friend," Emily retorted. "She's never been a friend of mine."

Hunter walked over to Emily and put his hands on her shoulders. "None of that matters now. The point is that she'll be here tomorrow, and I don't want to be alone with her."

"You won't be alone," Kimi said. "I'm not going anywhere if Ixchel and Emily cut me out of the bargain."

"Enough!" Ixchel said. "Maggie can stay here with Emily's husband. Kimi will extend his powers to Emily, including control of Jaguar Night and Red Jaguar, and teach her how to vanquish the demons. If she succeeds, she will be released from our bargain." Turning to Kimi, she added, "Once this mortal woman gets a taste of your power, she will beg you to take her as your own."

Emily rolled her eyes and offered a soft gagging sound by way of disagreement.

Ixchel ignored her. "Kimi, this is your chance to show her your strength. No woman can long resist a god who possesses power such as yours and twin jaguars of death. Emily will be bound to you, and you will have your way."

Kimi grinned in delight, "It will be done."

Ixchel clasped her hands together in victory. "Sleep well tonight," she said. "Tomorrow, we begin."

ABOUT THE AUTHOR

Lyla Cork was born and raised in Belize. As a child, she explored her native country with her family, and she enjoyed learning about the history of her homeland. The daughter of multicultural parents, she has always been interested in Belize's multicultural aspects and international appeal. Lyla has a BA in creative writing, and she has published nonfiction works as a writer and an editor. *The Sky Place* is her first novel.

If you enjoyed this book, please consider leaving a review on Amazon.

APPENDIX

A note on diction:

Maya/Mayan: Maya is used as a singular noun, a plural noun, and an adjective to describe the people and their culture. Mayan is used to describe their language.

Example 1: The Maya of Belize speak different Mayan languages.
Example 2: This ancient Maya pot was used during Maya rituals.

Mayan Pronunciation Guide:

Usually, the last syllable is stressed. Mayan vowels and consonants are generally pronounced as in Spanish. A few letters require special note:

A is pronounced as in father.
C is always hard.
Ch is pronounced as in church.
I is pronounced /ee/ as in knee.
J is pronounced /h/ as in his (soft) or as in Bach (hard).
U is pronounced /oo/ as in fool or /w/ before another vowel, as in woe.
X is pronounced /sh/ as in she.

Ajq'ij: ah kee
Buluk Chabtan: boo luke chahb tahn
Chac: chahk
Itzamna: eet zahm nah

Ixazaluoh: ee shah zah loo
Ixchel: eesh chel
Ixtab: eesh tahb
Kimi: kee mee
Kinich Ahau: kee neech ahwah
One Hunahpu: one hoo nahpoo
Xibalba: shee balba
Xmucane: shmookah nay
Xpiyacoc: shpee yahkawk

Definitions:

Ajq'ij: Mayan for daykeeper, see below.
Buluk Chabtan: The god of war and sacrifice. Buluk Chabtan is also spelled Buluc Chabtan.
Chac: The god of rain, lightning, and thunder. Chac is also spelled Chaac, Chaak, or Chak.
Ch'ak: "Axe" event against another city, such as the murder of a member of the nobility or an important battle.
Caracol: Caracol was known as Ox Witz Ha or Uxwitzá during the Classic period.
Daykeeper: Maya noble who keeps track of the Maya calendar and performs rituals.
Great Star: The Great Star is Venus. The ancient Maya tracked the cycle of Venus. When translated from Mayan to English, Venus was referenced as a star rather than a planet (during the Classic period).
Ixtab: The goddess of suicide. The ancient Maya believed that suicide was honorable.
Kimi: Kimi is one of many death gods in the Maya pantheon.
Kinich Ahau: The god of the sun, nobility, and the Maya monarchy. Kinich Ahau is also spelled K'inich Ajaw.
Landa: The Spanish Bishop Diego de Landa. He burned books, statues, and paintings of the Yucatan Maya in 1562. This was done to bring the Maya over to the Roman Catholic faith. This religious campaign included an inquisition that employed physical abuse. After the arrival of the

Spanish, the Maya worldview was influenced by Christian teachings. The Popul Vuh, the Maya book of creation, was written by the Maya during this time.

Lord Double Bird: King Wak Chan K'awiil of Tikal, approximately A.D. 537-562.

Lord Sky Witness: King of Calakmul, approximately A.D. 561-752. Calakmul was also known as the Snake Kingdom.

Lord Water: King Yajaw Te' K'inich II of Caracol, approximately A.D. 553-593.

Middleworld: Earth or the land of the living. The ancient Maya believed the earth was flat with four sides. At each of the four corners, a god supported the sky. Middleworld is located between the upperworld and the underworld.

Noble Ancestors: The ancient Maya believed that human beings could become gods. Many Maya gods were venerated ancestors, or forefathers with glorious achievements, who were deified and worshiped. These gods could be called upon for help through sacred rituals.

Night Sun: The jaguar god of the underworld. This is the form taken by the sun god when he descends into the underworld each night and becomes a jaguar.

One Hunahpu: Celestial being who became a god. Father of the Hero Twins.

Sacred tree: The sacred tree of the Maya is the ceiba tree. According to ancient Maya lore, a version of the ceiba tree, the World Tree, is at the center of the universe and runs through the three levels of the Maya cosmos, the upperworld, the middleworld (earth), and the underworld.

Sky-earth: Earth or the land of the living.

Sky Place: The Sky Place (Caana) is the tallest temple at Caracol. It is also known as the Sky Palace or the Sky Temple.

Tikal: Tikal was known as Yax Mutal or Mutul during the Classic period.

Underworld: The underworld or Xibalba is a fearsome place below the land of the living that the dead must traverse. It is filled with trials, tricks, and challenges, and it is home to various nefarious gods, such as the lords of Xibalba. The ancient Maya believed the sun descended into the underworld at night and was reborn each day as it emerged from the underworld.

Upperworld: The heavens or the celestial realm above the land of the living. The upperworld is home to benevolent gods, mystical beings, and deified ancestors.

Xibalba: See Underworld.

Xmucane: First divine grandmother and wife of Xpiyacoc. Mother of One Hunahpu.

Xpiyacoc: First divine grandfather and husband of Xmucane. Father of One Hunahpu.

Printed in Great Britain
by Amazon

26950204R00128